SPECTER OF BETRAYAL, THE GHOST II

A Vietnam War Story

RICK DESTEFANIS

SPECTER OF BETRAYAL, THE GHOST II
A Vietnam War Story

ISBN: 978-1-7367120-8-5

Acknowledgments

My special thanks and appreciation to my friends who helped me with the historical and technical aspects of this story. These include military veterans, Robert (Doc) Enzenauer, Edward G. (Buddy) Klein, Lee Thomas, Robert (Bob) Walker, and W.P. (a Special Forces Operator). Special thanks also go to my fabulous editors, story editor Carol Carlson (Author of: *Life as a Police Mom: Guidance and Support for Mothers of Police Officers from Behind the Thin Blue Line*), line editor Elisabeth Hallett, format editor Jennifer Johnson, and cover designer Todd Hebertson.

A Note from the Author

This is the second book in the two-part story about *The Ghost*. If you haven't read Book #1 (*The Ghost, Rumors from the Central Highlands of Vietnam*), I strongly recommend that you read it first. Much of what is written in this second book (Specter of Betrayal) is a continuation of that story, and it will make this one more understandable and enjoyable.

PROLOGUE

Lieutenant Martin Shadows was happy to be home from Vietnam, but he was deeply frustrated and saddened by the needless loss of friends and brothers in a war with no strategy and failed tactics. He and his fellow soldiers had fought hard, with many of their brothers killed or maimed for life. They had given their best. Now, the end was in sight. President Nixon's new "Vietnamization Program" was going full bore and the commander of the Military Assistance Command—Vietnam (MAC-V) said the Army of the Republic of Vietnam (ARVN) was steadily improving and ready to face the North Vietnamese Army—a laughable concept for the grunts who had fought beside them.

Martin had read everything he could about events surrounding the war prior to his going and since returning from Nam. It was now 1970, and it seemed the United States Military in Vietnam was facing the inevitable, something the Joint Chiefs of Staff years before had warned President Lyndon Johnson would happen.

That discussion occurred six years earlier on December 13, 1963, three weeks after JFK was shot dead in Dallas. The Joint

Chiefs of Staff told Johnson that a limited involvement in Vietnam with gradual expansion had a 100% guaranteed expectation of failure. Yes, Kennedy knew this early on and, frightened by a world at the brink of nuclear war during the Cuban Missile Crisis, he was about to announce a different course—one of peace, but that no longer mattered. He was dead, and Johnson became the head honcho.

The Joint Chiefs favored an all-or-nothing approach, telling Johnson they would rather get out altogether than fight the war with gradual escalation. They said it would be a debacle, but it didn't matter to Johnson. He didn't trust them, and there was an election to be won, along with greater powers to be assuaged. The more he read, the more Martin was appalled by this president.

LBJ defeated his opponent in the presidential election, and when he wasn't exposing his privates to journalists or chest-bumping congressmen, the vulgar Texan went against America's best military leaders by sending troops piecemeal to Vietnam. After all, power was power, and for the eyes of those who favored peace, this gradual escalation provided a reasonable façade of compromise. Now, a new president was facing bleak realities while wrestling with a way to exit the war without total capitulation.

Most South Vietnamese soldiers were conscripts from poor farm families, while a large portion of their officers were well-to-do political appointees lacking leadership and tactical skills. They had been promoted far above their competence levels and clung to their positions at the expense of their men and their country. The only reliable units were the Vietnamese Rangers, Special Forces, and paratroops, and though still fighting fiercely, these brave troops had been severely depleted.

Every American soldier below the rank of Colonel knew the Army of the Republic of Vietnam (ARVN) was a paper tiger and inept without American support. And when Martin returned home from his tour of duty in '69 he had no intention of returning, yet he sought to understand his time there, its meaning, and the meaning of his participation. His grandfather, Two Shadows, a revered Lakota Sioux Medicine Man, sent his spiritually bankrupt grandson on a quest to search for a new path in this life. It took him out on the cold winter plains of Montana.

Martin never understood what it was to be both native American and Anglo until he visited his grandfather that previous year before going to Vietnam. Now, he was suspended above an abyss between the spirits of his Lakota blood and his duties as a United States Army commissioned officer. And if there was a safety net, his experiences in Vietnam had removed it. If there came a conflict between those worlds he wasn't certain which he would choose.

After nearly twelve days alone on the high plains, Martin reached a state of exhaustion in which he was met with aberrations of thought he would rather have ignored. Yet, these thoughts spoke to his soul, saying he had but one way to find answers to his questions. That was to return to Vietnam. This seemed impossible.

Returning to the madness of that war would solve nothing. He put it from his mind and spent the following day far out on the Fort Peck reservation. Wrapped in a buffalo robe against the winter cold, he sat in meditation until a huge evening sun squatted on the western horizon, its shimmering rays dancing across the far plains.

It was quiet except for the distant calls of birds roosting in the trees, but as he listened, he realized it wasn't birds at all. It was the distant voices of people calling for help—people not unlike his Lakota ancestors—people who were suffering. This was when he saw the billowing flames of napalm spreading across the evening horizon. And only at that moment did he realize it wasn't a dream or his imagination, but something so real it could only be a vision.

Despite the winter cold, a hot wind blew in his face. And people—women and children—he sensed more than heard, were screaming somewhere in mountainous jungles—screaming as some evil specter came to wipe them from the earth. They were thousands of miles away, but Martin heard them and smelled the odor of burning napalm drifting across the vast Pacific Ocean. Fear gripped him and he wanted to act, only to realize he was merely an observer.

The strangest part came when he thought all was lost, but there appeared the faraway silhouette of a woman standing in an open doorway. It seemed she was holding something in her arms but turned away when she saw him. The vision of chaos and confusion had suddenly morphed into something mysterious and beautiful, and perhaps sad if he failed to follow his instincts. Yet understanding it seemed all but impossible, except for one realization.

He was now facing a new path and compelled to follow it. It was telling him that he must return to the war because kindred spirits were calling for his help. And his poorly understood vision ended in a sudden and stark silence as the night took the day and the orange afterglow remained on the clouded horizon—this time no longer terrifying but magnificently beautiful.

He inhaled deeply and came away from his trance as the hot wind of the napalm gave way to a winter breeze. He shivered, not from the cold, but from the realization of what lay ahead. He was going back to Vietnam, and his vision had been akin to nothing he expected—too real to be a dream, too real to be ignored. Telling his family of his decision would be painful, but only his Grandfather Two Shadows could possibly make sense of it.

CHAPTER ONE

Voices Calling from the Highlands
Fort Peck Indian Reservation, Montana

The three men stared at one another in silence. Martin had just told his father and grandfather he was returning to Nam, yet neither seemed surprised. The tepee walls were buffeted by the Montana winter wind, but the air inside remained still and was filled with the pungent odor of burning cedar. Thousands of years on these plains had allowed their ancestors to develop a lodge that withstood most of what the high plains offered. The current silence was a void begging for a voice, and Martin wanted to ask how they already knew of his decision, but he remained locked in puzzled silence. It was their turn to speak.

George Shadows, Martin's father, passed the pipe to Two Shadows and nodded to Martin. "Your grandfather has already shared his visions with me—visions which have told us of your intentions. He has seen many things, including this quest to help your fellow warriors. It will be a dangerous journey, filled with the bitterness of loss. I worry about you going back to the war, but my biggest fear is telling your mother. She will not be happy about this."

George Shadows turned and gazed at his father. Two Shadows stared across the fire with unfocused eyes.

"Martin, what your father tells you is important because you must not lose your will to be a warrior when these things come to pass. You must continue to fight and trust Wakȟáŋ Tȟáŋka will help you choose the best path. I have seen many more things—things that I do not understand but are a part of this journey you must take. I saw you walk to a faraway land where you killed your enemies with your knife and threw their bodies from the mountain. And I saw another vision of you giving the body of one of your warriors to a great eagle that took him into the sky, and another when you freed tigers from their grave.

"These and many more visions have come to me since your return, and I cannot explain their meanings. I can only say this: You will meet men worthy of your trust, while you will meet others worthy only of your knife's blade, yet in the end you will not use your knife to slay your greatest enemy. The spirits of those who have gone before you will dictate the way he must die."

The skepticism that once plagued him when he heard such things no longer remained. If there had been the slightest remnant of doubt in his mind, it was gone. Martin knew he was in the presence of two men who truly saw beyond the conscious world, beyond the realities of everyday life. They saw deep into a spiritual world that was visible to only a few of the chosen. It was clear that his father and grandfather were of these men, and he wondered why his father had never shared this with him.

It was late Saturday afternoon when Martin did something he had never done before while visiting his grandfather. He left the ranch and began driving—alone. His father had returned to Kentucky, and with two weeks remaining on his leave of absence, Martin would soon follow to bid farewell to his mother. Yet some unseen mover was now telling him to take his old pickup and drive it across the Montana high plains. He needed to listen to the soothing rumble of the gravel beneath its wheels. Heading east on a gravel road, he was in no hurry and unsure of where he was going—only that he was being driven by an unexplainable compulsion.

After a while he realized he was lost somewhere far out on the reservation, but he spotted a sign that said he was on the Powder River Road. Gazing into the rearview mirror, he watched the sun sinking into the prairie behind him. It would be dark soon, and he needed someplace warm where he could sit alone and think about what was coming.

Eventually the Powder River Road turned south, and a while later he found himself back on a familiar highway. Turning on the headlights, he headed west toward the town of Wolf Point, until he spotted neon lights off the highway. It was a bar, and by Montana standards a fairly large one. Sitting and thinking a while might help him unclutter his mind and help him to better understand this strange spiritual vision that was sending him back to the war.

His Lakota blood had already taken him places he never imagined existed, and now, he needed to calm his mind before his thirty-day leave ended. A shot of good Kentucky Bourbon might help him relax and perhaps calm the spirits clamoring at his door.

The parking lot was full when he arrived, and the thumping sound of a jukebox came from inside. The neon lights reflected blue and red across the vehicle windshields, dimming the stars in the Montana sky. The chill of the evening breeze quickly drove Martin inside, where Glen Campbell was singing "Wichita Lineman" on the jukebox. Several heads turned as he walked to the bar and took a stool.

The atmosphere seemed friendly enough with several couples dancing while others sat around the tables. Several women at one table affected appearances of boredom, while the cowboys circled them like buzzards, but they quickly succumbed when another slow song began. This time it was Jack Green singing "Almost Persuaded."

Martin ordered a shot of bourbon over ice while the music became an opiate for his worries. The couples swayed and the cowboys clung to their girls as if they'd been in love all their lives. He would have traded places with any of them, but not tonight. He had too much on his mind. Besides, approaching a girl in a bar was something foreign to his nature. If his past experiences with women were any indicator, he figured on dying a bachelor.

Relaxing, he watched the dancers in a mirror that extended along the wall behind the shelves of liquor bottles. After a few minutes he ordered another bourbon. This time he held up two fingers for a double. His mind was begging for understanding and filled with doubts about his decision to return to Vietnam. The warm buzz of the first drink had already relaxed him, and he was lost in the music. Some clever cowboy had filled the jukebox queue with nothing but slow love songs. This time it was another one by Glen Campbell, "By the Time I get to Phoenix."

At least he didn't have that concern. Leaving someone behind besides his mother and father was a burden he didn't need. There had been a few girls in his life—a couple in high school and three more in college, but he figured a combination of shyness and setting his sights too high had left him without a steady—probably a good thing because he didn't have to worry about a Dear John letter when he returned to Nam.

A girl stood up at one of the tables, and Martin watched her in the mirror as she walked up beside him. They faced one another in the mirror. She smiled. He smiled back at her.

"My name is Emma Birdsong. What's yours?"

"My name is Martin. Good to meet you."

"Would you like to dance?" she asked.

She was a pretty girl, and any other time he would have jumped at the invitation, but tonight he needed time alone—time without a distraction like Emma Birdsong. His mind raced to find the words that wouldn't hurt her feelings.

"Thanks, but I only came here to have a drink or two."

"Oh, you must have a steady girl."

"No. It's just that I wouldn't be good company tonight. Maybe another time."

He gazed into the mirror as she walked back to the crowded table and sat down. A moment later two young cowboys stood and walked up on either side of him. Both had beers in hand and wore gargoyle grins as they leaned against the bar.

"Howdy," one said.

"Howdy," Martin replied.

"Haven't seen you around here before."

They weren't big men, but they were both wiry and browned by the prairie sun. One was wearing an eye-watering after shave. Both had Indian blood showing in their faces. Like him, they were of mixed blood.

"No, I'm from Kentucky."

One of them glanced over his shoulder. Martin watched in the mirror as a man still sitting at the table raised his beer and grinned. There were several others with him, including Emma Birdsong. All were watching the two men at the bar, except for one woman who was staring down at her glass and frowning.

"So, how come you're not dancing with the girls?"

"Because I didn't come here to dance. I came here to drink."

"You don't like women?"

Martin sized them up. They were up to no good. He could make roadkill out of both in three seconds, but he was outnumbered by the bunch back at the table.

"Look, why don't I buy each of you boys a beer, and y'all go back to your table and tell your friends I didn't come in here to entertain them."

"Well hell! That's a pretty good offer," one said. "How 'bout you buy a round for our friends, too?"

The other's face reddened. "I'm not letting a queer buy my beer."

Knowing he might leave them both wearing the jagged edge of a beer bottle in the next few seconds, Martin gave them a disarming smile.

"Fellas, I didn't come all the way from Kentucky looking for trouble, so why—"

"So why did you come here?" the angry one snarled.

"I came to visit my grandfather before I leave for Nam."

"Where does *he* live?"

"On the res up near Wolf Creek."

"Who's your grandfather?"

"His name is Two Shadows."

The smiling one's face morphed to a mask of incredulity while the angry one's face paled.

"You're Two Shadows's grandson?"

"That's right."

The angry one gave a nervous laugh.

"We knew that. We were just messing with you, man. Why don't you come sit with us at our table?"

"Thanks, but I'm going to finish my drink and go."

"Hey Bill, set this man up with another of whatever he's drinking, and it's on me." He turned to face Martin. "Look man, we were just horsing around. I mean we…well hell, what I'm saying is *everybody* around these parts knows your grandfather."

Martin continued watching them in the mirror as they rejoined their friends at the table and began trading hissing whispers. As his adrenaline flow subsided, he killed the drink and the bartender set another double in front of him. It was two more shots than he intended to drink, but the roads on the reservation were all but empty this time of night. A few moments later, the two Lakota cowboys left the bar with their hats pulled down low, but the girl who had seemed disgusted stood and walked toward Martin.

MAC-V Headquarters
Saigon, Republic of Vietnam

Martin walked down a long hallway at MAC-V that day until he saw the name on the door—Major Steven J. Ramseld, the officer to whom he was ordered to report. He knocked lightly at the door.

"Enter!" a voice boomed from inside.

He pushed the door open. The major remained seated behind his desk.

"Lieutenant Martin Shadows, reporting, Sir."

The major didn't return his salute.

"Take a seat."

No eye contact—nothing but a motion of his hand. *Another self-absorbed hardass* was Martin's first thought. The major shuffled through several folders on his desk before drawing one out and opening it atop the others. Tight-lipped and stone-faced, he thumbed through the contents. Nearly a minute passed before he raised his head and nodded with a grim countenance.

"I'm Major Ramseld, adjutant to Colonel Krieger. The colonel told me to meet with you, issue you your orders, and give you fair warning. I don't have time for a lot of small talk, so let me get to the point. The colonel believes you're a maverick and said if there's any more freelancing on his watch, your next job will be as a cook at the Long Binh Stockade. We're sending you to Recondo school. After that you will—"

"Sir, my understanding is that Recondo School is voluntary."

"Yes and thank you for volunteering."

"Now, as I was saying, you will be assigned as commanding officer of a special advisory unit up in I-Corps. This job comes with a promotion to the rank of Captain."

"Commanding officer? Captain?"

"Don't let it go to your head. You'll only have a small contingent of American advisors under your command. The rest are indigenous Montagnard—a former CIDG unit that was under the command of Army Special Forces. They now report to an ARVN outfit near Phu Bai. You and your advisors and the Yards will work with the South Vietnamese and a company of their Rangers. I assume it's mostly reconnaissance duty, but where you're going there are enough NVA to keep you busy for the rest of your tour. And who knows? Maybe you can convince the little bastards you really *are* a ghost."

Martin saw red. "If the colonel believes I—"

"At ease, Captain! Don't raise your voice with me."

Martin drew a deep breath and quelled his temper.

"Sir, those *little bastards* as you call them, fought both the Japanese and the French, and I don't see a lot of Japanese or Frenchmen around here right now. And this 'ghost' business isn't something I made—"

"That's enough, Captain. It would be in your best interest to remain silent and listen. My understanding is that you were assigned a very specific mission when you disappeared for several months. Most of your personal records are now classified, and parts of them are redacted because during that time a Chinese national was supposedly killed while in your custody. Whether or not this is true, you can be assured that the colonel and his boss don't tolerate soldiers who violate the Military Code of Conduct.

"The same type of thing happened last year, when Project Gamma went off the rails and we had to relieve some Special Forces top brass, but we're not going to wait around for more fuckups and the possibility of another embarrassment for the military. All Special Forces units are being deactivated in the next year and their indigenous troops put under the command of the South Vietnamese. You need to understand that you are a commissioned officer in the United States Army and will conduct yourself as such."

Martin saw clearly that he was a marked man and there was nothing he could say that would make a difference.

"You also need to understand that you are to discuss with no one anything that pertains to your previous tour of duty. That includes any after-action reports and other related documentation."

"Sir, regardless of what you or the colonel think of my performance, I'm not qualified to be a company commander."

"Why do you say that, Captain?"

"I don't have the time in grade."

"I wouldn't worry about that. You'll have some experienced advisors working with you and most of your command will be Montagnards. Besides, your previous CO, Captain Palmer, gave you a pretty glowing Officer Efficiency Report—not that the colonel or I agree with it, but if you can cut it, the Recondo school where you're going will provide the advanced training you need."

He shoved a brown envelope across the desk.

"Those are your orders. You're assigned to a transient BOQ

here in Saigon until we get you a slot at the Recondo School in Nha Trang. After that you'll report to Colonel Duggin in Phu Bai. He's the advisor liaison for the ARVN units we're supporting in I Corps. You're dismissed."

There were a hundred more questions Martin could ask, but he gritted his teeth instead and said nothing more. It was useless. This major was a jerk, and these people had their minds made up about him. He stood and saluted. Ramseld gazed down at the papers on his desk and after a pause reciprocated with a terse salute.

Martin had heard much about Saigon, but the descriptions little matched the reality he was now experiencing. Colorful ribbons and paper lanterns hung among towering green trees along crowded thoroughfares where exotic women in silk áo dàis and bar girls in red vinyl miniskirts clashed in a meeting of eastern and western cultures. The afternoon streets of the city were already crowded with aging Citroen cabs, bicycles, small Honda motorcycles, pedicabs, rickshaws, and myriad other means of transportation, including occasional military jeeps, manned by white-helmeted Vietnamese M.P.s, sarcastically referred to as *the white mice* by American G.I.s.

The bus driver, who resembled a high school kid, remained silent as he patiently wove his way through the streets to an officers' bachelors' quarters near the Continental Palace Hotel. Martin pressed his forehead against the barred window and gazed out at the battle-damaged buildings, some now only charred piles of rubble. During the 1968 Tet Offensive, the VC had failed to capture the city, and most were killed in the attempt, but they had left their mark.

The old colonial beauty of Saigon, once called *The Pearl of the Orient*, now bore scars inflicted by her own people who were either subjugated or ignored by the French. Martin saw clearly from both points of view, and it only lent more doubt and confusion to his purpose for being here.

The big green bus, mostly empty, hissed to a stop and the baby-faced driver gazed into the rearview mirror—making eye contact with him. "This is your BOQ, Sir." He pointed to a building with an MP standing at a sandbagged guard station out front. "And up there on that next block is the hotel you asked about, the Continental Palace. Is this your first time in Saigon?"

The Spec-4 driver stared at him through the mirror and only now did Martin realize he was no cherry.

"This is my second tour, but I haven't spent any time here."

The driver nodded. "Don't mean to be preachy, Sir, but treat it like the boonies. Don't go out at night without a friend. This ain't a nice place after dark."

Martin shouldered his duffle bag and walked up the aisle to the door.

"I read you Lima Charlie, Specialist. Thanks."

As he exited the bus, he glanced back at the driver. Above the left pocket of the soldier's fatigue shirt was a CIB patch. The boy had been there. He had stared the beast in the eye.

After registering at the BOQ, Martin walked up Tu Do Street and made his way to the Continental Palace Hotel—a place he had heard old vets talk about with a hint of respect. Part of its mystique was how one might walk into its bars and restaurants and sit down beside anyone from a guerrilla to an international diplomat, or from a war correspondent to a general. Martin opted for the rooftop bar where he might find fresh air.

With a hazy view of the city stretching away below in a hodgepodge of avenues, structures, and trees, Martin was beginning to relax when a dull *"thump"* came from somewhere far away, then another—the distant impacts of artillery shells. The sounds were barely audible, almost as if the war was a thousand miles away. No one around him seemed to notice or care.

Studying them, he tried to guess who they might be—soldiers, businessmen, news correspondents, diplomats—the possibilities were endless. Most wore civilian clothes, but there were two sitting on the far end of the bar that caught his eye. They wore army dress khakis with Special Forces insignia and green berets. It was a long shot, but perhaps they might know something about Luis Ravera and what had happened to him.

Ravera was the American Special Forces soldier he had rescued from the island prison along with five Montagnards. Sergeant Ravera had submitted himself as a witness for the commendations the army had so reluctantly awarded Martin. Finding Ravera and his Montagnard warriors seemed to be a part of his quest, and it was unlikely the two soldiers at the bar could help, but he had to start somewhere. Martin stood and walked across the restaurant toward them.

"I see you men are Army Special Forces."

Despite Martin's jeans and casual shirt, they seemed to realize he too was likely military.

"Yes, Sir. We are."

"I know this is a long shot with SF scattered all over Nam, but would you happen to know a Sergeant Luis Ravera?"

The two Green Berets made eye contact with one another. They knew something.

"I've heard his name," one said, "but that's about it. He was supposed to have escaped from a North Vietnamese prison, but that's all been rumor. If it really happened, the whole affair's been kept pretty hush-hush for some reason."

"Is he still in Vietnam?" Martin asked.

"They say Ravera is with MAC-V SOG, but we really don't know much about him. Those people operate in the shadows, but there's a spook—an agency type—who comes around here. We've seen him a couple times this week. Sometimes he wears camo fatigues and sometimes he wears a Jungle Jim outfit. Name's Liegeman. He might be able to tell you more about Ravera."

"How is it you know Liegeman?"

The two green berets shuffled their feet nervously.

"Look, we're leaving for Fort Bragg in the morning, and we don't really know much of anything for certain. Like I said, it's all hearsay. Find Liegeman, but don't tell him you spoke with us. He may know more about Ravera, but don't be surprised if he doesn't."

"Okay, but can you give me a better description of him?"

"Five-foot-eight, blond hair, blue eyes, thin-boned face—kind of an Ivy League type. Likes to wear aviator sunglasses, but when he doesn't, he likes to stare you in the eye and talk in a low monotone. Takes all that spook shit to a new level. Know what I mean?"

Martin nodded. He was certain the men knew Liegeman well, but they weren't going to say more than they already had. He had pushed his luck far enough. After thanking them, he walked back to his table.

———

Two days later Martin was at the Continental's streetside patio when his man showed up. The Green Berets' description was spot-on—Jungle Jim outfit with gold-rimmed aviators. The only thing missing was a safari hat and Tamba the chimp. After Liegeman was seated and had his first drink in hand, Martin walked to his table.

"Mr. Liegeman?"

Without raising his head, Liegeman removed the sunglasses and cut his ice blue eyes up at Martin.

"Who's asking?"

"My name is Martin Shadows. I'm an army intelligence officer and hoping you might help me find someone."

Liegeman curled his lip and stared down into his drink.

"Army intelligence—that's an oxymoron, isn't it?"

Despite the snarky remark, Martin effected a good-natured grin. "Depends on who's asking."

"State your business," Liegeman snapped. "I don't have time for bullshit."

Schizo was his first thought, and it was clear that "*nice*" wasn't going to work. With his patience fizzling on a short fuse, Martin tried again.

"Like I said, I'm looking for someone, a soldier."

"It's pretty pathetic when army intelligence needs help finding one of their own."

"Do you go armed, Sir?" Martin asked.

With a sarcastic devil-may-care air, Liegeman cocked his head to one side. "Should I?"

"With a mouth like yours, you should consider the option."

His face folded inward, and for the first time, Liegeman seemed uneasy as he pulled his hands to the edge of the table.

"If you're contemplating drawing a weapon, there's no need," Martin said. "I'm not carrying a firearm."

"Then state your business. I'm trying to relax and have a drink before dinner."

"I'm looking for someone named Sergeant Luis Ravera."

Listening to birds and observing wildlife back home in

Kentucky had given Martin an uncanny ability to recognize subtle nuances in animal behavior—something that worked equally well with humans. Liegeman hadn't blinked, but it was a forced thing. It was a sign where there was none, and his crystal blue eyes had betrayed him. He knew Ravera.

"And why in the world would you think I knew this—what did you say his name was, Ravera?"

"Because you do."

"Okay, I'll humor you. Let's just assume I do. What do you want with him?"

"We're friends. He saved my life, and I want to look him up and thank him."

"What did you say your name was, Shadow—something?"

"It's Martin Shadows. Do I need to write it down for you?"

Liegeman gripped his now empty glass as if he would crush it. His face reddened and the tendons on his neck grew rigid.

"Do you have any clue who you're fucking with?"

"I'm not fucking with anyone. I ask you about Sergeant Ravera, but if you're too paranoid to talk, maybe you can simply tell him I'm back in country and going up to Nha Trang to the Recondo School."

The waiter set another glass of whiskey in front of Liegeman. "Another double, Sir. May I get you anything else?"

Liegeman waved him away and killed the second glass of whiskey.

"I work for the Office of the Special Assistant, and since you claim to be army intelligence, I'm certain you must know we are the most powerful organization in the world. They pay me to be paranoid."

It was becoming clear that Liegeman wasn't going to tell him anything.

"Who sent you to me?" he asked.

"Had you shown me some respect, I might have answered your question, but I'm done talking. Good day."

Martin didn't return to his table but walked out to the street instead. As always, it was busy with traffic. When he reached the BOQ he was given an envelope. Inside were his orders. He was to report to Tan Son Nhut the following morning for a flight to Nha Trang. The orders came sooner than expected but were welcomed. He didn't care to cross paths again with Liegeman. If Sergeant Ravera was still in Nam, he would find him another way.

CHAPTER TWO

MAC-V Recondo School
Nha Trang, Republic of Vietnam

The C-130 Martin took to Nha Trang did one of those ten-thousand-foot spiraling nose dives into the airstrip to avoid ground fire. He wasn't quite sure why, except that it was SOP. After all, the view of the palms on the coastal islands and the sparkling emerald South China Sea was a helluva change from the ravages of war-torn Saigon. What appeared below looked more like paradise. MAC-V Recondo school was set in an idyllic location that looked more like Hawaii than Nam.

At ground level, the perception was immediately altered. The sandy dirt road leading up to the gate at the Recondo school was closer to reality. And the walled compound was laced with barbed wire. A Nung guard wearing tiger-striped fatigues and armed with a Thompson submachine gun waved the driver through. Martin already knew he was in for three weeks of intense jungle warfare training, and he was quickly coming to understand the C-130 pilot's nosedive for the airstrip was probably warranted.

The officer behind the desk was lean with a deeply burned-in tan. He may have been behind a desk, but he was no REMF.

Standing, he extended his hand. "Captain Lee Topper, 5th Special Forces training command. It's an honor to meet you, Shadows. We've been expecting you."

Martin was caught off guard. It had been a long time since he received such an amicable greeting.

"It's good to be here."

"Yeah, in case you're wondering we have someone on our training staff who's already told us a lot about you—Staff Sergeant Luis Ravera. He saw your name on the new candidate roster and shared some incredible stories with us."

"Sergeant Ravera, yeah, I owe him a lot."

"It sounds like he might owe you a lot as well. You can look him up tomorrow at orientation. Let's get your gear and get you to your quarters. You've got three tough weeks of training ahead."

At orientation the following morning Martin spotted Ravera. He was standing at the front of the classroom with several other training cadre, including Captain Topper. The sergeant had gained weight but was still lean and looked healthy again.

Martin filed in with the other students and took a seat at one of the wooden desks. Ravera saw him and walked his way. After flashing a quick salute, he extended his hand. "And you didn't even come up front to say hello."

Martin stood and shook his hand.

"I didn't want to make any assumptions—I mean being as I'm a student."

"Well, it's damned good to see you again, Sir. And I'm not sure what we can teach a man who escaped an NVA prison and crawled into an NVA basecamp to save some of his men."

Several students cast curious glances at them. Ravera glanced over his shoulder.

"I believe the CO is about ready to get started, but we need to drink a cold one and catch up on things when we have time."

Martin had heard rumors about MAC-V Recondo training. Sergeant Stoneman, who had been through the Ranger school at Benning, said it was the toughest three weeks he'd ever experienced. Martin assumed some of it was hyperbole, but the first day began at oh-four-thirty hours with a run of several miles while carrying a one-hundred-pound rucksack. The distance increased daily. Eighteen-hour days packed with classroom training were backed with intense hands-on experience, and the Special Forces cadre were excellent teachers with high standards.

Introduction to the McGuire and STABO extraction rigs was followed by ladder training under a hovering Huey. And while it wasn't quite the adrenaline rush he'd experienced sliding down the rope from the island prison, rappelling from the sixty-foot tower and later from a hovering helicopter didn't come without some degree of terror. He handled and fired every type of weapon the enemy employed, plus a few others the Special Forces Spike Teams preferred.

And after several days they choppered out to Hon Tre Island, five miles off the coast, where they learned patrolling techniques, ambush tactics, and quick reaction drills. The third week would be spent on an actual long-range patrol deep into enemy territory—the sort of final exam no one wanted to fail. Organized in six-man teams, they were to be accompanied by a training cadre member who would coach and grade them. Martin prepared his gear the afternoon before departure, while he and Ravera talked. It was the first time they had actually found more than a few minutes together.

"So, tell me, Sir, why in the world did you come back to Nam?" Ravera asked.

"Save the protocol for when we're around other troops, Luis. You can call me Martin or Shadows."

"Fair enough, but I think I'm dubbing you 'The Ghost.' I've heard that's what they're calling you up in I-Corps now, and if you don't mind, my call sign is Encore—got that tag after escaping that damned prison. And my question remains: why are you here?"

"I think it's for the same reason you didn't go home."

"Oh, really, and what do you think that is?"

"Let me ask you something first."

Martin began laying out his gear—rucksack, eight freeze-dried meals, three frags, three smokes, one willy peter, a claymore, eighteen magazines of ammo, pen flares, two canteens, purification tabs, heat tabs, poncho with liner, extra socks, extra camo grease, speed tabs, blood expander, LBE harness with ammo pouches, a CAR-15, and his K-bar.

"Do you know an OSA spook named Liegeman?"

Ravera's eyes grew wide, and he laughed aloud. "Did that clown interrogate you, too?"

"Not exactly, but when I mentioned your name to him a few days ago he started foaming at the mouth. What was that about?"

"Well, first of all, you need to put it in perspective. Liegeman and the spooks got their panties in a wad when MAC-V snatched the Phoenix Program away from them and put it under Army supervision. The top brass got tired of the bad press they were getting with stories of torture and arrests of innocent civilians. Then Project Gamma went sideways, and Liegeman and the spooks were implicated, along with our boys. Of course, the spooks claimed total innocence, and Liegeman blames anyone wearing a green beret—hates us all and MAC-V, too. There's more I could tell you about my involvement with Liegeman, but it's highly classified."

"I believe it. He acted like a twenty-four-karat asshole when I asked about you."

"So, you're saying they never interrogated you about our escape from the island or what happened to Colonel Linh or his Chinese buddy Chang?"

"No. After I filed my After-Action Report, I thought they would come back with questions, but it never happened. Why?"

"Did you mention Linh or Chang in the report?" Ravera asked.

"I said they both went overboard and escaped. That's it—nothing more."

"Ha! They must have thought we collaborated on our stories."

"Why?"

"Because I told them the same thing."

"And you think they believed you?"

"Oh, hell no! It was Liegeman and some CID REMF that kept tag-teaming me with questions, but I told them I was delirious and seasick most of the time and couldn't remember much."

"That was it? They left you alone after that?"

"Not exactly. They sent my men, Khonsu, Brau, Katu, and Guia to an old CIDG camp up near Phu Bai. It's run by the ARVNs, and they sent me down here to Nha Trang. I was going to get them into a program up at FOB-1, but I've been pretty much restricted to this base. Hell, rumor is they're gonna shut down the Recondo school and send us all back to Bragg. Anyway, God only knows what kind of treatment Khonsu and my guys are getting from the ARVNs. The South Vietnamese hate the Montagnards, you know? Hell, they might even be dead by now."

"I think not."

"How do you know?"

"This may sound a little crazy, but do you remember on the boat when we talked about our beliefs in spirits?"

"You made a believer out of me," Ravera said.

Martin began explaining to him about his vision and his grandfather's recent visions, and how they were his reason for returning to Nam. When he was done, Ravera seemed lost in thought as he stared out at nothing.

Martin began packing the rucksack. "My next duty station when I leave here is an ARVN firebase up near Phu Bai. I'm supposed to have a company of Montagnards reporting to me."

Ravera snapped from his trance.

"No shit?"

"No shit. I'll see if I can track them down when I get there."

"Look, I need to tell you something, but I want your word you won't repeat it. It's the classified incident I mentioned, but the reason I'm telling you is for your own protection."

"Okay, you have my word."

"The night I was captured with my men, we were involved in a bad situation. I was led to believe it was a well-planned prisoner snatch, but it resulted in a bunch of civilians being murdered by an ARVN outfit supporting us. That asshole Liegeman was the OSA special advisor in charge of the mission, but he was duped by a VC informant.

"It was a setup, and when the whole thing went sideways the Vietnamese colonel providing backup panicked and started killing people in the village. Liegeman had no idea we survived and were taken prisoner. We had been listed as missing in action until we escaped that prison. That's when he started trying to cover his tracks. He's the reason they split us up and sent Khonsu and the others up north.

"I'm telling you this because you mentioned Liegeman and my Montagnards together. I'm afraid for both you and them, and if I were you, I'd watch my back where Liegeman is involved. If he could, the sonofabitch would see that me and my Montagnards are killed, because of what we know about that night. I could tell you a lot more, but bottom-line is watch out for yourself and trust no one."

Later that night Martin lay on his cot thinking about what Ravera had said, and he wondered if this was related to his visions of helping the Montagnard peoples. It certainly seemed so. His tour of duty was taking a serious turn into the unknown, but he suddenly saw another figure there smiling at him. It was the second girl at the bar that night in Wolf Point.

She was a welcome memory, and he recalled when she walked up and stood beside him at the bar. Unlike the first girl, Emma Birdsong, this girl wasn't smiling. Blinking self-consciously, she glanced down, then up again as their eyes were drawn together in the mirror.

"I only wanted to come apologize for those guys' behavior. They're immature and bored—get their kicks messing around with folks. I'm Kania Miles."

Her hair was the color of caramel, but her eyes were dark brown, expressive, and revealed her Indian blood. Her beauty left him momentarily mesmerized, and he suddenly wished he hadn't drunk so much. Saying something intelligent was impossible as the sight of her left him dumbstruck. She was one of the most alluring women he had ever seen, and what little makeup she wore wasn't needed.

If only he could think of something special to say—he closed his eyes for a moment, but his head spun, and he steadied himself against the bar.

"Martin Shadows. Pleased to meet you, ma'am."

He hated himself. He sounded like the Lone Ranger and felt like an instant fool.

"So, you really *are* kin to Two Shadows?"

"Like I told your friends, he's my grandfather."

"They aren't my friends—just acquaintances of sorts. So, are you staying up at your grandfather's place?"

"Yeah, why?"

"Just asking."

Someone fed more quarters into the jukebox, and another slow love song began playing—the Casinos singing "You Can Tell Me Goodbye." It was one of his favorites, and Martin turned to look directly into her eyes—eyes that would make a fool out of any man, especially a drunk one.

"You wanna dance?"

He had never danced a lick in his life and immediately wished he hadn't asked. After all, it was taking every ounce of concentration he could muster just to stay on the barstool.

She laid her hand on his. "I'm assuming you've got a vehicle out in the parking lot, right?"

"Yeah, why?"

"Tell you what, promise me you'll save that dance for me another time, and I'll walk outside with you to get some fresh air. What do you say?"

He did little more than nod. She smiled.

"I pro-promise," he stuttered. "My next dance will be with you."

Martin's relief was only momentary as he slid off the stool and pulled his wallet from his jeans. The bartender stood patiently as he fumbled with several twenty-dollar bills. Squeezing his eyes shut, he tried to clear his head, but his fingers wouldn't cooperate. The girl gently took his wallet and glanced at the tab. She fished out a twenty, laid it on the bar, and handed him his wallet.

The cold night air was a relief of sorts, but Martin knew he was in no shape to drive. He pointed to his pickup, and she fished the keys from his pocket. After climbing in, he held his hand out for the keys.

"No, you move on over," she said. "I'm driving you home, but first, I have to go back inside and tell the girl I came here with to come pick me up at your grandfather's house."

It was a memorable night—one he wanted to believe was equally as important to her, but the question had returned too many times since: Why Kania? Why was she so important to him? Was it because he needed a girl to weep at his funeral? He didn't plan on dying, but any soldier would appreciate such a farewell—a beautiful woman sitting beside his mother, gazing through tear-glazed eyes at the Stars and Stripes draped over the casket while Taps echoed across a cemetery. But such weren't his thoughts. Kania was more—much more, but what was it about her? Why was she so important to him?

She had occupied his thoughts continuously since that night, but there was the haunting reality that their first meeting was likely no more to her than it was to most young women her age—an infatuating romantic adventure. And he wondered if that's what it was for him as well—a hormonally driven infatuation for the opposite sex. It didn't seem so, but going off to war did strange things to a man's mind.

———————

Early the following morning, Martin and five of his fellow Recondo trainees, along with Special Forces trainer Sergeant Sam Saber, were onboard a Huey flying over the Central Highlands. It was their Recondo School third-week baptism of fire—a four-to-six-day long-range reconnaissance patrol deep into enemy territory. The morning mists filled the valleys below and the rushing wind was cool as they sat in the doorway while the chopper dove earthward and skimmed the treetops, making several false insertions.

Saber had appointed Martin to begin the day as team leader, a position that would rotate to another student each day. The Huey's main rotor thundered as it again dropped into a tiny clearing on the side of a steep mountain ridge. This time the seven men jumped from the skids, and the chopper quickly climbed out and disappeared down the valley. The sudden silence was eerie.

Martin keyed the radio handset twice to signal the helicopter.

The chopper pilot replied, "Roger, Romeo Tango Two, I have you Lima Charlie. Good hunting. Out."

No one moved. Martin twirled his index finger, pointed at the designated point-man, then up the ridge. Silently, the point man moved out, followed by his slack man. Martin followed with the first radio, trailed by the Recondo school advisor and the remainder of the team. Everyone was on their game as the team moved with stealth.

Martin didn't exactly relish his "Ghost" label, but today he felt like one—moving as a phantom in the shadows. He inhaled deeply through his nostrils taking in the scent of the jungle and the crisp mountain air. No one wore insect repellent or anything that emitted an unnatural odor. Their faces were painted with green camo stick, and their equipment was taped for silence. Hand signals were used whenever possible. This was what guerrilla warfare was about, and though some were yet unproven, the men with him seemed confident.

Two hundred meters up the ridge he stopped the point man and signaled the team into a tight perimeter. There they waited and listened. Not a word was spoken, and not a sound was made. The minutes passed slowly as the jungle came back to life. Monkeys chattered on a ridge across a small valley, a parrot squawked, and birds began chirping. Sweat dripped down his face as Martin eyed his wristwatch. Nearly a quarter hour passed before he again motioned for the point man to begin moving on the predesignated azimuth. This time they turned west, paralleling the ridge.

They were deep in the heart of bad-guy territory, where there were no villages, no people, and supposedly no roads, but there were enemy trails, rutted and wide, snaking beneath the double- and triple-canopied jungle. These were avoided, except where they intersected. In the next valley five klicks away, intelligence reported that two main trails coming out of Cambodia virtually disappeared and air recon had failed to determine where they went. It could be they simply dispersed into numerous smaller trails, or it could be they led to a hidden enemy basecamp. As yet no one had penetrated far enough into the valley to determine the answer. Team Two's mission was to recon up the valley, searching for trails and possible river crossings.

By noon the team was perched on a rock precipice above the valley. Far below the trilling leaves sparkled in the sunlight, while high above them billowing towers of white cumulus climbed into an eternally blue sky. The haze normally encountered along the coast was absent, except along the farthest mountains on the horizon. It was views like this that sometimes made Martin forget he was in a war-torn country until he remembered that the beautiful blanket of greenery stretching away for miles hid thousands of enemy troops.

"What's your plan?" Sergeant Saber asked.

Martin unfolded his map and split his fingers to reference two different locations.

"These are where you said those two main trails come over the mountain from Cambodia and drop into the valley. Do you see anything similar about them?"

"Yeah, they both cross through saddles on the main ridge—easier to cross."

"That's true, but there are several more saddles. These two are different because they have streams flowing down to the river in the valley. Thus, the trees and other vegetation are heavier and hide the trails better. Now, follow the blue lines into the main valley. See how the streams provide extra heavy cover all the way down?"

Saber nodded. "Yeah, we pretty much know this, but the question is where do they go from there?"

"The theory has always been that the trails either split into several more or else come together and continue coming eastward somewhere up this ridge and on toward the coast. You said Recondo teams have searched for them for months, but I don't think they exist. I think the trails cross the river and intersect separately with a north-south trail somewhere on this mountainside below us. That way they can send men and supplies either north to I-Corps or south toward Saigon."

Saber cocked his head to one side and raised his eyebrows.

"All this time we've been looking for a trail coming eastward up this mountain. It's always seemed the obvious direction for them to come, but you're saying it doesn't exist. And your logic makes perfect sense. Why would the enemy do the obvious?"

"Exactly, and I want to take a look at the saddle to the north first. I think with all the activity that's been going on up in I-Corps that's likely where we'll find the most traffic."

"That's pretty good, Shadows. So, what's your next move?"

"I want to stay up high for now. Let's call in a sit-rep and give the TOC our location and destination. Hopefully they'll agree with our plan. Then we'll move north till we're across the valley from that saddle. We'll decide our next move when we get there."

"Sounds good. Brief your team and let's get moving."

By late afternoon the team lay in heavy cover waiting while Sergeant Saber studied the second saddle across the valley. He handed the binoculars to Martin.

"You look a while. S2 says it's there, but I don't see anything that looks like a road."

Martin lay prone and propped the binoculars on his rucksack. It was three or four kilometers across the valley, and the refracting heat waves shimmered against the distant slope. He studied the heavier vegetation along the stream—glassing it carefully all the way down to the base of the mountain. The strong winds swirled in the distant treetops creating momentary openings that quickly closed. Drifting shadows from the clouds added to the visual distractions. He was about to give up when a copse of trees near the base of the mountain suddenly bent and swirled about, creating an opening which quickly disappeared.

What he had seen was little more than a snapshot glimpse of what appeared to be rocks stacked in the streambed. Rock outcroppings were scattered up and down the valley, but these stones seemed to be stacked in an orderly manner, perhaps as a culvert or low-water bridge crossing the stream. He lowered the binoculars and squinted.

"See something?" Saber whispered.

"Maybe. The wind separated the trees down there and for a moment I thought I saw a bunch of stones stacked across that stream—didn't look natural."

"What's your plan?"

"I say, while we're still up high here, we scan the valley for a couple of possible extraction points, mark them on the map and call them in to the TOC with our next sit-rep. At dusk we'll ease down and set up our NDP somewhere below. After daylight, we can recon along the river to see if we can find where they're crossing."

Saber gazed out across the valley.

"Sounds like a good plan, but I'd also request flyovers every two hours tomorrow. Once we get down into that valley, we're going to need them for radio contact with the TOC."

"I thought this was a training mission," a young lieutenant said.

"It is," Saber answered, "but like we told you a couple weeks ago, we aren't testing you. We're letting you show us you can do the job. Are you up for it?"

Lieutenant Gainer looked like a rosy-cheeked frat-boy, but he'd been an infantry platoon leader for six months and wouldn't have been allowed in Recondo school without some decent creds.

"I'm in," he said. "I just didn't realize we would—" he paused.

"Poke our head into the lion's den?" Saber said.

Gainer laughed. "Yeah, I suppose."

"No problem. I'm not going to let us do anything stupid. We'll recon a day or two and get the hell out of Dodge."

CHAPTER THREE

Recondo, The Final Exam
A Mountain Valley on the Cambodian Border

Martin decided the Greek god of war Ares was either severely pissed off at the little reconnaissance team or else was giving them a full-on pass-fail final exam. Right after dark Ares teased them with the distant sounds of squeaking brakes and rumbling tires coming from the other side of the valley. The team lay in a tight circle, straining to hear and attempting to count what sounded like heavy trucks coming down the far mountainside. Except there was something missing. There were no sounds coming from their engines.

"What's that about?" Martin whispered.

"I heard them do that sort of thing once before," Saber answered. "It took me a while to figure it out, but they're coasting downhill to save fuel. Their engines aren't running. When they get lower on the mountain, they'll need them. You'll see."

And a few minutes later a motor rumbled to life, and the LRRP team began counting as each vehicle reached that point and the driver cranked its engine. The night air had grown still, and the sky was clotted with high clouds moving in overhead. Beyond the far horizon somewhere in the mountains of Cambodia the reflection of bright flashes lit the night sky—Arc Light strikes, Martin figured—high level bombing of supply routes by flights of B-52 Stratofortresses. Flying thirty thousand feet above the jungle, their jet engines were never heard. You never heard anything until the earth shook under your feet and the jungle exploded in thundering devastation, leaving pond-size craters, piles of broken and shredded timber, and a mile-long swath of almost demonic destruction where nothing survived.

"Looks like we're in for some rain," Saber whispered.

"Rain?"

"Don't you see that lightning reflecting out there?"

"I thought it might be an Arc Light strike."

"If that was the case, they'd be closer, bombing along the Ho Chi Minh trail, and we'd hear them. I think it's thunderstorms, but they're still a long way off."

Saber, like the other Recondo instructors, was Army Special Forces with extensive jungle warfare experience. He knew his craft. The team slept in snatches until sometime after midnight when a crack of lightning had them all pulling ponchos over their heads. The hair on Martin's arms tingled with static electricity as another deafening lightning bolt struck nearby. The crack and pop of lightning across the mountain became so intense, until a barrage of 120-millimeter rockets couldn't have been much worse.

The wind came next, followed by the rain—a monstrous downpour that blotted out everything and flowed around them in gushing torrents running down the mountainside. There was no staying dry, and by the first graying of dawn, the team huddled together, soaked to the bone, shivering, and spooning down cold lurp rations. A heavy fog shrouded the dripping vegetation, its thick mist hiding everything beyond five meters.

"Well, men, it's a beautiful day in the Nam," Saber whispered, "and our first flyover is scheduled to occur in thirty minutes, but I doubt that's going to happen. The Birddogs won't fly in these mountains with this kind of cloud cover."

"So, what are we going to do?" Lieutenant Gainer asked.

"Nothing. We're going to lay dog and wait for the weather to break. We change team leaders today, and I want you to take over, Lieutenant."

Gainer shrugged. "Not much leading to be done today."

"That's okay, Sir. You never know what might come up later."

Martin realized Saber hadn't made a random choice. The lieutenant had shown some anxiety and lack of confidence. That didn't make him a bad soldier or necessarily one to be discounted from Recondo duties, but perhaps one who needed more seasoning. Assigning him team leader on a day with no particularly critical decisions to make would likely benefit both him and the team. A while later there came a new sound from down in the valley—the metal-on-metal squeaking clank of tracked vehicles.

"Is that tanks?" the lieutenant asked.

Martin sat listening as Gainer and Saber talked.

"That's about the only tracked vehicle the NVA will bring this far south. They used them at Lang Vei. They're taking advantage of this cloud cover to move them. How many do you hear?"

"Hard to tell," Gainer said.

The fog hid everything, but the distant whine of the engines grew louder as they came across the valley floor. They were still at least two klicks away.

"Listen for a pattern. Every once in a while they sound like they're really straining."

"Yeah, I hear it," Gainer answered.

"That's where they're crossing the river," Saber said. He turned to Martin. "You agree, Ghost?"

"I agree."

The radio handset hissed quietly as it broke static. Gainer picked it up and keyed the mic. "Bravo Delta One-Niner, this is Romeo Tango Two, Over."

"Roger, Bravo Delta One Niner, location remains same as previous. We have identified by sound approximately twelve motorized vehicles and three additional tracked vehicles, location from Papa Oscar Romeo Juliet three, up four...."

The lieutenant continued the situation report, identifying the two alternate extraction points. When he was done, the Birddog pilot told him to standby. From high overhead came the faint buzz of the spotter plane. He was likely flying at ten or twelve thousand feet, staying above the cloud bank.

A couple minutes later Gainer again held the handset close to his ear and communicated with the spotter plane.

"He says the TOC wants us to relocate up the valley three clicks north of here."

"Well, crap. They must know something we don't. Did you forget anything?" Saber asked.

The young lieutenant stared blank-faced at the trainer.

"I figure I must have, or you wouldn't be asking."

"If they're telling us to relocate, they must figure this ground fog is about to break up. Ask him for a weather update."

The forecast from the TOC was for the cloud bank to move off the AO before noon, leaving moderately good weather for the next two or three days. Martin glanced at his watch. It was only oh-eight-hundred hours when Lieutenant Gainer put him on point and signaled the team to move out. Saber said nothing. Perhaps he was simply following orders, but stumbling about in a mountain fog was an easy way to get yourself killed. As point man, it was now on his shoulders, and Martin shot an azimuth, but without any visible landmarks, it was an exercise in futility. By going neither up nor downhill, he hoped to use the terrain to walk a relatively straight line.

Walking slack behind him was Sergeant Junior Mansfield, and following Junior was the current team leader, Lieutenant Gainer, or so Martin hoped, because Gainer and the rest of the team to his rear were invisible in the thick fog. He led the team slowly and deliberately for nearly two hours, using his ears and sense of smell as much as he did his eyes. After a while the fog thinned ever so slightly, and he could see nearly twenty meters before everything became lost in the misty shadows. He glanced back. Most of the team members were now visible.

It was time for the next flyover when Martin spotted movement barely twenty-five meters ahead. He froze as did his slack man. The others in the column behind him stopped only at the last moment. Gainer and Saber were only a few meters to his rear. One by one the shadowy silhouettes of enemy soldiers wearing pith helmets crossed to their front. Standing fully exposed, Martin moved only his thumb against the CAR-15's receiver and pushed the selector switch to auto.

He had counted thirty-six men when there came the buzz of the Birddog aircraft, this time sounding like it was considerably lower. The enemy leaders began calling muffled commands, which were followed by the sucking sound of boots in the mud and the rustling of vegetation as they took cover all around Martin and the recon team. It was a gamble, but Martin turned and signaled for the team to take cover as well, as shadowy groups of enemy soldiers dove to the ground on the surrounding hillside.

The quiet voices of excited enemy soldiers came from all around, some barely ten meters away. Martin reached into the lieutenant's rucksack and switched off the radio. Even though the radio handset was barely audible when held close, he was taking no chances. Saber gave a barely detectable nod of approval. The little spotter aircraft circled over the mountainside for several minutes before drifting off to the north.

Another quarter-hour dragged agonizingly by before an enemy soldier somewhere in the fog barked a command and the NVA troops began reassembling. More shadows appeared around the team, but none seemed to notice as they moved rapidly toward an apparent trail. Saber reached into Gainer's rucksack, switched on the radio, and slowly broke squelch three times. This was the signal to indicate close contact without speaking. It was normally used for just such circumstances.

The team waited. It had been twenty minutes since they last heard the spotter aircraft, and the enemy had begun moving again. Before the last of them passed, Martin counted a hundred and fifty soldiers. The recon team remained in place. No one moved, and after a while the surrounding jungle again grew quiet and still. An occasional bird called, and the monotonous dripping sound of the vegetation again became noticeable. Saber and Gainer crawled up beside Martin. It had been nearly an hour without further movement.

"How about you and me ease up there and take a look at that trail?" Saber said.

Apparently class-time was on hold. Martin nodded and they crept ahead to find what looked more like a well-traveled road. Fresh wheel ruts indicated the enemy had non-motorized wheeled weapons and carts likely containing ammunition. As predicted, the fog was now dissipating, and Saber motioned for Martin to follow him back to the team, but there came sounds of boots sucking mud from just down the trail. The two men froze in place as an NVA soldier with an AK-47 slung across his back came trotting up the road.

Spotting them, the soldier waved and continued toward them, apparently mistaking them for his own people. With an entire NVA company having just passed, shooting the soldier was out of the question. Martin handed Saber his CAR-15 and lunged as the man realized too late they weren't his friends. Clamping a palm over his mouth, he wrestled him to the ground and pushed a knee into his back while Saber quickly stuffed a field dressing in the soldier's mouth. After tying his hands behind his back, they led him back to the team and searched through a courier pouch he was carrying. Inside was a map, a firebase drawing, and several more documents.

"Holy shit!" Saber muttered. "I recognize this firebase. It's one of our Special Forces outposts several klicks north of here. And look at this." He pointed to three small squares with arrows leading into the firebase. "These are tanks. The bastards are going for a repeat of Lang Vei. We need to call for extraction and get these documents to our S2 shop ASAP."

"We know the ground behind us was clear," the lieutenant said. "I suggest we move back toward our original planned extraction point."

"I concur," Martin said, "and I think we should move to the top of this ridge before we head south. We can make better time that way."

"Okay, but this guy is a courier and I'm betting they'll come looking for him," Saber said. "We've got to make some good time and put down powdered CS on our back trail."

Junior pulled a can of powdered CS from his rucksack. "I have us covered. I'll walk drag."

"Let's get the hell outta Dodge," Saber whispered. "Lead out, Ghost."

Martin glanced at his watch. It would be dark in six hours.

By mid-afternoon the Birddog returned, and the team notified him of their request for extraction. The TOC wanted a reason, and Saber responded with code Medusa.

"That'll get their attention," he said. "Means we can't transmit in the open because we've opened a can of snakes."

By dusk they arrived at the extraction point, and the choppers were inbound. Thirty minutes earlier they heard the painful squalls of a tracker dog apparently after it snorted a nose full of CS powder. The NVA had been tracking them and were within a thousand meters as the first Hueys thundered in and settled on the LZ. A thin line of green tracers arced across the ridgetop. The enemy was too far away and merely shooting in the direction of the LZ—a bad mistake. A Cobra gunship shot past overhead as it released a salvo of rockets.

It was dark when they landed at Nha Trang. Standing beside a jeep were a colonel and sergeant major. The team stooped and ran to the edge of the chopper pad, where they squatted and waited while the choppers hovered down the airstrip to their sandbagged revetments. Saber slapped the courier's canvas bag across Martin's belly.

"You captured it. You deliver it to the colonel and tell him what we got."

"But—"

"As you know, Captain, there's no rank on our teams, except for the acting team leader and the instructor. Take the bag to the colonel."

After the Recondo graduation ceremony, Martin joined a gathering of students and training cadre sitting under a palm bough cabana on the beach. An onshore breeze made for a comfortable day while the men drank beer and cooked steaks over an open grill. He and Luis Ravera were sitting in beat-up aluminum lawn chairs staring out at the beautiful South China Sea. Martin shook a cigarette from his pack.

"You want one?"

Ravera laughed.

"You Indians are always wanting someone to smoke a pipe or something. Yeah, give me one."

Martin flipped open his Zippo and lit the cigarette. He handed it to Ravera.

"I'm only half Lakota. A full-blooded Indian would have offered you peyote or maybe some special prairie weed."

"That might be pretty good about now—help me forget about the coming shitshow."

"What do you mean?"

"Well, you do realize the government is giving up on this war, right? We're turning it over to the South Vietnamese. Once all our troops pull out, I figure the South Vietnamese will last maybe three or four years at best. And yet we're still here training men like you and plugging them into the breach. Doesn't make much sense."

"Yeah, I know. So, what do you think they're up to?"

"There's all sorts of scuttlebutt floating around, but I think the idiots in Washington are still micromanaging the war with a crap game mentality."

"I'm not sure I know what you mean."

"That's just it. It doesn't mean anything. They're like a chimpanzee with a half-loaded revolver—never knowing when it's gonna go off, but they keep pulling the trigger."

"Hey!" a voice came from back at the cabana. It was Sergeant Saber. "Are you two going to eat a steak with us?"

"On the way," Ravera shouted.

There was more Martin wanted to talk about, but Ravera seemed reluctant.

"Maybe we can talk later," Martin said. "I think there's more you can tell me."

"Let's go eat a steak and forget about this shit for a while."

And it was clear the Special Forces Sergeant had said all he was going to say. That's the way it was with this war—dark ops stories with no endings, unfinished missions, unfulfilled expectations, and the unrealized dreams of those who would never go home.

CHAPTER FOUR

Into The Breach
Phu Bai, Republic of Vietnam

The camouflage painted C-130 dove steeply through the clouds to the runway at Phu Bai, and when the ramp was lowered, Martin felt an instant difference. Unlike the blazing heat back in Saigon and Nha Trang, the air here was cool and damp, and a light mist was falling. By late afternoon he had found his way to a compound guarded by American MPs. The mist had stopped falling, but there was no breeze to stir the thick blanket of humidity. They pointed out his destination.

Colonel Duggin's office was one of several located in a fairly large concrete building surrounded by a cinderblock wall topped with concertina. There was no signage, only the Stars and Stripes and the red and yellow Republic of Vietnam flag hanging limply from poles at the front of the building. With the help of another MP at the building entrance, he found the colonel's office.

Duggin was all business but infinitely more respectful than Ramseld. He returned Martin's salute and invited him to take a seat.

"So, Captain Shadows, how did you end up here in my unit?"

Martin bit his lower lip. The colonel's question was ambiguous, and his tone was loaded with innuendo. It seemed Krieger and Ramseld had forewarned everyone in Nam about him.

"I'm not sure what you're asking me, Sir. This is the unit my orders say I'm assigned to."

"I'll cut to the chase, Captain Shadows. MAC-V has been assigning men and officers to my unit because most have somehow managed to piss off a superior. I've been studying your records, but I can't make heads or tails out of them. They're redacted to hell and back, and you've got an Officer Evaluation Report that's pretty damned good. You've also received some of the highest decorations this army awards its men, and they're accompanied by some damned incredible descriptions of valor."

The colonel glanced up at him, but Martin remained silent.

"And then there's this investigative report that reads like some sort of spy novel, except it's so heavily redacted, I can't figure why they even bothered to put it in your file. Most of the AARs read the same way. So, who the hell are you and who did you piss off?"

Major Ramseld had made it clear that much of Martin's army record was considered classified and to be shared with no one outside of MAC-V. It would be poor form to avoid his new commander's questions, but he had to be careful with what he said.

"A few days before I departed Saigon, Colonel Krieger had his adjutant brief me. He said that much of what I was involved with during my previous tour is still considered highly classified. I don't mind telling you what I can, but I don't want to violate the Military Code of Conduct."

"Were you associated with the Phoenix Program or the Gamma Project, Captain? They've really got their stingers out for those boys."

"No Sir. My involvement was strictly with an Army Intelligence operation."

The colonel nodded slowly.

"Yes, an obviously classified one, and it involved no one from the Office of the Special Assistant or the Vietnamese Government or their army, right?"

"As far as I know, Sir, my original mission did not directly involve any of those entities."

The colonel's lips turned down at the corners, and he squinted one eye. It was clear he was frustrated and believed Martin was withholding information.

"As best as I can decipher from your records, you were a POW and you managed to escape and free other POWs. Something happened during that operation, but it's redacted. So, what *can* you tell me?"

"Both statements are true, Sir."

The colonel's face grew purple as the veins on his forehead bulged. After a few moments he seemed to calm himself and took a deep breath.

"I understand your reluctance to say more, Captain, but you may need to trust me at some point. We will leave it there for now. Here's what I know. Your MOS is Army Intelligence, and you were trained at Fort Holabird. You also recently finished Recondo training. That much I can decipher from your file. I'll work forward from there. Do you know anything about this unit to which you're assigned?"

"No Sir, only that Colonel Krieger alluded to it as a recon outfit."

"Well, I'm going to share a lot more with you than you have with me. You're taking command of a group of bastards—boonie bastards for the most part. I suppose you could say they're my 'leper colony' and I'm their General Savage. But don't get me wrong—these are some damned fine soldiers. Most of them came out of SOG. They're all decorated, and they know how to fight.

"It's just that the current leadership at MAC-V has little use for them because of their past involvement in certain situations involving special ops. The new commander at MAC-V is trying to clean up the army's image and is currently at odds with Special Forces and any specialized units outside of the Army Rangers. If a Green Beret or any other soldier gets sideways with MAC-V for any reason, he is sent here where it's my job to keep him out of trouble until his DEROS.

"About two weeks ago, the outfit you're assigned to was caught in a major firefight and overrun by NVA regulars. The company commander and two other advisors were killed in action and three others were wounded. The temporary acting commander is a Lieutenant Postiche. He wrote the AAR, and reports unit morale is not very good, especially among the Montagnards. The lieutenant also said some of the Montagnards ran away during the engagement. I'm not sure about that. That group has been one of the best we've had in I-Corps. so you will have to get in there, determine the issues, and rebuild that team.

"All the Montagnard troops will be under your direct command. They were an old Provincial Reconnaissance Unit and now live in a relocation camp southwest of the ARVN firebase. The Yards are some damned good soldiers, so I'm not sure why they ran, or if in fact they did. Several of them worked with our Special Forces down at Chu Lai before being placed under ARVN control and have been extremely loyal. I just don't think running is in their blood.

"Our primary mission involves supporting ARVN line units mostly in advisory and reconnaissance support roles. Your group works closely with one of the Ranger units. Their CO is Captain Truong. He's a good man and a competent leader. His Ranger

Company and four ARVN armored cav companies make up the battalion to which you'll be attached. The battalion commander is Colonel Pham. He's somewhat of a pompous ass, but I'll leave it at that. You can make up your own mind about him. Questions?"

"Where are my advisors billeted?"

"You and your men will be billeted on the ARVN firebase with the Ranger company."

"I'm assuming my ARVN counterpart is fluent in English, correct?"

"You were at Holabird. Are you telling me you don't speak Vietnamese?"

"Studied culture, customs, history, and some phraseology, but that's it."

"Figures. Well, you're not the first. It happens that your counterpart, the ranger CO Captain Truong speaks English, but I'd brush up on the phraseology every chance you get. You'll need it."

"Will do, Sir."

"Your unit works out of the ARVN firebase. It's south of here a few klicks west of Highway One. You'll catch a chopper out of here first thing in the morning. We have some bunks available, and you'll spend the night here on the compound. I'd advise you to stay out of town."

The following morning Martin rode a chopper southward to a sprawling ARVN firebase west of Highway 1. He planned to meet with his men and the Vietnamese Rangers first thing after arriving. At an airstrip outside the firebase, he met his Vietnamese counterpart Captain Thuan Truong, the ARVN Ranger company commander. As they drove up a berm and through the main gate at the firebase they were met with lethargic salutes and surly stares from the ARVN sentries. These guys' give-a-shit meters were hovering near zero, but the stern-faced Captain Truong returned a rigid military salute.

After driving further into the firebase, Truong stopped the jeep at a second gate. Extending from either side of this gate were rolls of concertina wire that surrounded an array of sandbagged Quonset huts and other small buildings and bunkers. It seemed to be a base within the base. The guards here came to attention and delivered snappy salutes which Truong returned.

"This is our compound," Captain Truong said. "Only your advisors and my Rangers are permitted inside these gates."

"So, this is where the battalion command and control center is located?"

"No. Everything else around you is the battalion commander Colonel Pham's compound. This wire is only meant to keep others from coming into our area."

It seemed odd the Ranger unit was segregated from their own ARVN line troops, but more questions seemed imprudent for the moment. Martin nodded and remained silent.

"I will have your men assemble in formation with mine for your introduction, Captain Shadows."

"My PRU troops are billeted here as well?"

"No Sir. The Montagnard stay in their own village five kilometers from here. It is one of the old CIDG camps, but they are now under Colonel Pham's authority."

Truong had remained reserved since their introduction, something not necessarily unusual for the Vietnamese nor for a meeting with a new counterpart. Martin realized it would take time to gain his respect. This man had likely been fighting the Communists since he was a child and probably knew a whole lot more about war than he did.

"Uh, Captain, after we meet with our men together, is there

someplace I can gather with my advisors and get to know them?"

Truong remained pokerfaced and nodded. "I will show you a place with some shade."

Truong was a young man, early thirties at best. His face was smooth and without scars or signs of injury. His eyes though said he was a combat veteran. Still, Martin couldn't help but wonder if he was just another political appointee—one who had gotten a job for which he had no real qualifications. After all, commander of a Vietnamese Ranger company was likely a golden stepping-stone to bigger and better things in his army. Time would soon tell.

As they assembled, a skinny and sunburned American Sergeant First-Class stepped up, saluted, and introduced himself. His rip-stop jungle fatigues had more repairs than a Raggedy Ann doll and his jungle boots were worn to raw leather. Despite the wear and tear on his uniform he stood with a rigid military bearing.

"Sergeant First Class Gautier, reporting, Sir. I'm the unit First Sergeant. All the men are present and accounted for."

Martin returned his salute. "Pleasure to meet you, First Sergeant. I'll be needing your help to guide me through this liaison advisory role."

"Will do, Sir. We usually let Captain Truong tell us what's needed and plan our missions from there."

Truong had one of his lieutenants call the troops to attention. There were fewer than a hundred of them and only fourteen American advisors—slim numbers for what was supposed to be an entire company.

Truong turned to him. "While you speak to my Rangers, Captain, I will translate if you wish."

"Is this your entire company and all of my advisors?"

"You have three men in the hospital at Phu Bai. They should return any day, but we lost thirty-one other men two weeks ago.

Three of them were Americans. One was your predecessor—Captain Watson. He was a good officer. We lost eight Rangers and twenty of your Montagnard tribesmen. Your Montagnard reconnaissance group now numbers less than sixty men."

And this, perhaps, was the hinge pin on which hung the somber, if not surly demeanors of the men before him. They had been through hell. The American advisors and the Vietnamese Rangers stood in grim silence. There was a lot of work to be done.

"Thanks, Captain. We'll talk more later. Let's get started." He turned to the troops. "At ease, men. My name is Captain Martin Shadows. I am not here to chan—"

Truong began translating, and after a brief pause, Martin continued.

"I am not here to change what you are already doing, nor am I here to make a name for myself. I am here to join with you, to learn from you, and to accomplish our mission jointly along with our PRU troops. I intend to do this without undue risk. I've already been informed by Colonel Duggins that you all have extensive combat experience, and that you are some of the best fighters this war has produced."

He paused while Truong seemed to struggle with the translation. A ripple of murmurs flowed across the formation. He'd hit on a sore spot—but what was it? It was time to shut up and listen. Saying too much could lead him into a verbal minefield.

"I am not a man to talk a lot, so I'll say simply this: I am proud to be working with you Vietnamese Rangers and with you, my American advisors, and I hope we can continue working jointly to accomplish our mission. Right now, the advisors and I are going to relax and get to know one another better."

Martin turned to Truong and thanked him. Ten minutes later Truong showed them to the scraggly remains of several artillery-wrecked trees.

"I'm figuring shade must be a scarcity around here," Martin said, gazing up at the mangled tree limbs.

"It is the best I can do, Captain."

"No worries, Captain. I wouldn't want my men to think I'm going to spoil them."

A ripple of cynical laughs passed through the group.

"This is strictly informal, men. Smoke 'em if you got 'em. I'm going to ask some questions. When I call on you, I'd like for you to introduce yourself with your name, rank, time in country, and your previous unit. You can also tell me where you're from back in the world if you want."

Martin studied the group. There was one first lieutenant and two Specialist Fourth Class soldiers. The rest were NCOs of various ranks.

"Men, what we say here, stays here. That doesn't mean I won't judge you by it. It simply means whatever you say doesn't go beyond me. I want to know what you're thinking. I want the truth, not some bullshit song and dance about duty, honor, and apple pie. You have my permission to speak freely. I want to know what's bugging you. I won't promise you the moon, but I will listen."

Several men traded clandestine stares.

"Each of us has a mission here. I want to know yours. Lieutenant, what's your mission?"

The young officer looked as if he'd been slapped in the face.

"Uh, sir, my mission is to…." He paused. The only sound was that of a slight breeze rattling the dead leaves overhead. "Lieutenant Mason Postiche, 1st Cavalry Division. I've been in-country six months. My mission is to follow your orders, finish my assignment, and go back to Sai…uh…home."

He raised his chin and stared directly into Martin's eyes. This guy was odd. He hadn't made eye contact until he was finished talking, and "finish my assignment" wasn't a term combat officers normally used.

"Thanks, LT."

He pointed to a staff sergeant, another lean man with intense eyes who appeared to be Hispanic.

"What's your mission, Sergeant?"

"Sergeant Lugo, 75th Rangers. Two months into my second tour. My mission is to teach these boys how to avoid getting their asses greased in this worthless shitshow of a war, Sir."

"Thank you, Sergeant Lugo. I appreciate your frankness."

Martin didn't want to be pushy, but getting these men to say much of anything was going to take more than this first shuck and jive session.

"Might as well go for three out of three," he muttered under his breath.

He pointed to a soldier who didn't look a day over sixteen years old—except for those eyes. They were staring past him at something a million miles away. "You there, Specialist, what's your mission?"

The young soldier's eyes never focused as he spoke. "Spec-4 Thibodaux, Sir. They call me T-Bo. I'm from Lafayette, Louisiana. I was with the 4th Infantry up near Pleiku before my platoon got wiped out. Then they sent me to a recon outfit. Hell, I don't know. I reckon maybe my mission is to survive the rest of this war with my nuts, arms, and legs in the same place they was when I got here by not taking orders from idiots."

"That's enough, Thibodaux!" Sergeant Gautier said.

Martin raised his hand. "No, First Sergeant. Let him speak. I want these men to tell me what's on their minds, and I want to hear what this man has to say. Tell me about these idiots, Specialist."

T-Bo seemed struck with a sudden case of lockjaw. His eyes remained unfocused as the group's silence became paralyzing and begging for someone's intervention.

"It's okay. Say what you're thinking. Whether or not I agree with you, I won't hold it against you. Tell me about the idiots."

"Sir, no disrespect intended, but it's the dumbass officers who order us to do stupid shit that gets us blown away when it wasn't never necessary in the first place. It's this damned army that don't want to win the war. They're just making us go through the motions, and for what? I think those hippie fuckers back home got it right."

"I appreciate your honesty, T-Bo. You say that's what they call you?"

"Yes, Sir."

Martin turned to another sergeant sitting at his feet.

"Sergeant, why do you think Specialist T-Bo feels this way?"

"Sergeant Zeke Anderson, Sir. Second Special Forces, FOB-1, Phu Bai. I go by Bushmaster, and this is my third tour. I got sent to this outfit 'cause they said I killed an enemy prisoner. What I did was kill an armed VC who had just executed some innocent village elders. My team and my CO stood with me, but here I am.

"I'm from south Alabama. I reckon the specialist feels that way because we cycle men through here like pawns on a checkerboard. And it seems sometimes the politicians back in Washington don't really give a shit how many of them are dying. So, what if some of us are WIA or KIA? As long as they have their dumbass body-count showing the gooks are losing more men than we are, they act like that's all that matters."

"What do you mean, Sergeant?"

Martin wanted to hear more of what the sergeant had to say.

"Where are you from, Sir?"

"Kentucky. Why?"

"Well, like I said, I'm from Alabama, and we've got these little bitty bastards down there called fire ants. There's thousands and thousands of them everywhere. They build these big mounds, and after one bites you, somebody can ask you if you'd rather have a lighted match stuck up your ass, and you'll choose the match every time. We burn off entire pastures thinking we've killed them, but they go to building new mounds the next day because they live deep in the ground. You see, we've been over here for years killin' fire ants a few at a time, and every time we kill a few dozen, hundreds more come up out of the ground the next night."

"Damned good point, Sergeant. Thank you."

Martin lit a cigarette and gazed at his group of advisors. Every eye was on him. He was surrounded by men who were jungle warfare experts, men with combat experience, and he'd apparently gotten their attention. These were good soldiers—severely demoralized perhaps—but competent. The only one who didn't quite seem to fit was Lieutenant Postiche. He was somewhat of an anomaly—not easily pegged and perhaps not totally honest. There was something about him that set those little subconscious red flags to waving.

"Men, I appreciate your honesty. Just so you know, I've already seen some bad things during my first tour here in the Nam, and I wish I had more time today to talk with you, but I have to keep moving. It's clear we have a morale problem, and I'll do my damnedest to get a better understanding of the things you've said here this morning. My door is open to any of you anytime you need to see me. In the meantime, I'll try to avoid becoming one of Specialists Thibodaux's idiots.

"Give First Sergeant Gautier a list of your needs, including uniform parts, gear, and anything else you may want—short of an early-out. Just don't hold me to getting it overnight. I'll do what I can. For now, I want you to go back to your hooches, make sure they're clean and ready for inspection. The same goes for your weapons and gear. Have them laid out on your cots.

"As I said, the unit HQ hooch remains open anytime you need

to meet with me. Just clear it through First Sergeant Gautier to make sure I'm available. My inspection will be this afternoon before chow. And don't worry, I won't chickenshit you on things that don't matter—only things that can make you sick or get you killed. I want your quarters to be clean and sanitary. I want your gear clean and functional. Other than that, I don't think *Playboy* centerfolds and such will get you killed."

A less cynical ripple of laughter crossed through the group.

"Uh, Sir. Can I say something?"

Another soldier raised his hand.

"You sure can, troop. What's your name and what unit were you with before you got here?"

"Uh, well, Sir. Yeah. So, I know I'm supposed to say something intelligent here, but I just want to second what our men are saying."

Martin studied him. He was lean, wore a green bandanna around his head, and his faded fatigues were well beyond worn. His matted hair was also beyond regulation, but he had the green eyes of a cat. This was a warrior, what the men called a Boonie Rat. Despite his catlike eyes, he seemed focused on something deep within himself or perhaps it was far beyond the horizon—something perhaps only he could see.

"You look like a soldier with a lot of experience, and I want to hear what you have to say."

"Yes Sir. So, here it is. Everybody is tiptoeing around the real problem, like they're afraid to speak up. Me, I don't give a flying fuck."

"Before you continue, give me your name, rank, and your previous unit."

"Sergeant Whit Porterfield. They call me Sky Soldier 'cause I was with the 173rd Airborne in '67, and later with the 101st. I worked mostly with long range recon teams when I was with the Hundred and First. Sir, this is my third tour of duty, and I'm willing to fight with these men who are stuck here like me till our tours are up, but I'm not charging up any more hills. I did that in '67 on Hill 875 at Dak To and again in '69 on Hamburger Hill with the Hundred and First.

"We lost a lot of good men and gave both hills back to the enemy within days. That's why I'm here now. I got sick of the shit and requested a 1049. We're wasting a lot of men's lives for what? The army doesn't want to win, and far as I can tell, they never have.

"The colonels make us attack fortified enemy positions on these hills and our men get shot to shit. Then we walk away and let the NVA have them back. And the South Vietnamese Army won't fight. They showboat around and shoot up their own villages, then run when the real shit hits the fan. I'll admit the Vietnamese Rangers we're working with here are tough bastards, and they know their shit. I like them, but the ARVN line companies on this firebase are pussies. They run at the sound of a firecracker. That's what happened to Captain Watson, Boogie, and Gomer, and a bunch of our Yards. They got hung out to dry. Now, that's the damned truth."

He paused and for a moment there was silence broken only by the rhythmic thump of a Huey passing somewhere in the distance.

"I read you loud and clear, Sergeant Porterfield, and I believe you are speaking about something I intend to address. I've been told by our battalion commander, Colonel Duggin, that our mission here is advisory and recon, and I intend to keep it that way, but I'm going to find out why the ARVN troops did not come to the aid of our men that day. All I ask of you experienced NCOs is that you keep me from making mistakes that needlessly risk the lives of our men."

The soldiers sat in stony silence.

"Men, I'm not going to blow smoke up your ass and promise

you free bubble-up and rainbow pie, but I can assure you that whatever we do, I will be at the front leading you."

Martin turned to the company first sergeant.

"First Sergeant Gautier, I'm meeting with Captain Truong for the next few hours. Tomorrow, I'm going to visit our Montagnard troops at their camp. After that, I want to meet with you and the senior NCOs to discuss these and more of your concerns. I also want an update on our hospitalized men. I have to go now. After you get a list of uniform and equipment needs, you can dismiss the men."

"How did your meeting with your men go, Captain?" Truong asked.

"Morale is rock-bottom, Captain, and I'm hoping you can tell me more about the incident that caused it."

The Vietnamese Ranger captain shook a Salem menthol from a pack and offered one to Martin.

"Thanks, but I'll pass. I prefer these."

Martin took a pack of unfiltered Camels from his shirt pocket and shook one out. Truong lit his Salem and extended the lit Zippo while Martin bent over and held his cigarette to the flame.

"You are speaking of the incident two weeks ago when the previous CO and two of his advisors were killed?"

"And twenty of our Montagnard troops."

"Yes, and twenty Montagnard militia and eight of my Rangers. Before we continue, let me say this: I and my Rangers are in the same situation as you. We must follow orders. We did what we could to support them, but we were overruled by my superior."

"Your battalion commander, Colonel Pham?"

"That is correct."

"What the hell happened?"

"First, I must ask that you not repeat any of what I tell you here. My relationship with the colonel is what you might describe as 'tenuous.' And the political climate of our army is such that it could lead to a great deal of trouble for me."

"You have my word. Tell me what happened."

"Your predecessor Captain Watson, two American advisors, and a Montagnard Provincial Reconnaissance unit were in the hills near the highway leading into the highlands. Their mission was reconnaissance, and they identified a large enemy force near a village. Our ARVN battalion was brought in on the highway and forced the NVA to retreat into the hills. Captain Watson and his men became trapped between these and another NVA force that flanked them from behind.

"My Ranger company was less than a kilometer from them when they called for Colonel Pham to come to their aid. I immediately sent one squad to help and began organizing the remainder of my men to move against the enemy, but the colonel ordered me to remain in position. He also held his men near the village. The two enemy forces overran Captain Watson and his forces as well as my squad of Rangers, killing all but the few who were able to escape."

"Why in hell did Pham do that?"

"I later asked Colonel Pham why he chose to remain near the village, and he said he feared an ambush and would not risk his men for the Montagnard. He claimed he didn't know at the time that Captain Watson or my Rangers were with them, but I do not believe that is true. The colonel had a radio and likely heard the captain's requests for support."

"So, all these men were killed because this spineless bastard was scared?"

"Actually, we only recovered twenty-two bodies. Six of the

Montagnards and two of my Rangers are still listed as missing. They may have been captured, but we did not search for them because of large enemy units remaining in the area. I also do not think the colonel was frightened as much as he simply did not care because these men were Montagnard."

Martin furiously sucked his cigarette to a nub and shook another from the pack.

"And do you feel the same way as your colonel?"

"Captain Shadows, I and my Rangers will stand with you. I believe the Montagnard are our allies and good fighters. It is my superior who interferes, but there is nothing I can do about that. I must follow his orders."

"Oh, but there *is* something you *can* do."

Truong's brows narrowed as he gazed at Martin.

"The next time that worthless bastard orders you to stand down, you don't. You do what is right."

"But Captain—"

"There's no 'but' to it, Captain. You stand with me or don't. I can be your best ally or your worst nightmare. You decide."

Truong was no pushover. A hardcore Ranger, he now fixed Martin with a stony stare. After a few moments he looked away as he ground his cigarette into an ashtray.

"I have heard many rumors about you, Captain Shadows, and some seem somewhat…" Truong paused.

"Believe what you want, Captain, but leave me or my men out to dry like you did Watson and his PRU, and the enemy will be the least of your worries."

Their eyes met, and Truong gave him a nod.

"Remember, Captain Shadows, that I lost eight of my men, but you have my word, when the time comes for that decision, I will do what is right. Have you met with your Montagnards, yet?"

"No. Why?"

"I suggest that you take your men with you and be prepared. The Montagnards are not happy. I would be very careful around them. Colonel Pham believes they have revolted, and he plans to arrest their leaders and take their weapons in order to prevent an uprising."

"When does he plan to do this?"

"Very soon, I believe. Perhaps in the next few days."

"Do any of the Montagnards speak English?"

"Two or three, yes. Their leader is a man named Khonsu who speaks your language well."

Khonsu—the name was a stroke of lightning to Martin's psyche, but it brought him an immediate sense of hope. He was one of Sergeant Ravera's men who escaped the island prison with them. If the Montagnards were contemplating a revolt, talking with him would be the key, but it had to happen quickly.

CHAPTER FIVE

The Montagnards
A Relocation Camp West of Phu Bai

Martin timed his arrival at the old relocation camp for first light the next morning. Only Zeke Anderson accompanied him. Despite Truong's warning, he knew the Montagnards would respect him more if he didn't show up with a contingent of bodyguards. Leaving the jeep outside the camp, he and Zeke approached the two guards at the gate. Both guards held M-1 carbines at the ready, but when the Montagnards recognized their uniforms, they lowered their weapons.

Behind them, the camp sprawled along a shallow river and adjacent hillside for a couple hundred meters. Some few of the structures were old American-built ones, but the hillside was lined with dozens more of the traditional Montagnard thatched huts. Built on raised stilts, the elongated huts seemed to float on the foggy morning mist drifting up from the river. The village was quiet.

"I am here to meet with your leader," Martin said.

The wide-eyed guards nodded rapidly, but it was clear they didn't understand what he was saying. One took him by the hand

and began leading him into the camp. Hand holding was a gesture common among the Montagnard, a gentle people who held none of the taboos of western culture. Zeke followed while the other guard remained at the gate. A pig squealed, and several chickens in a cage fluttered and clucked as the men walked through the rows of huts. An old man appeared on a raised platform outside of one of the huts and began shouting and pointing at them. It was clear whatever he was saying wasn't praise. A boy ran out and pulled the old man back inside.

The implications were ominous, and Martin's doubts grew as they stopped at the center of the village. He had to find Khonsu quickly. Casting a glance at Zeke, he hoped for some sort of sign, but the Special Forces sergeant simply shrugged. Perhaps, the two of them coming here alone wasn't one of Martin's better ideas, but Zeke didn't seem particularly concerned. If it hadn't been for the Green Beret reputation for unflinching bravery, he would have trusted this reaction. The Montagnard guard signaled for them to wait while he climbed a ladder to one of the huts.

Martin gazed about while frogs croaked along the river and birds called from the mountainside behind them. At the center of the village stood a totem pole and he did a double take. He had long ago recognized the similarities between the Montagnards and some American Indian tribes, but the totem pole left him enthralled as he studied an intricately carved bird, a monkey, a fish, and a huge snake. At the top there was what appeared to be a Christian cross carved into a circular halo of wood.

"It represents their beliefs in the spirits," Zeke murmured. "They see the spirits in everything, even trees, rocks, and the mountains."

"I know," Martin said. "That's the same thing many Indians back home believe, but what's with the cross at the top?"

"The French Catholic Missionaries converted many of the

Montagnard tribes, but the French government screwed them over and pushed them off their land and back into the highlands."

A long minute had passed when streams of Montagnard warriors began coming from doors on opposite ends of the long hut. All were armed with a variety of weapons ranging from M-1 Carbines to AK-47s. They stood glaring down at Martin and Zeke. One man stepped forward. An obvious elder, his thin gray hair glistened, and is only weapon was a spear he brandished above his head.

"That's the CMFIC," Zeke muttered.

"The who?" Martin whispered.

"The Chief Mother Fucker in Charge."

"Who you?" the old man shouted in a shrill voice.

"Better speak up fast," Zeke muttered. "I think these boys mean business."

"I am Captain Shadows. I am replacing Captain Watson, and I came to talk with you."

Several of the warriors traded glances while the old man pointed his spear back toward the gate.

"You go, now," he shouted. "We no talk."

The hair tingled on Martin's neck as he recognized their hostility and its explosive potential. One misspoken word, one misinterpreted movement, and the Montagnards could kill him and Zeke in an instant. Khonsu was his only hope.

"Khonsu, is he here?"

The Montagnard's aggressive demeanor grew suddenly hesitant as they traded glances.

"Khonsu?" the old man repeated.

"Yes, Khonsu."

It was a glimmer of hope.

"Khonsu no here. You go! No American come to camp now."

Despite the man's broken English, his message was clear. He wanted nothing to do with them.

"But I know Khonsu. He—"

"No!"

The old man raised his spear, while the variety of well-worn M-1 Carbines, M-16s, and AK-47s were brought to bear.

"You go. No American talk. We no more friend."

Martin raised his hands. "Okay. I'll go but tell Khonsu that Martin Shadows came to see him. Do you understand?"

"No talk. You go."

"I am going but tell Khonsu…" and it occurred to him. "Tell Khonsu *the Ghost* came here to see him. Do you understand?"

The old Montagnard's hostility suddenly morphed to wild-eyed doubt, as he studied Martin carefully.

"You go, now. I tell Khonsu Ghost come." The old man's voice was considerably calmer, but Martin realized this conversation was over. He would return to the firebase and come up with plan B. He and Zeke walked back to the jeep on the road outside the village gate. Jumping into the driver's seat, he was about to start the engine when a dozen or more men brandishing weapons emerged from the dew-soaked undergrowth. Their weapons were trained on them, and his first thought was he was about to be taken prisoner again by the Vietcong.

With both his and Zeke's CAR-15s propped between the seats, Martin eyed his weapon. His right hand rested inches from it. Death now seemed a better option than another trip to an enemy prison camp. This time he might not be so lucky. His captors advanced rapidly from the morning mist.

"Don't do it," Zeke muttered. "They're Montagnards."

Only then did Martin realize they were carrying American weapons. He and Zeke raised their hands.

"We're Americans," Martin shouted.

Standing either side of the jeep, the Montagnards pressed their rifle muzzles against each man's head. That these boys were no longer loyal to the Americans was obvious. They had been screwed one too many times. Even if it was by Colonel Pham and the ARVN troops, the Montagnards somehow believed the Americans were complicit. This was one fucked-up war, and Martin wondered how he ever thought he could make a difference.

The indigenous mountain tribes had been lied to, enslaved, abused, and subjected to mass annihilation. Eighty-five percent of their villages had been destroyed, and they were now beggars and nomads in their own country. These had seen enough. They wanted nothing more to do with the Americans, the South Vietnamese, or anyone promising them anything. And these had seen the worst of it when they were transferred away from their Green Beret friends to the control of their worst abusers—the South Vietnamese Army.

The others stepped back as a single Montagnard walked out of the mist. Their apparent leader, he waved the others back, as he approached but suddenly stopped. Still several meters away, he squinted at Martin. It was Khonsu.

"Khonsu!" Martin said.

The Montagnard's face lit with recognition.

"Ghost!"

Turning toward the others, he barked commands as they quickly lowered their weapons and backed away.

"Bushmaster, Ghost, I sorry my men treat you not good." He noticed the black Captain's bars on Martin's collar and reached out to touch them. "Ah, you Đại úy now." He nodded with satisfaction.

"We need to sit down and talk, Khonsu."

"Yes, Khonsu talk with Ghost, but not with Vietnamese army. You come now. We go back to village."

Martin pointed to the man holding his CAR-15. "Can we have our weapons?"

Khonsu barked an order and the man quickly scrambled

forward and extended the rifle with bowed head. Martin put his gun between the seats and motioned for Khonsu to get in.

"Come ride with us."

As they pulled away and drove back inside the camp gate, he noticed Khonsu's men double-timing behind the jeep. Seemingly un-winded, they ran with their weapons at the ready. These were hardcore fighters—men he would be proud to have in his command.

Martin and Khonsu sat in the shade while the Montagnard leader told how the ARVN troops had abandoned them to be overrun by the NVA. Khonsu's deep-seated anger was evident, but he spoke quietly, showing little outward emotion as he explained how he and four of his men were able to retrieve the bodies of the Americans and escape while the remainder of his platoon fought to the death.

Martin drew a quavering breath. A prejudicial dislike for a people might be human nature, but to act on it by abandoning men who were fighting with you was unforgiveable. It came from the darkest corners of humanity, and Colonel Pham was an apparent chartered member.

Khonsu explained how he went back to the firebase to get the second PRU platoon and return to the ambush site, but the South Vietnamese wouldn't allow him to go.

"He Captain Truong say we not go. Give order, but when he leave, we go anyway. I find my men. NVA tie to trees. They torture, kill them. I hunt NVA now, VC too, but do not help ARVN soldiers. They cowards."

Khonsu trusted him, but Martin was careful with his words.

"I need to talk with your elders. You need to come and join with me and my men. If you don't, I believe the ARVN battalion commander will come here and take your weapons. Come with me, and I will tell them you are again fighting with us, and I won't let them put you or your men in a position like that again. I give you my word. I will fight with you."

Khonsu looked away into the misty jungle.

"I think we go Cambodia, maybe Thailand someday. They say it beautiful country."

It was the dream of all oppressed, a promised land.

"That's six hundred miles, Khonsu. You'll never make it."

"We go to Laos and Cambodia first."

"But what about the Khmer Rouge?"

The genocide of the Cambodians at the hands of the Khmer Rouge was an ill-kept secret by the Communists.

Khonsu continued staring into the endless jungle that began only a few meters away. Martin remained silent while the little man contemplated his options. And Martin had no idea what was best. He only knew he wanted to help. Whatever path Khonsu chose, he would support.

"Okay. I talk with my people. You come back tonight. I tell you what they say."

An hour before sunset Martin returned to the Montagnard Village. Sergeant Anderson, the Bushmaster, was driving the jeep and sitting in back was Sky Soldier, Whit Porterfield. Sky Soldier had seen some of the worst combat of the war with the 173rd and later with the 101st. Bushmaster had been an A-team leader with the Special Forces. He had conducted missions across the fence on the Ho Chi Minh Trail. If Khonsu accepted his offer, these two were Martin's choices to work with the Montagnards. The guard at the village gate motioned them through without hesitation.

The aroma of meat roasting over a wood fire filled his nostrils. The Yards were about to have a feast, and this time the guards at the gate were smiling as the three Americans passed through in their jeep. The smiles and the preparation of the feast were good signs. Martin remained hopeful as Zeke brought the jeep to a stop at the center of the village. Khonsu was standing with one of the elders in front of the totem pole. Both were smiling.

"Let them do the talking," Bushmaster said. His experience working with the Montagnards in the highlands was invaluable. "We will eat and probably drink some rice wine first. When they're ready, they'll tell us what they're thinking, but I can already tell you we wouldn't have gotten this far if they weren't ready to rejoin the unit."

The feast came with chopped fish mixed with rice and hot peppers wrapped in leaves, along with a second course of bowls of rice with roasted meat and more hot peppers. Additional courses came in bowls filled with fermented fruits passed around the circle of men. It was a feast—one Martin realized these poor mountain people had sacrificed much to put in front of them.

Later, a large gourd was placed at the center of the hooch. Martin already knew of the Montagnard fondness for this community toast. From the gourd sprouted a cluster of hollowed reeds—straws, and the men took turns sharing something that tasted like sake. The only problem was it possessed a liquor-on-steroids effect. Martin was feeling no pain when three more men joined them, sitting in the circle surrounding the gourd. It was Brau, Katu, and Guia, the other three men he had freed from the NVA prison.

This was the first time he had seen them since their escape from the island. Khonsu motioned for the three to sit beside him as others gave up their straws to the newcomers. It was a reunion Martin had never imagined would happen. The Bru wine made his mind wander, reminding him of another improbable reunion—one he doubted would ever occur—seeing Kania again. He still expected a "Dear John" letter from her any day. It seemed inevitable. One of those smart-assed cowboys from the bar would woo her affections and she would be lost forever. His head swam in the pleasant world of the Montagnard wine as he thought again of that night in Wolf Point.

The warmth in the truck and the alcohol worked together to drive him into a deep sleep while she drove his pickup to Grandfather Two Shadows's house up on the res. When Martin opened his eyes, he was looking out at a gravel road dimly lit by the pickup's headlights. Kania was beside him clinging to the steering wheel with both hands, and the truck radio was playing the scratchy remnants of a country song that faded in and out. Gravel popped beneath the floorboard, and he was tempted to go back to sleep, but she noticed he was awake.

"Do you drink often?" she asked.

"No. This is the first time since I got back from Nam."

She pursed her lips and continued staring ahead into the night.

"Vietnam. Well, that explains some things."

"Where are we?" Martin asked.

"On the res—Powder River Road."

"How do you know my grandfather?"

"The same way everyone else in this corner of Montana does. He helped my mother and father when they lost their cattle several winters back, and he got me some financial aid when I went to school in Missoula. Matter of fact, he got me a full scholarship. He helps everyone."

"Why did those guys in the bar seem afraid of him?"

"Your grandfather is a powerful man. He's a medicine man. Some say he's a shapeshifter. They call them Skinwalkers down south. Whatever his spirit may be, he has the highest respect from everyone on the res. He's our North Star."

The bare winter crop rows fluttered past in a dizzying blur, and Martin closed his eyes as he tried to continue an intelligible conversation.

"So, do your parents live on the reservation?" he asked.

The girl didn't reply for a long minute. He had apparently done it again—stuck his dumbass foot in his mouth.

"No. My mother died last year, and I came home to look after my father. I moved him into town because he's not in good health."

Women did that to him. He was a bumbling fool who could never say the right thing. Better to remain silent, and Martin again closed his eyes, but it seemed only moments until a sudden flood of fresh air awakened him. He sat up. They'd arrived at his grandfather's house, and the girl had opened the truck door to step out. After walking around to his side, she opened his and he slid out on rubbery legs. She grasped his arm.

"Come on," she whispered, pulling his arm across her shoulders. "Let's get you inside."

"No! I don't want my grandfather to see me like this."

The night air was still, and an owl called from down on Wolf Creek. The girl stopped and her hand tightened around his wrist.

"What's wrong?" he asked.

"Something important is about to happen."

"What?"

"I don't know."

"So, when is your friend coming to get you?"

"Some cowboy has her attention. She said it'd be at least an hour."

The girl motioned toward the old couch on the front porch. "We can wait out here till she gets here."

"It's too cold."

"It's only forty degrees," she said. "We'll use those wool blankets."

The night air made him shiver as he pulled the thick blankets from the back of the couch. Unfolding them, he wrapped himself and Kania in a tight cocoon and rested his head against her shoulder. The warmth of her body was inviting as he snuggled closer, and after a while he slipped into another dream. It was only natural that he dreamt of their lips meeting with passion. It was a pleasant fantasy, and it seemed so real as her breathing became heavy. He smiled to himself and snuggled closer. If only real life was as good as dreams.

After a while he pushed her blouse upward along with her bra, freeing her breasts. They were hot against his bare chest, and he felt her hands scratching his back as he loosened her jeans. Pushing his hand gently into the soft and moist part of her body, he heard her moan quietly and it all seemed so real. This girl was about to give herself to him, and—with a jolt of reality he awakened. The dream ended.

It had been all too good to be true, but now that he was awake, he realized it wasn't a dream at all, and neither was the passion of the moment. They were about to consummate their all-too-brief relationship in an especially important way. He paused, but she pushed her jeans down and kicked them free before unbuckling his belt. His every instinct said she wasn't an easy woman, and he worried that he had been too pushy in his drunken stupor.

"Are you sure?" he whispered between breaths.

Kania Miles paused and tried to catch her breath.

"Has your grandfather…has he ever talked with you about the spirits that guide us?"

"Yes."

"Then you know, and so do I. I've never been so sure of anything in all of my life as I am this moment."

When he again awakened, dawn had grayed out the nighttime stars and Kania was sleeping in his arms. It was cold, but her face was one of absolute peace. A beautiful face, the stresses he had seen there that night at the bar were wiped away, replaced by a calm he envied. Gently he ran his palm over her hair and with his fingers, pulled it away from her eyes. She stirred. His life had taken a major turn down a new path, and he dreaded telling her he was soon returning to Nam.

After a while, Martin came out of his reverie and realized he hadn't said anything to his Montagnard friends as they continued sipping the wine from the gourd. He glanced at Khonsu who smiled and nodded. The others nodded as well, and it seemed a mutual signal of sorts as Khonsu stood. Something was about to happen. Martin's head was swimming, but he forced himself to attain some degree of sobriety, such as it was.

"Đại úy, we talk." Khonsu motioned toward the others in the hooch. "You our new leader. We follow. We also follow Bushmaster and Sky Soldier."

With that Khonsu bowed and gave brass bracelets to each of them. They were engraved with various symbols of the sun, moon, and animals. Bushmaster already wore two from his previous tours. He added this one to his wrist as well. There was no discussion, no debate—only this quick and certain affirmation of their loyalty.

"The Montagnard don't give these to just anyone," Bushmaster said. "You are highly regarded by them, Captain."

Martin's military mind clicked into gear as he nodded his thanks to Khonsu.

"We will train together and be ready to fight. And I will be there to lead you."

Khonsu nodded and translated it to the others. They too smiled and nodded. After a few minutes Brau, Katu, and Guia departed, but the gourd was far from empty. Khonsu began speaking slowly in broken English then in his native tongue as he told the others about the Ghost who had rescued him and his comrades from the

NVA island prison and how he brought them south to freedom. The Ghost was a spirit man, a man they should follow, he told them.

This was the first time Bushmaster and Sky Soldier had heard this story, and they listened with rapt attention. Martin was pleased to be spoken of so highly, but there had been luck involved in that venture. He knew the coming days could be as difficult and again require a tremendous amount of that same luck. That would begin when he met with Colonel Pham.

He would return to the firebase, find Captain Truong, and arrange a meeting with the ARVN base commander. Everything afterward was beyond his control. Both of his sergeants, Zeke and Whit, were shit-faced when they bade their farewells to the Montagnard that evening. Martin wasn't much better off when he sat behind the wheel of the jeep. It was late and probably better to spend the night inside the protective perimeter of the village, but he needed to meet with Colonel Pham first thing in the morning. He had to pre-empt any action the colonel planned against the Montagnards.

CHAPTER SIX

The Loyalty of the Montagnard
The Highway West of the ARVN Firebase

As they walked to the jeep that night, Martin admired his bracelet, knowing it was an honor the Montagnard gave to only their most highly respected friends. Their ways were indeed much like his father's Lakota ancestors, and he wondered about something else he had observed. All the Montagnard warriors wore amulets around their necks—small wrinkled brown objects that resembled a piece of carved wood. All were similar and suspended from a single leather lace. He poked Bushmaster to get his attention.

"Hey, what were those little brown things the Yards were wearing around their necks? I mean, what do they symbolize?"

Bushmaster stopped at the back of the jeep and steadied himself as he turned to face Martin.

"You're half Lakota Sioux, and I'm assuming you know about the respect the Indians have for the spirits of their slain enemies, right? They took their scalps for a reason."

"Yeah?"

"The Montagnards do the same."

Martin closed his eyes. Scalps? And it came to him, and he wondered how he could have been such a dumbass. Even in his current drunken state, it was now obvious. Whatever they were, these amulets were similar in nature to the scalps taken by Indian warriors. He no longer wanted to know what they were, but it was too late. The subject was broached.

"The Montagnards believe the spirits of their enemies are powerful and must be held at bay after death by wearing those around their necks. That's the simplest explanation."

"Trophies?" Martin asked, but he really didn't want to know.

Bushmaster wagged his head emphatically.

"No. No way. I know that for certain. It's not their nature. The Yards are fierce fighters, but they're humble people. It's strictly a spiritual matter for them. It's complicated, and I've never fully understood all there is to know about it, but they wear those ears as channels to the spiritual afterlife."

"Ears?"

"Yeah. Those are Vietcong ears they're wearing, and each man wears one for protection."

The more he learned, the more Martin grew to understand his grandfather's world, and the more he wondered what else had been omitted from his studies on world religions.

The red-filtered headlights barely lit the roadway as Martin held the jeep's accelerator to the floor. Driving the five kilometers back to the firebase wasn't one of his better decisions, but the VC probably figured anyone in his right mind wouldn't be stupid enough to try it. The engine roared, but top speed was barely 45 MPH, and the nighttime shadows loomed over the roadway. The Montagnard brew had negated whatever judgement he had, and he was now driving blind through bad-guy territory—a place the VC owned at night.

With two klicks down, they had only three more to go to the firebase when the road ahead exploded with the bright flashes of hand grenades and clashing showers of red and green tracers. Martin mashed the brake, sliding the jeep to a stop as he doused the lights. His two sergeants, now wide awake and sobered with floods of adrenaline, held their CAR-15s at the ready. Bushmaster stepped from the passenger seat and ran to the side of the road where he knelt. Martin did the same on his side, while Sky Soldier knelt behind the jeep. Stray bullets cracked and whined through the night air, and more grenades exploded with brilliant white flashes. With the firefight less than fifty meters ahead, they had a front row seat.

And just as suddenly as it began, the automatic gunfire subsided. There were two more shots, then one, until an uneasy silence returned to the night. The sweat ran into his eyes and Martin used his fatigue shirt to wipe his face. Two minutes passed, then five as they watched and waited. It could have been an eternity. The only sound was that of his heart thumping in his chest. No one moved. He strained to listen, but there was now only the impenetrable darkness and absolute silence.

Leaving the village after dark was a colossally stupid idea. He knew that now, and the only reasonable option was to turn back and spend the night there. He gazed across the road where Bushmaster knelt. He was just another jungle shadow, silent and unmoving. Sky Soldier remained behind the jeep but held his palm outward toward Martin, telling him not to move. For the moment, this was just fine with him. His night vision was only now beginning to return, and he studied the road ahead. Something moved.

The moon had not yet risen, and the only point of reference was the open space of the sky above the road ahead. It was black, but not as black as the surrounding jungle. Again, Martin thought he saw something moving, but it was no more than a shadow. His imagination was red-lined with adrenaline, and he cut his eyes over at Bushmaster then to Sky Soldier. Experienced warriors, both were frozen, unmoving, but alert, and with their weapons at the ready.

Martin's primal senses told him there was someone coming up the road toward them. And he remembered his training about night vision and using peripheral vision to see what wasn't readily visible in the darkness. Another movement became the shadow of a man. Someone was standing less than twenty meters away. *How had he gotten so close? Why had the others not seen him?* Martin pointed his CAR-15 at the shadow but hesitated. Who was it?

Hesitation got people killed in combat, but killing a friend or ally would leave a mark on his soul he could never forget. He waited.

"Đại úy, I Katu. I am here."

Martin exhaled.

"We kill VC. You go to firebase, now. Is good."

"Damned," he cursed and sucked down another breath of relief.

It was Katu, one of the Montagnards he had been drinking with less than an hour ago. The three Americans met him at the center of the road.

"What happened?" Martin asked.

Katu's teeth gleamed in the darkness as he smiled.

"We kill many VC."

"How many got away?" Sky Soldier asked.

"We kill all," Katu said. "You go now. My men watch road."

Martin put his hand on the little man's shoulder.

"Thanks."

"Katu happy help. You go before more come."

Martin and his two non-coms jumped into the jeep and sped

toward the firebase. Sky Soldier leaned forward and spoke into Martin's ear. "I'm not sure we can teach those boys anything they don't already know. They came out here two klicks in the dead of night and found that enemy ambush. They know their shit."

He was right, and now more than ever, Martin had to make certain Colonel Pham stood behind them. If the colonel thought the VC and NVA were tough opponents, he didn't want to make enemies of these mountain tribesmen.

CHAPTER SEVEN

Meeting with Pham
The ARVN Firebase Southwest of Phu Bai

Before departing for his meeting with Captain Truong and Colonel Pham, Martin met with his NCOs and instructed them to begin training the Montagnards. Telling them to focus on immediate reaction drills and escape and evasion techniques, he doubted more would be necessary. Team organization and communication SOPs could be determined during the training. When his advisors departed for the Montagnard village, Martin went to the ARVN Ranger billets and joined Captain Truong. They walked across the firebase to the battalion HQ.

"You aren't saying much today," Martin said. "I assume you're not looking forward to meeting with the colonel."

"He is not an easy man with whom I can discuss problems."

"Tell me more about him. Was Colonel Pham promoted through the ranks?"

At that moment the battery of one-five-five Howitzers on the north side of the firebase let loose a thundering barrage that shook the ground beneath their feet. Truong shrugged as if to say talking was useless. The barrage ended ten minutes later as they arrived at the ARVN commander's office. The building's whitewashed block exterior was heavily reinforced with a sandbagged Marston mat steel roof, all of which belied its interior. The outer office resembled something from back in Saigon with vinyl chairs, lacquered ashtray stands, and bamboo framed prints of tigers and peacocks on the walls.

A young officer announced their arrival, but it was several minutes before they were escorted to the inner sanctum. An unlikely affair, it was even more out of character for a firebase HQ, with a lamp, throw rug and amenities befitting an attorney's office. After setting his cigarette on the edge of a jade ashtray, Pham returned their salute as he stood and extended his hand. His actions were more those of a patrician appointee than a hardened military colonel.

"Please, sit, Captain Shadows. I am happy you finally came to visit me."

It was the third day since Martin's arrival, and Pham's poorly disguised complaint was understandable. A battalion commander, he probably expected the commander of his American advisors would report to him first, except Martin had no intention of becoming his lackey. Having already learned more than he wanted to know about this man, he intended to keep a buffer between himself and Pham.

"I hope you will forgive me, Colonel, but I wanted to meet with my men first and introduce myself to them. It took longer than I expected."

"And what did you learn, Captain?"

"I've learned that we have some serious problems."

"Oh, and what are these *problems*?"

Captain Truong, who was now sitting beside Martin, remained stoically passive and silent.

"The low morale among the Montagnards and my advisor

group is probably the biggest issue. I've met with both groups and already begun rebuilding their confidence."

"The tribesmen have revolted, Captain Shadows, and I intend to correct that problem. We are going to disarm them and arrest their leaders."

"I believe you're mistaken, Colonel. Why would they revolt? They're our allies."

"How should I know? Perhaps they have gone over to the Vietcong."

"No, they haven't, but they are angry because your troops abandoned them when they were surrounded by the NVA."

"That is not true! Your own advisor said it would be unwise to commit my troops to save them."

"My own advisor?"

"It no longer matters. These people have chosen their destiny and I intend to deliver it to them."

"But they haven't revolted. I met with their leaders just yesterday, and they're committed to working with my advisors and providing the reconnaissance your battalion needs."

The colonel's face hardened, and his eyes glared. "How did you meet with them?"

Pham turned toward Captain Truong, but he refused to meet the colonel's glare. The colonel turned back to Martin.

"It would have been wise to consult with me first, Captain, and seek my permission. You are fortunate they did not kill you."

"The Montagnards told me of their concerns and how no one came to their support when they were surrounded by the NVA, but I assured them it would not happen again."

The colonel wagged his head. "No. You do not speak for me. They are *moi*—savages! They do not understand the intricacies of military warfare. You should not make promises for what you cannot provide. The tribesmen made their own problems. I did only what was militarily wise, but they have made threats against my troops, and I feel they are misleading you. After we disarm them and arrest their leaders, you may determine who among them is telling the truth. We have ways of obtaining it."

It was clear the colonel was implying the use of torture, but that would never happen. The Montagnards would never surrender, and there would be no torture on Martin's watch. He would see to it.

"I believe that would be a bad mistake, Colonel. The Montagnards are strong and capable allies, and my superiors will never agree to such an action. I'm sure we can resolve this matter. Perhaps you can talk with Colonel Duggin and with the Montagnards to assure them yourself."

Pham displayed a tight-lipped facade as he took the cigarette from the ashtray and inhaled the last of it. He gazed up at a wall map of Vietnam, and after a moment exhaled the smoke toward the ceiling.

"Perhaps you are right, Captain, but I do not need to meet with Colonel Duggin. I will meet with the Montagnard leaders. I will make certain that they understand my concern for their loyalty."

"I can go with you, Colonel. That way we can assure—"

"That will not be necessary, Captain. I would rather meet with them alone."

If the truth in Pham's voice was a bell, it was cracked. There was something awry. Martin's every instinct was telling him the colonel still planned to arrest the Montagnards.

"When is our next mission, Colonel?"

"I will meet with you and Captain Truong in a few days, Tuesday perhaps. Your advisors and Truong's Rangers will patrol the mountains near the abandoned village at Thon Ben Tau before my troops move up the highway. You will make certain the highway is clear of enemy troops."

As he and Truong stood to walk out, Martin noticed a roughly sketched map pinned to the back of the door. The layout was familiar. It was the Montagnard village, and arrows were drawn indicating troop movements surrounding and entering the village proper. He pretended not to notice as he departed.

The morning sun had risen high in the sky as he and Truong walked back across the firebase to the Ranger compound. A string of Hueys passed to the south, heading into the highlands. They were likely American Marines coming out of Da Nang. Truong had yet to say a word as they walked in silence.

"Do you think the colonel will do as he said and simply talk with the Montagnard leaders?"

Truong continued walking in silence. Martin waited.

"I cannot speak for the colonel, Captain Shadows."

"I'm sure you saw that map on his door," Martin said.

"I did."

"I think he plans to attack the village."

"Captain Shadows, I have my family and my men whom I must protect. I have no choice but to live here in this country under men like Colonel Pham, and he already suspects my dissatisfaction with his actions. You have no such problems."

"Okay, I see your point, but I have one question for you."

Martin paused as he carefully formulated his question.

"If I go to my superiors about this and also warn the Montagnards, will you support me?"

"I and my Rangers consider the Montagnard our allies, but there is only so much I can do. I will support you with my silence. That is all I can promise. Do as you must. I will not interfere."

"I'm contacting Colonel Duggin. Hopefully, he can reason with Pham."

"There is only one secure communication line in the battalion command center, and it is available only with Colonel Pham's permission."

"I'll go back to visit Pham later today and tell him I need to send my weekly report."

"The colonel will not be easily deceived. He is a man of many faces. You should tread lightly, Captain Shadows. He works for powerful people outside of the military and can cause you a great deal of trouble."

The advice was well placed, and Martin wanted to ask about these "powerful people" Truong referenced, but being too aggressive might shut him down. Contacting Colonel Duggin was his best option.

Captain Truong was right. Pham would likely prevent Martin from sending his weekly report to Duggin. To avoid Pham's interference, he went to the battalion TOC late that evening. With Pham's battalion on standdown, the Vietnamese duty officer and a couple of his NCOs were the only ones present. The young lieutenant saluted as he entered. Martin returned the salute and went to the Telex machine where he began typing in his report.

A moment later, he noticed when the officer picked up a telephone and turned his back to him. He began talking quietly on the phone. It was less than a minute before the ARVN lieutenant turned to him and held the telephone receiver out to him. "Colonel Pham would like to speak with you," he said.

Martin took the phone. "This is Captain Shadows."

"What is your use of the secure line, Captain?"

"I'm sending my weekly update to my commander in Phu Bai."

"Use of that line is only with my authorization, Captain. Leave your message with the duty officer, and I will have it sent tomorrow."

The stakes in this chess game were growing, but Martin

couldn't disobey Pham's order without repercussions. He had to buy time.

"Will do, Colonel, but I'll need to return later with a written copy."

"Thank you, Captain. Please do so. Now, return the telephone to my duty officer."

Martin handed the phone to the lieutenant and started toward the door, but paused to watch as the lieutenant went behind the Telex machine and disconnected the cord. With all that was happening along Highways One, Twelve, Nine, and the NVA movements throughout I-Corps, disconnecting the secure communication line was beyond irresponsible. What if an urgent message was sent to the TOC while the machine was unplugged? And there were so many other things that could happen, it could endanger the safety of the entire firebase. This was the pinnacle of stupidity.

He wanted to tell Pham as much, but it now seemed certain the colonel planned to follow through with his plan to disarm the Montagnards and arrest their leaders. Martin refused to stand idly by and let this happen because the Montagnards would fight, and there would be bloodshed. He had to meet with his men when they returned from the village.

CHAPTER EIGHT

Between a Rock and a Hard Place
Ranger Compound at the ARVN Firebase

Despite his deep frustration, Martin explained the situation to his men as dispassionately as possible. The people of South Vietnam were at war as much with one another as they were with the Communists. Internal spy networks, special police, military entities of all sorts vied for political advantages while factions of Catholics, Buddhists, the PLA, and others vied for power or at the least, survival. Colonel Pham's planned attack on the Montagnard Village was a prime example of one of these old hatreds.

The urban South Vietnamese and the French colonialists had taken the ancestral lands of the tribes, displacing the Montagnard, and pushing them back into the highlands. The Vietnamese looked down on them as lower-class humans and treated them as such. Now, Martin and his men were faced with a situation with no easy solution.

There was no doubt Pham would attack the village when the Montagnard refused to surrender their weapons. Without direction from Colonel Duggin, Martin had only his conscience to follow. His team of advisors gathered around him that afternoon as they discussed the best way to protect the villagers. They'd chosen a Quonset hut for privacy, and the lethargic rotation of a couple of ceiling fans did little to dissipate the heat.

"Anyone wanting to standdown for this one is free to do so," Martin said. "There'll be nothing said, and no one will think less of you. I am still hoping to hear from my CO in Phu Bai before anything happens, but I'm going to stand between the South Vietnamese troops and that Montagnard village. I don't want another massacre—not on my watch."

"If we all go with you, Sir, we'll have less than sixty men, even with the Montagnards," First Sergeant Gautier said. "There's not much we can do against a mechanized infantry battalion with mortars and recoilless rifles. You need to think about this, before we get our men hurt."

"With a half-dozen men, I can take out their heavy weapons pretty fast," Bushmaster said.

"No!" Martin snapped. "I mean—hold on. Let's think this through carefully."

He'd been too quick with his objection, and the men grew quiet. Bushmaster shrugged. He had worked extensively with the Montagnards as a Special Forces A-team leader, and he could no doubt do as he said, but violence had to be the last option.

"I'm not dismissing your suggestion, Sergeant, but let's try to come up with ideas that will make that unnecessary. I've met with Colonel Pham. I'm not exactly sure why he wants to do this, but I think he's more worried about his reputation. I believe he'll back down if we stand in his way."

"Hail yeayuss!" T-Bo shouted. "We'll have a high noon showdown with a whole battalion of gooks. I mean, really? We'd be crazy to do that."

"Yeah," Sergeant Lugo said. "I'm all for protecting the Yards, but this shit could go sideways in a heartbeat."

There were more head wags, and expressions of doubt.

"Hang on, men," Martin said. "Don't get all worked up just yet. Let's talk this through."

More mutters and grumbles came from the men.

"At ease!" Bushmaster shouted.

They grew quiet. If there was one NCO everyone respected, it was Bushmaster. Three tours, all with Army Special Forces, he still wore his green beret with pride. He'd been on more missions than anyone in the room—Cambodia, Laos, and even up into North Vietnam. He was an iconic symbol of what most of them wanted to be. He walked to the front of the group.

"We all know this war has become a shitshow, and our government is pussyfooting around, so nobody wants to be the last man KIA in this place. But I believe we owe the Yards our loyalty. They have stood with us in this country. Listen to the captain, and we'll make a plan with as little risk as possible."

"So, what are you thinking?" Lugo asked.

"We can go to the village tonight," Bushmaster said, "and tell them to move all their men and weapons. We'll take them to those ridges on the other side of the river. They can watch the village from the high ground while the ARVNs search it."

"And just what the hell are we gonna be doin' while all this is happening?" T-Bo asked.

Martin liked this kid. Specialist Thibodaux was a country bumpkin from Louisiana Cajun country, but he was smart. He asked questions that mattered.

"We'll be with the Montagnard troops, T-Bo," Martin said. "We need to keep them from engaging the ARVNs, and hopefully we'll be well hidden, so I don't expect they'll find us."

"What do you expect the South Vietnamese to do, Sir?" Lugo asked.

"I'm hoping for intervention from Colonel Duggin before it

goes that far. Lieutenant Postiche left here a little while ago on a resupply chopper. He has with him a full written report of this situation and my request for immediate support. He should reach the colonel's HQ in a few hours. If he's successful and Colonel Duggin can intercede, we'll standdown tomorrow. Leastwise that's what I'm hoping will happen. Regardless, if this fails, I believe Pham will standdown when he finds the Montagnard fighters are no longer in the village."

The men seemed to relax, and Martin didn't want to say too much more, but he had to plan contingencies. The command staff back at MAC-V had already read the riot act to him, but here he was again left to his own resources. And with no guidance other than his own sense of morality, he intended to support the military code of conduct by preventing another village massacre. When Pham discovered only women and children were in the village, Martin planned to then approach him and ask for a peaceful resolution.

His men departed quietly that night to warn the Montagnards and lead them from their village. Only the women, children, and elderly would be left behind. They would present no threat to Pham and his troops. After that, it was up to Martin to negotiate with him.

If the colonel didn't want the Montagnards in his AO, Martin would ensure they departed, but they would likely end up at another relocation camp. He hoped that wouldn't happen. Captain Truong had to make the colonel realize these were his allies and a potent reconnaissance force that could provide invaluable support. But there was a missing piece to this puzzle. Even with the old prejudices, Pham's determination to destroy them defied reason. There had been past Montagnard revolts, but he had no reason to believe this was one. And the more he thought about it, the more Martin wondered if Pham was somehow directly connected to Sergeant Ravera's ill-fated prisoner snatch.

It was near midnight when the sit-reps came in from Martin's men. Using pre-planned alternate radio frequencies and coded language, they updated him. Thirty-five Montagnard guerrillas and eight advisors had crossed the river and taken up positions on a high ridge overlooking the village. Khonsu had argued they were leaving his people unprotected, but Martin assured him he would not allow the South Vietnamese to harm them.

Twenty more Montagnards along with Bushmaster and four more American advisors were also positioned on a high ridge back up the road closer to the firebase. If the ARVNs brought up mortars or recoilless rifles to fire on the village, Zeke and his men would stop them. This was a worst-case scenario and unlikely, but one that had to be considered. He had his men in place, well hidden, and ready for what he prayed would be a successful bluff. If Duggin didn't show up, or the bluff failed, tomorrow could be a bloody day. It was after midnight when he lay on his cot and closed his eyes for what he hoped would be a few hours' sleep.

Martin felt someone grasp his shoulder and shake him.

"Captain."

It was First Sergeant Gautier.

"Bushmaster and Sky Soldier are both reporting movement near their positions, and it's not the South Vietnamese."

Martin sat upright.

"Shit!"

He had slept in his boots and fatigues. Stumbling across the HQ hooch, he grabbed the radio handset but turned back to Gautier.

"VC?"

"Bushmaster thinks they're NVA."

"What'd they report?"

"A column of infantry is following the trail on the northside of the ridge, paralleling the highway. They're heading east, coming this way."

"Any estimates of their numbers?"

"Best guess is around two hundred men."

"Holy crap!"

Martin grabbed his rucksack and a radio.

"I need to get out there. You stay here and monitor the radios. Has there been any movement from the ARVN troops here on the firebase?"

The first sergeant gave him a grim nod.

"I'm afraid so. They positioned a column of APCs and several deuce-and-a-halfs over at the main gate a couple hours ago. The vehicles were idling and making a lot of racket, so they shut them down. I suspect they're planning to go into the Montagnard village at first light."

Martin shook his head in resignation. "And the NVA somehow already know this. That's why they're moving our way to set up an ambush. They've got to have a spy on this firebase. Go to Captain Truong's hooch, and y'all go together to warn Colonel Pham. Tell him if his troops move toward the village the NVA will be waiting on them. I'm going to see if we can secure the village until this thing is resolved."

"It's five klicks to the village, Sir. How are you getting there?"

"I'll take our jeep as far as that old woodcutter's shed two and a half klicks up the highway. I'll hoof it from there."

"Sir." There was an uncomfortable pause as the first sergeant dropped his chin and wagged his head. "You can't save the world. Let's use the radio. You've got some of the best combat soldiers this war has produced out there. They can handle it."

"I appreciate your concern, First Sergeant, but I belong out there with my men."

After securing the radio inside his rucksack, Martin grabbed his CAR-15 along with his K-bar, several frags, and smoke, before stepping into the doorway. It was late, but the stars were still out, and the sky was clear. A quarter-moon shone brightly overhead. He had one intention: to protect the Montagnard villagers and his men until he heard from Colonel Duggin at Phu Bai. Hopefully, Lieutenant Postiche had reached him, and he was in contact with Colonel Pham. But only then did he remember the unplugged teletype machine.

With the jeep hidden behind the woodcutter's shed, Martin set out on foot. Finding his men and the Montagnard fighters in the jungle at night was a dangerous proposition, but he'd been there before. Creeping up the shoulder of the road, he stopped to listen and search the shadows, but there were only the sounds of insects and the sweet smell of the jungle. He continued moving, covering ground as rapidly as possible.

With the NVA in the area, finding Sky Soldier's main force near the village was out of the question. He opted instead to search for Bushmaster. Zeke and his platoon would be closer and likely on this side of the approaching NVA troops. After another hundred meters, Martin stopped. He was as far down the highway as he dared go without making contact.

He whispered Bushmaster's call sign into the radio. "Bushmaster, this is Night Shadow. Sit-rep. Over."

The response was almost immediate as the radio handset hissed. "Night Shadow, this is Bushmaster. We're one-hundred mics to the November of about sixty of the bad guys. I think they're positioning to greet anyone whiskey-bound coming from the firebase. Over."

"Roger, Bushmaster. I'm coming your way. Are you able to give me coordinates? Over."

"Standby, Night Shadow."

There came a minute's pause, before the quiet hiss of static again came from Martin's radio handset.

"Night Shadow, this is Bushmaster. Count from Papa Oscar Blue Two, seven klicks plus eight hundred mikes right and two hundred and fifty mikes up. Approach my pos from the echo but stay on top of the ridge. The bad guys are down below between us and the highway."

Martin crawled into a deep ravine, pulled his poncho liner over his head, and unfolded his map. Counting from the point of origin designated as Blue Two, he pinpointed Zeke's position. He was less than two hundred meters away, up a steep ridge northwest of the highway. The enemy soldiers were even closer, just below him.

After extinguishing his light, Martin keyed the radio handset. "Bushmaster, this is Night Shadow. I'm coming into your perimeter from the echo in about twenty or thirty mikes. Make sure your boys know I'm coming. Over."

"Roger, Night Shadow. Out."

Although his gear was taped, the radio in the rucksack with the other equipment made it difficult to maintain silence. This forced Martin to move slowly as he eased along the roadway searching in the darkness until he found a trail leading up the ridge. Drawing a deep breath, he started up the slope. Somewhere, not too far to his left, were at least sixty NVA regulars waiting in ambush for whoever came up the highway. One misstep and he'd be in a world of hurt. Carefully, he placed each step to avoid breaking a stick or rustling a leaf.

After nearly twenty minutes he had taken one hundred and eighty steps and stopped. Having reached the approximate coordinates sent by Bushmaster, Martin inhaled deeply through his nostrils. The faint odor of a human hung in the warm night air, and the moonlight silhouetted two shadows less than twenty feet away. They had to be Bushmaster's men, squatting side by side at the edge of a ravine.

"Green," Martin whispered the password challenge.

"Moon," came the response.

As he eased past them, he caught a glint of moonlight in one soldier's eyes.

"Bushmaster," the man whispered, and pointed toward a jumble of shadows only a few meters farther up the ridge.

Martin nodded and continued in that direction until he heard someone whispering. They were only a few feet away. He listened and recognized Thibodaux's Cajun drawl. Easing closer, he took a knee beside him. The other man was Bushmaster. Neither had detected his presence, or else they thought he was one of their own.

"What'cha think the captain's gonna do?" T-Bo whispered to Bushmaster.

"I suppose we'll find out when he gets up here."

"I'm here," Martin whispered.

"Jesus, Mary, and Joseph!" T-Bo hissed. "You scared da shit outta me, Sir."

"Keep it down," Martin whispered.

"I see how you got labeled the Ghost," Bushmaster said.

"Where's the enemy from here?"

"Right down there, maybe sixty or seventy meters, watching the highway. They were making all kinds of racket a few minutes ago, but they're settled in now. We heard them walking down the ridge. I think they set out claymores along the roadway."

"Yeah," T-Bo said, "and we heard a clanking sound like maybe a mortar plate being set up back northwest of here."

"So, what's the plan?" Bushmaster asked.

"That bunch down there is only a quarter of the enemy troops that Sky Soldier said passed his position," Martin whispered. "Where are the others?"

Bushmaster rolled on his side and pointed into the darkness down the ridge. "These assholes down below us are a secondary ambush. They're going to let the main ARVN column pass through so their main force closer to the ville can ambush them. This bunch here is a secondary ambush for any relief troops that come from the firebase. So, the question remains, Sir. We need a plan, 'cause this shit is gonna get pretty hairy when daylight comes."

"We were right about Pham. He has a convoy ready to leave the firebase at first light. First Sergeant Gautier is going to find Captain Truong, and they're going to warn Pham about the ambush."

"Yeah, I don't think these enemy troops showing up is a coincidence," Bushmaster said. "I think Pham has a spy in his outfit. I'm just hoping Postiche can get Colonel Duggin involved before this thing gets any worse."

"Yeah, I know. Duggin is bound to show up pretty soon."

"And if he doesn't?"

"Well, right now, I'm going down to the roadway, find those enemy claymores, and turn them to aim back up the ridge."

Bushmaster gave an audible grunt. "With all due respect, Sir, you must be out of your damned mind."

"Maybe so, but we're caught between a rock and a hard place right now, and I'm doing everything possible to put the odds in our favor. We're going to take this thing one step at a time as it plays out. I'll be back in an hour. Move over there and tell your Yards what I'm doing so they don't mistake me for one of the enemy."

CHAPTER NINE

A Lesson in Guerrilla Tactics
The Highway West of the ARVN Firebase

A mist floated high in the trees, and the birds were singing as if they were in paradise. Daylight had broken over the hills, and the tension was grinding Martin's last nerve to a pulp. If Pham had any sense at all, he would heed Gautier's warning and not send his men up this highway today, but it seemed inevitable. It was the ancient parable of the turtle and the scorpion, and Pham was most certainly the scorpion.

Pham was a prima donna who likely imagined himself to someday be in the upper echelons of the South Vietnamese government. He would mistrust his American advisors, and his hatred for the Montagnards had clouded his mind. He would overthink matters and believe he was being misled. Pham would use his stinger even if he killed himself.

The radio handset hissed quietly as it broke static, and the voice of First Sergeant Gautier came from the command center. "Night Shadow One, this is Charley-Charley One. Over."

Other than the cacophony of birds high above, the hillside remained still. Not so much as a leaf stirred, and it was hard to believe sixty or more heavily armed NVA troops were just down the ridge, hidden in the undergrowth. Another barely audible hiss came from the radio handset as Martin picked it up and pressed it to his ear.

"Night Shadow, this is Charley-Charley One. Over."

"Night Shadow, they didn't believe the information we gave them. Lotus Five requests you come up on his ops frequency ASAP. Over."

Lotus Five was Captain Truong—probably wanting to get an update on what was going to be a giant clusterfuck if Pham didn't back off.

"Roger, Charley-Charley. Will do. Out."

Martin twisted the nobs on the PRC-25 to the ARVN ops frequency. It was quiet.

"Lotus Five, this is Night Shadow. Over."

The response was immediate.

"I roger you, Night Shadow. I am ordered to lead the convoy to the village. Request your location. Over."

"Where is your CO?" Martin asked, breaking protocol.

With time running out, he made no pretense of coding the message.

"I am with my men, Captain Shadows." It was Pham. "We are going to the village to collect weapons and make arrests. I am ordering you to assist or standdown. I will not tolerate your interference."

If the enemy was listening, they were surely enjoying the exchange and preparing for a turkey shoot.

"Colonel, if your convoy continues toward the village, you're going to be ambushed by the NVA. I suggest *you* standdown."

"Night Shadow, this is Lotus Five, my Rangers are escorting the convoy. Can you tell me where the enemy ambush is located?"

Pham had put his best men at the front of his column—cannon

fodder for the NVA. Truong had predicted as much.

"Bastard," Martin murmured. He keyed the handset. "Colonel, you and your troops are about to get chopped to pieces."

"Night Shadow Charley-Charley Two. I have TAC air on standby," Gautier said.

Normally good news, this time it wasn't. Martin couldn't use air support without endangering his own men who were on the ridges behind the enemy.

"This whole mission is going to shit," he muttered.

Now that it was daylight, Bushmaster had leaned against a tree and lit a cigarette.

"I concur with your assessment, Sir. So, let's think this through."

Back to the east on the highway came the whine of diesel engines as the convoy approached. Time was running out.

"What are you thinking, Zeke?" Martin asked.

"I prefer Bushmaster, Sir, and I'm thinking we hook up with Captain Truong and light-up the bastards on the ridge below us. Then Sky Soldier and the rest of the Yards can flank that other ambush."

"Sounds pretty good," Martin said, "but what if we tell Sky and his men to drop off the back of that ridge and set up an ambush on the trail the NVA used getting here? I think as soon as they realize they've been compromised and we have the drop on them, they'll use that trail to get the hell out of Dodge."

Bushmaster grinned. "Sounds even better, Sir."

"Okay. Call them and give them the plan. I've got to get down to the road and stop Truong and his people. I'll try to get them to spread out and move up the highway toward the ambush. Hold our men up here on the ridge when the shooting starts. Tell them to stay down and find cover. We don't want to end up shooting at one another. As soon as the enemy begins to retreat, you and Gia can hit them from this side. I'll get Captain Truong to move up the highway to the second ambush. If we keep the heat on them, the enemy will break contact and go back the way they came. That's when Sky Soldier and his men will hit them."

"Well…" Bushmaster paused. "It might be a damned good plan, but I'm worried about what Pham is going to do if and when the NVA retreat."

Bushmaster was right. Pham was a wild card, but there was no time for further talk. Martin sprinted wildly back east, then down the ridge to the highway, where he stopped breathlessly in the middle of the road. The lead APC rounded the curve two hundred meters away. He raised his CAR-15 over his head, and the vehicle jolted to a stop while an officer peered at him through binoculars. It was probably Truong. Martin began walking his way.

Truong jumped down from the APC as several of his Rangers ran to his side with weapons at the ready. He raised his hand and signaled for them to stop while he walked toward Martin. Truong had already shown he was a man of honor. Martin could only hope he wouldn't mortgage his soul for the likes of Pham. But Truong was Vietnamese, and despite their mutual goals, he possessed Asian philosophy and logic. Martin approached with caution and met Truong in the middle of the road.

"What's your mission, Captain?" Martin asked.

"Colonel Pham has ordered me and my men to escort the convoy to the Montagnard village. His APCs follow mine. He has brought out two companies."

"And with an enemy ambush just up this highway behind me, what will you do?"

"Captain Shadows, I believe you and I are caught in the same snare."

"Then let me free you. A little farther up this highway on this ridge behind me is an NVA ambush, and about another click farther is a second one. Inform your colonel if he continues up this road, your men and his will be slaughtered."

"Colonel Pham has already heard this, but he believes it is a ploy. He believes there is no enemy ambush. He believes you are attempting to stop our troops from going into the Montagnard village."

"And you, Captain, what do you believe?"

Truong stood almost sad-eyed as he faced Martin.

"I have no choice but to do as I am ordered."

Realizing his efforts to save them had failed, Martin shook his head in resignation.

"I won't stand in your way, but you and your men will likely die. Hopefully, Colonel Pham will come to your aid, but if past practice continues, he will let you die."

"What would you have me do, Captain?"

"Don't you see that you're nothing more than a helmet on a stick for Pham? Give me time to go back up the ridge to my men who are behind those enemy troops. In a few minutes, you can proceed around that curve, but have your men in attack mode. We will work together to take out this first enemy ambush, then regroup. My second group has already flanked the second enemy ambush and is ready to move against them."

"Yours is a risky plan, Captain, but I will inform the colonel of our intentions."

"I wouldn't tell him shit, Captain, but that's your call. Good Luck."

After Martin climbed back up the ridge to Bushmaster and his platoon of Montagnards, Captain Truong brought his APCs up the road, stopping and turning their guns up the ridge. The NVA realizing they'd been discovered detonated their claymores—the same claymores Martin had reversed to face up the ridge. The firefight was again furious but brief as the communist troops were devastated. Martin's only casualty came from one of Truong's fifty calibers firing too high up the ridge. A Montagnard soldier had been severely wounded.

While Truong's men and his APCs turned to drive up the ridge, more ARVN APCs rumbled up the highway. It was Pham with his main armored cav force. By the time Martin again reached the road, Pham was standing atop his APC berating Captain Truong. The colonel spotted Martin approaching and leapt to the ground, charging toward him with his forty-five caliber Colt in hand. Two Montagnard guerrillas stepped from the jungle beside Martin and leveled their weapons at the colonel who stopped and looked back at his men. None of them moved.

"Colonel," Martin shouted. "I am only trying to keep you from making a mistake."

Pham seemed dazed as he spun about, pointing his forty-five toward the jungle.

"We just wiped out an enemy ambush that would have destroyed your men."

The Vietnamese colonel seemed to slowly regather his wits.

"My mission is to protect this road all the way back to Highway One, and the railroad that is there as well. Highway 12 is mine, and you and these Nguoi Thuong are interfering. You must move aside and tell them to surrender their weapons."

Martin turned to one of the Montagnards standing beside him. It was Katu. "Go back and tell our men to take cover further up the ridge." In a flash the two Montagnards disappeared back into the jungle. Martin again turned to face Pham.

"I've already informed Colonel Duggin what is happening, and I've told you the Montagnard are not revolting and intend to work with us, but if you attack them, they're prepared and they're waiting for you. There are no combatants in the village, only women and children. If you harm anyone in their village, you will have their blood on your hands, as well as that of your men. Are you ready to face responsibility for a massacre of innocent civilians?"

Martin read people well, and Pham looked as if he'd been gut-shot. It was part bluff, but it was working. Pham now seemed more bewildered than ever. His eyes darted about, and he glanced back at his armored column before turning again to face Martin.

"You believe you are clever, Captain Shadows, but I know better. You will regret this interference. Move your advisors aside, or risk becoming casualties."

Reasoning with the mad fool was useless. Martin intended now only to protect his men and the Montagnard people, but the second NVA ambush only a click up the highway might well help him.

"We will not stand in your way, Colonel. Go, but don't say I didn't warn you."

From the direction of Phu Bai came the thumping sounds of approaching helicopter gunships. Martin prayed it was Colonel Duggin. Pham returned to his APC and the diesel engines whined and spewed black exhaust as the ARVN column continued up the highway. Truong remained behind as he recalled and reorganized his Rangers. Martin ran up the ridge and radioed Sky Soldier to move his men and evacuate the entire village. His only remaining hope was that the Montagnard villagers could flee into the highlands and escape before Pham and his troops arrived.

When the last of the ARVN vehicles passed, Martin led his men back down to the highway and across the river. As they reached the opposite bank, the sound of the second NVA ambush exploded and echoed downriver. Pham had charged into the kill zone as a daisy chain of detonating claymores thundered and echoed against the far ridge. The NVA followed with rocket-propelled grenades and what sounded like a fifty-one-caliber machine gun. The ARVN helicopter gunships unleashed their rockets into the enemy positions, but it was too late. Pham was getting his ass handed to him piecemeal by the NVA.

Continuing parallel to the river, Martin and his group bypassed the ambush on the other side and arrived at the village to find Sky Soldier and Khonsu's men rushing the women and children through a back gate. The sounds of the firefight back up the highway had abated—replaced by the clank of treads and whining diesel engines. The remaining ARVN APCs were approaching. Having been badly mauled, Pham and his troops would no doubt be hell-bent on vengeance, and the village inhabitants were easy targets.

"What's the plan, Sir?" Bushmaster asked.

The advisors surrounded Martin, panting and sucking water from their canteens. Several hundred meters away, east of the main gate, the ARVN troops began deploying across the highway and along the ridge to the north. A jeep with a recoilless rifle spun about in a cloud of dust, and the gun crew began loading the weapon.

"We need to delay them, but we can't fire on them," Martin said.

"Why not?" T-Bo asked.

"Because shooting allied troops will get us locked up in Leavenworth," Bushmaster answered.

Only then did Martin notice several Montagnard guerrillas were still in the village below. Two were carrying the village totem on their shoulders as they ran toward the back gate. Two others were squatted in a ditch, watching the South Vietnamese troops as they spread in an extended line either side of the main gate.

"What in the hell are they doing down there?" Martin muttered.

"Rescuing their totem pole," Bushmaster said. "It's important to them."

"I know, but I'm talking about those two over there in that ditch."

"They wait for all the Vietnamese troops to come, then have special surprise for them."

Martin turned to find Khonsu standing behind him.

"Surprise?"

"Foo gas," Khonsu said.

"How in hell did you get foo gas?"

Bushmaster cleared his throat and scratched his head. "Well, Sir, we, I mean, I have some friends up at Phu Bai who helped me get the JP-4 and naphtha, and there's empty 55-gallon drums all over the ARVN firebase, I mean, just sayin', it was meant to defend the village against the VC and NVA attacks, but well...." He shrugged.

Foo gas was a first cousin to napalm and provided a devastatingly effective perimeter defense.

"And let me guess, those boys down there in the village are about to blow that shit all over Pham and the ARVN troops, right?"

"Well, Sir, not if Pham and his people don't fire first. Like I said, it was meant for the NVA, but these people are fighting for their lives."

Bushmaster's words were punctuated by an echoing boom, as the ARVN gun crew fired the recoilless rifle. A Montagnard hooch exploded in a shower of straw and poles. The South Vietnamese troops opened fire, and their tracer rounds began setting more huts afire. The worst possibility was happening before his eyes as Martin watched helplessly.

"What are your orders, Sir?" Bushmaster shouted.

Martin turned to his team leader. "Take all our advisors back downriver and circle back to the firebase. I'm staying with the Montagnards and try to get them somewhere safe, maybe another firebase. Recover my jeep from the woodcutter's shed on your way back."

Bushmaster motioned to Sky Soldier. "Get at it!"

"No!" Martin shouted. "You go too."

"Hear me out, Captain. I'm not only better qualified, but you can cover for me. Let me take these people south toward the Laotian border."

"You don't have to do this, Zeke. Get out of this godforsaken war while you can."

"Sir, you can book this. Someday, I'm gonna come knocking at your door again. Now, listen. List me as MIA, and I'll take care of the rest."

There came a thundering explosion near the main gate as a 55-gallon drum rocketed skyward, nearly a hundred feet into the air. A secondary explosion ignited an orange mushroom cloud of foo-gas, sending napalm's first cousin spreading in a lethal blanket over the ARVN troops.

"Okay, go. Take them. Get the hell out of here before they recover. I'll go back to the firebase with the men. You can come visit me at Leavenworth."

CHAPTER TEN

New Spirits Calling
The ARVN Firebase

Before Martin departed for Vietnam, Two Shadows had told him he saw bitterness and loss in his vision. It now left Martin wondering if Bushmaster and the Montagnard villagers would survive. The odds of a group that size successfully crossing hundreds of miles through the Central Highlands to reach the border were slim at best. The trackless mountains and valleys were crawling with NVA troops, American troops, and LRRP teams—not to mention constant flyovers by surveillance aircraft. The highland trails were also subject to monstrous B-52 Arc Light Strikes, known to wipe out miles of jungle in a single attack.

When he arrived back at the ARVN firebase that afternoon, Martin saw an American loach on the helicopter pad outside the main gate. Colonel Duggin had flown down from Phu Bai. He was with First Sergeant Gautier at the HQ hooch. The colonel's crisply starched fatigues and spit-shined boots stood in contrast to Martin's muddy, torn, and sweat-soaked tiger-stripes. The two officers traded salutes.

Martin set his CAR-15 in a corner rack and shed his rucksack while the colonel lit a cigarette. He handed it to Martin and lit another.

"Did Lieutenant Postiche fill you in on what's been happening?" Martin asked.

"I haven't seen the lieutenant," Duggin said, "but First Sergeant Gautier has given me a detailed situation report. So, tell me what the hell happened out there today?"

"You haven't spoken to Lieutenant Postiche?"

"No. Was I supposed to?"

"Sir, after Colonel Pham refused to let me send my report to you on the secure line, I sent Postiche back on the supply chopper to Phu Bai. He was supposed to inform you and—"

"I haven't seen or spoken with him. Sit down, and let's take this thing from the top."

Martin's mind raced with the possibilities. From their very first meeting, Postiche had seemed strangely oblique in many ways. Yet, there was also the possibility that he somehow had been detained by Pham's people. Duggin began taking notes as Martin recounted the events of recent days. The colonel did not interrupt or ask questions, but his legal pad was rapidly filling with notes and sentences punctuated with question marks. When he was done, Martin sat in silence.

"So, you have one CIDG soldier badly wounded, one of your men MIA, an estimated thirty to forty enemy KIA, and nearly two hundred Montagnard villagers scattered to the winds?"

"That's the gist of it, Sir."

"What about Colonel Pham and his battalion?"

"They took heavy casualties—first when the NVA ambushed them, and again when they attacked the Montagnard village."

"Attacked?"

"Yes, Sir. They fired into the village with a recoilless rifle and numerous small arms."

"Were they fired on first from the village?"

"No Sir. The South Vietnamese opened fire first and without provocation. That's when the two Montagnards who stayed behind detonated the foo-gas on the village perimeter."

"Foo-gas!? You've got to be— Where in hell did they get foo-gas?"

"It was part of their village defenses for possible enemy attacks."

Duggin exhaled and shook his head in resignation.

"I want a full and detailed after-action report ASAP. And just so you know, I found out about this matter only a few hours ago when I got a call from Colonel Krieger at MAC-V. He said he got a classified intelligence report from the OSA saying there was a Montagnard revolt, and our advisors were in some way involved. He told me to look into it."

From somewhere outside the firebase came the whine of diesel engines. Pham's troops were returning. Martin walked with Colonel Duggin toward the staging area near the main gate. When they arrived, they found Captain Truong wearily giving orders to men stacking rows of body bags and carrying the wounded on stretchers to the aid station.

"Where is Colonel Pham?" Duggin asked.

Truong stopped and stared at him for a moment. "The colonel is dead, as are thirty-eight of our troops. We have nearly twice that number wounded and many more missing."

"What about your Ranger company, Captain?" Martin asked.

"I have only two wounded. Most of the casualties were Colonel Pham's troops when they were ambushed by the NVA and when they attacked the village."

"I'll get you some more medevac choppers in here," Duggin said, "and I'll see if we can get some of our troops to scout the highway out to the Montagnard village for your missing men."

Martin and Truong locked eyes, but neither spoke. After several seconds Truong looked away.

"Thank you, Colonel. I will inform Colonel Pham's XO, Major Lahm."

———

At dusk, Martin walked with Colonel Duggin out to a bunker near the main gate. Just down the hill, his pilots were pre-tripping his chopper as the turbine began to whine to life. Duggin had met with Truong for a long while and was now preparing to return to Phu Bai. Martin's thoughts swirled in a vortex of confusion, with the biggest question being why Pham had been so hell-bent on destroying the Montagnard villagers.

"If you don't mind my asking, Sir, did Truong tell you anything about why Pham was so intent on attacking the Montagnards?"

"Captain, I know very little for certain, but there have been some strange things happening, and I intend to get to the bottom of just what in hell is going on."

"Strange things?"

"Did you know that Lieutenant Postiche and a OSA advisor named Liegeman have met with Colonel Pham at his HQ several times in the recent past?"

"No, Sir."

"So says Captain Truong, and he also told me that it was Postiche who advised Pham not to move to the aid of Captain Watson and his Montagnard troops that day when they were overrun by the NVA."

Stunned, Martin realized he'd been blind and should have followed his instincts. "Postiche? What the—! Who the hell *is* Postiche, and where is he now?"

"Something I'd like to know myself, Captain. If he shows up,

I want you to keep it low-key till I get back with you. Don't ask too many questions. Don't back him into a corner. Let him explain where he's been. Let him do all the talking and just keep an eye on him. We'll deal with the lieutenant later.

"Right now, I want you and your men to standdown until you receive further orders. I'm going back to Phu Bai and begin calling in some favors from old friends. I believe Captain Truong is on the up and up and can be trusted, but don't share too much information with him until we're certain. I'll be back in touch with you in a few days."

One of the pilots came trotting back up the hill to the gate. He had a green laundry bag over his shoulder.

"Oh hell!" Duggin said. "I almost forgot the mail. I'm also sending a resupply chopper down tomorrow with some steaks, potatoes, gravy, and all the fixins, along with some canned peaches and real ice cream. Oh, yeah, and there should be clean uniforms, new boots, and several cases of beer onboard as well. We'll talk soon."

At nightfall, when he returned to the advisors' hooch, Martin found most of his men lights-out on their cots, lost in a sleep of total exhaustion. He carried the mailbag back to his HQ hooch. Mail-call could wait till morning, but he wondered if the Dear John letter he was expecting from Kania might be in the bag. After all, he hadn't answered either of her previous letters and it had been over two months since they'd seen one another. The two weeks they spent together before he went home to Kentucky were an awkward and confusing time. Almost as two timid lovers wanting the other to make the first move, they'd not made love again, but it hadn't been for lack of desire.

They spent hours together talking while sitting on his grandparents' front porch, or riding in his pickup, or wrapped in blankets while sitting around a campfire. He had learned much about Kania in those last days before heading to Nam. She was one of those surprise babies who came late in the lives of her parents, and her sisters and a brother had moved away to distant parts of the country, leaving her heir to the parental care chores. He learned that Kania's father was full-blooded Lakota, and her mother was of Scandinavian blood. She also told him how she had begun her final year at the University of Montana when she was forced to return home to look after her ailing father.

Kania was a strong woman, a beautiful woman, and a woman with intelligence. It had taken a lot of willpower to bury his infatuation for her, but it was for the best—at least for now. Lifelong relationships weren't normally built on one-night stands where alcohol was involved, and despite those near misses, they'd remained close, and he had received two letters from her since returning to Nam. He had yet to finish the one he was writing—his first—but it wasn't for lack of care. Vietnam had made him a cynic. No woman would wait a year for a man she'd only known for two weeks. And no woman would remain long with a man who had raised cynicism to such a perfect art form.

Despite missing her senior year of college to nurse her elderly father, her letters were upbeat. She mentioned visiting Two Shadows and how Martin's grandmother had treated her as a daughter. The second letter alluded to their night together on his grandfather's porch, and she said for her it was as much of a commitment as he wanted it to be. She had stopped short of saying it was love at first sight, and he assumed the next move was his.

The most recent letter also told how she was now avoiding the bar, because she could no longer dance with the boys—it just wasn't in her heart. However, she was visiting the diner regularly for lunch with her girlfriends and getting fat. Martin opened the mailbag and dumped the pile of letters on his bunk. He spotted hers immediately and stuffed the rest back in the bag. Opening the envelope with his knife, he lay back on his cot.

March 1970

> *Dear Martin,*
>
> *I know you must be terribly busy and haven't had an opportunity to write, but I would at least like to know that you are okay. Just in case they haven't arrived yet, I want you to know I have sent you two previous letters. No matter what happens, I will be here for you when you come home. And don't forget that you promised me that next dance. I am looking forward to it. Other news here is not so good. Dad has again taken a turn for the worse, and it does not look good. He has always been such a strong man, and it's difficult to see him in this condition. Your grandfather and grandmother have been a tremendous help for me, even at their age. So, this letter has to be short because I've got to get back to Dad. Please write soon.*
>
> *And just for the record, after that first night with you and those few days we spent together before you went back home, you stole my heart. I am hopelessly in love with you.*
> *Always Faithful,*
> *Kania*

It wasn't at all what he expected. He had been lying to himself. He *did* care for her, and it was this letter that now made it seem losing her was something he couldn't bear. Perhaps that was why he'd been so reluctant to admit to his feelings. And if it truly was love, he now needed to exhume that mad infatuation he had so carefully buried.

He could no longer let her believe he didn't care, but there was a reality that would severely test her commitment. That was the seven thousand miles and ten more months in Vietnam that still separated them. Despite his exhaustion, he sat up and went to the table in the corner where he began writing.

March 1970

Dear Kania,

I apologize for not writing sooner. I already wrote one letter, but it got wet in my rucksack before I could send it. Anyway, you are right about being busy. I was promoted to Captain and went through Recondo training school here in Nam. It's probably the best army training I've had. I now command a group of advisors attached to a South Vietnamese Army unit. It's mostly reconnaissance, so it's not as dangerous as it could be, but it does have its interesting moments. Ten more months in this place seems like an eternity, and I am limited as to what I can write, but there's been a lot of talk about our country's part in this war coming to an end. I hope so because I still hope to have that dance with you someday. I am sorry to hear about your father and will offer a prayer for him and for you. If I come home in one piece and remain in possession of your heart, I hope we can pick up where we left off. Till then I will remain faithfully yours.

Martin

It seemed that giving her hope without giving her false hope was a delicate balance of words. When he was done, he folded the letter and slipped it into an envelope. Writing the Montana address on it made him think of every single one of those thousands of miles that separated them. Going home had never seemed quite so important as it did now, and it wasn't the loneliness or escaping the war that drove this feeling. It was Kania.

Kania was right about the guidance of the spirits. They and

God were now calling to him from both sides of the ocean. Here in Nam, it was Khonsu and the Montagnard people, and his men, but her voice was calling him from back home.

Martin lay back on the cot and read her letter again and again, before he felt the ground trembling and saw an orange sun from which flowed rivers of molten gold down through the mountains and valleys, to a place—a cabin perhaps. It seemed at once familiar and strange, and a lone figure was silhouetted there in the open doorway. It was the same mysterious figure he had seen in his first vision back in Montana.

After a while he found himself standing in front of a cabin as a sudden snowfall began. Huge snowflakes were driven by a cold wind that made him shiver, and the shadow of a face appeared staring out at him from the partially open cabin door. Martin felt as if he might cry out at the person, and he struggled to draw a breath only to realize he had awakened. The flowing golden light, the heavy snow, and the mysterious figure in the doorway were gone. It had all seemed so real, but it was only another dream.

This musty hooch in Vietnam was reality. He sat up on the side of the cot and rubbed his face. The dream was much like the vision he had months ago, except the flames of napalm had somehow evolved into an inviting golden light.

A spiritual power not unlike his grandfather's, although embryonic, seemed to be growing from within and he wondered what he had just seen, because he now realized his dream was just as real as the war outside. His mind toyed with the images, and only now did he realize his vision of several months ago and this dream had occurred in two places. Both had come from Vietnam and somewhere in Montana. It was all somehow related, yet he was frustrated because he had not yet found the wisdom to understand or interpret their meaning. This was something his grandfather had always done. Closing his eyes, he prayed for sleep.

CHAPTER ELEVEN

A People with No Home
FOB-1, Phu Bai, Republic of Vietnam

It was forty-eight hours later when Colonel Duggin ordered Martin and his advisory detachment to the Special Forces compound in Phu Bai. Known as Forward Operating Base-One, it was homebase for Army Special Forces teams operating in Laos, North Vietnam, and I-Corps. After transport by chopper, the advisors were ordered to standdown again and await orders, while Martin was called to Duggin's office. It was after sunset when he arrived, and Duggin had a bottle of bourbon and two glasses sitting on his desk.

"Have a seat, Captain."

The colonel studied the notes on his desk several moments before looking up.

"Shadows, I've uncovered a hell of a lot of crap that puts you up to your chin in a swamp full of gators. Much of what was redacted from your file and AARs was filled in by Sergeant Luis Ravera down at Nha Trang and Sergeant Stoneman with the 75th Rangers. It took a lot to find them, and even more to get Ravera to open up, but when I mentioned you and the Montagnard leader named Khonsu, he began talking. You have a choice. You can let me help you, and I'll tell you what I've learned, or you can stay clammed up, and we'll let the chips fall where they may."

"Do you mind if I smoke while we talk, Sir?"

It was an easy decision. There were no good options remaining other than putting his trust in Duggin. It was apparent the colonel had been kept in the dark, and this Lieutenant Postiche was acting under a false flag. As best he could determine, Postiche and Liegeman were working together to see that Khonsu and his men were destroyed by the South Vietnamese.

Duggin reached into his desk drawer and took out two cigars. Using his old paratrooper knife, he trimmed the ends off the cigars and handed one to Martin. "Try this."

Martin flipped open his Zippo and fired up the cigar. The colonel poured the glasses full.

"What either of us says here tonight is still classified military information and it cannot be discussed outside this office. Agreed?"

Martin nodded.

"I want you to tell me everything that happened at that prison and after you escaped, but first let me tell *you* a little about how Sergeant Ravera and his Montagnards got there. You see, Ravera and his CIDG became unknowingly involved in the Phoenix program when they were recruited by the OSA for an attempted prisoner snatch of two high-level VC cadre members. The VC were supposedly meeting with civilian PAVN sympathizers at an old French mansion near a village in Bình Định Province.

"It's splitting hairs when you're talking about the VC, but it was a mission better suited for the South Vietnamese Special Police—not the CIDG or our military. The problem was Liegeman, who coordinated the mission, had been unknowingly conned into believing this story concocted by a VC An Ninh Agent.

"The mission was compromised, and typical of a lot of OSA

capers, the whole shitshow went sideways. Ravera and his CIDG troops were ambushed. Those that weren't killed were captured. That's when the ARVN commander providing security backup ordered his men to begin shooting people in the village, claiming they were VC sympathizers. Afterward they reported it was Ravera and the Montagnards who slaughtered the villagers. No one knew anything different until you freed Ravera and the Montagnards from the NVA prison. Oh, and that ARVN commander that night was a then Major Pham."

Martin sat upright. Duggin had dropped the last piece of the puzzle in place. Pham had as much to lose as Liegeman if it was discovered he had ordered the massacre of the villagers.

"You seem surprised, Captain. You didn't know Pham was responsible for the massacre?"

"I suspected as much, but it didn't make sense how he managed to get assigned up here, and how—"

"Liegeman. He pulled the strings necessary to get Pham assigned to I-Corps and get the CIDG troops under his command.

"That's when Liegeman and the OSA began orchestrating a coverup by threatening to report Ravera to MAC-V for his part in the raid. And like I said, they also got the Montagnards placed under Pham's command with the implicit understanding he would silence them."

"When does MAC-V wake up and smell the coffee?" Martin asked.

"I think MAC-V failed to understand the Agency was undermining their efforts to end these dark ops, but they know now they were being manipulated—especially since I discussed Liegeman and Postiche with Colonel Krieger. He said his people had no knowledge of the lieutenant's location or involvement— only that he was on temporary duty, assigned to the Office of the Special Assistant as a military advisor. And it seems someone there gained approval for him to be inserted into my advisory command. We think his mission was to work secretly with Colonel Pham, but I was totally ignorant of that and signed off on it. The people at MAC-V are pretty pissed off about it right now, and I was able to wrangle a favor from them."

"Favor?"

"I've been given permission to send a unit of my advisors to find Bushmaster and the Montagnards. MAC-V wants to have them returned to an old CIDG camp that for now remains under American control. You will plan and execute the mission to search for them, but everything goes through me first for approval. In the meantime, the Special Forces people here at FOB-1 have agreed to provide equipment, transportation, and communication support for your unit."

"So, Liegeman and Postiche were working with Colonel Pham to have Khonsu and his men killed, but in the process Captain Watson and two American advisors, along with twenty other Montagnard troops were killed instead. Will they be held accountable?"

"That's the way it seems. We have Captain Truong's statement to that effect and everyone else's story puts the crosshairs on Liegeman, but we have to leave the investigation to MAC-V and the CID. Right now, I want you to give me a list of supplies you'll need, along with an ops plan. I've had messages sent to the Marines, the First Cav, the Hundred and First, and a couple other outfits in this area to keep an eye out for the Montagnards. I made sure everyone understands they are friendlies. I was also able to get SF to commit a Pink Team as needed for your transport and air cover."

"A Pink Team?"

"Two slicks, two Cobra gunships, and a C&C chopper."

"That's pretty generous. How'd you do that?"

"After I told their CO what I learned from Ravera, he was pretty pissed. The snake eaters are a hundred percent behind helping us find Bushmaster because he's one of their boys. They've assigned us our own radio frequencies and are running our communications through their TOC here at FOB-1. I will coordinate our movements with other units in the AO to avoid contact with them. Questions?"

"I need a day or two to organize my men. I want to do a flyover south of the old Montagnard village. I know they're likely gone, and a hell of a long way from there by now, but it'll give me a better idea of the terrain and the path they may have taken."

"I can provide my chopper for a flyover, but something else you need to know is that Pham's XO, Major Lahm, has already sent patrols out the highway toward the village. And the South Vietnamese have been doing flyovers of their own. I believe they're still searching for the Montagnards, but when I asked him about it, he said they're only searching for their own MIAs. It seems Liegeman may have already gotten to him."

"Bastard," Martin muttered.

"Don't worry about him or Lahm. They're wasting their time. We've already gotten intel from a SOG Alpha Team that spotted Sergeant Anderson and the Yards nearly a hundred kilometers south of the village. I don't know how they're doing it with that many people, but they're hauling ass due south and will likely cross into Laos before we can catch up with them. The worst of it is you'll be operating at the southernmost limits of our AO and dependent upon an X-ray radio relay team operating south of Da Nang. Commo may be problematic that far back in the highlands, but we'll do our best."

Thirty-six hours later Martin and his team boarded slicks bound for an LZ a hundred and fifty klicks southwest of Phu Bai. A mountainous area with few roads and fewer villages, it was double- and triple-canopied jungle cut by deep valleys and rocky streams. Finding a Special Forces soldier and Montagnard guerrillas would have been nearly impossible had they not been traveling with the entire village, including children, the elderly, and livestock. It also helped that they had been spotted again by a Birddog pilot, who thankfully reported them as apparent civilian refugees.

By midmorning the Ghost and his fifteen-man team were deployed on a desolate mountain slope near the Laotian border. It was during his flyover the previous evening that he spotted barely noticeable wisps of smoke filtering from the jungle below. This was in the same valley he now studied with binoculars. The smoke was likely the cook-fires of the Montagnard villagers, but it also could have been the NVA. He had requisitioned an M-60 machine gun for the team. The pig was a heavy weapon for a recon team, but the situation demanded it. Gautier and Sky Soldier sat beside him watching and waiting.

The Ghost pointed to a place in the valley that looked no different than the next. "Back that way about four or five klicks is where we saw the smoke yesterday evening. I think they're probably past here by now. We need to move down the mountain and see if we can pick up their trail. What do you think?"

"Sounds like a good move," the first sergeant whispered.

"I agree," Sky Soldier said. "I'll put T-Bo on point. Lugo can walk slack for him."

"Good enough. Let's move out."

Martin stood, but something he sensed more than heard made him freeze. The others noticed and paused, casting curious glances his way.

"What is it, Sir?" Gautier asked.

Martin held up his hand for silence and cocked his head to one side. It was a sound—a distant one. The peaceful warble of a bird came from somewhere in the jungle, and a gentle breeze riffled through the leaves overhead. He strained but only silence came in return. His grandfather's words reminded him: "Only few can hear the voices of the spirits when they call." The Ghost was a fanciful name, and he still wondered if he was one of the few. Turning about, he raised his hand to motion the men forward when it came again, this time with clarity—the rhythmic thump of a helicopter flying somewhere back to the northeast.

His men went instantly to ground, disappearing before his eyes. These were jungle fighters who knew their craft. They lay and waited, and after a while a lone helicopter came down the valley from the north. American military choppers seldom flew solo, and he watched this one with curiosity as it approached. It passed fewer than two hundred meters away, a black Huey, either a SOG or OSA asset. No one moved, and the chopper seemed it would continue southward but it didn't. It flared up and away as it began circling the valley. And there came another sound.

From somewhere in the valley below the distinct crow of a rooster came loud and clear. With no villages within miles, it had to be the Montagnards. The bird crowed again, and Martin refocused his binoculars, but he couldn't penetrate the jungle canopy. The helicopter had apparently spotted something as it slowed and its occupants stood in the open door, searching the ground below. After a few moments the chopper crossed the valley and turned back north.

"Do you think they spotted them?" T-Bo whispered.

"Not sure," Sky Soldier answered. "They saw something."

The chopper disappeared as it flew back north up the valley.

"Let's move out," Martin said. "Bushmaster won't let them stay there for long."

"Hell," T-Bo muttered. "They're probably halfway over that mountain by now."

CHAPTER TWELVE

Don't Tread on Me
A Mountain Valley Seventy Miles South of Phu Bai

After calling in a sit-rep to the X-ray team, Martin moved the patrol as rapidly as he dared down the mountainside toward the valley. The helicopter had no doubt spooked the Montagnards, who were likely moving fast. Martin hoped to intercept them before they disappeared, but T-Bo was nervous. Continually stopping, he surveyed the surrounding jungle. It was to be expected. This was the way he was trained. Martin refused to push him. No one would be rescued if they blundered into an enemy ambush.

For the next half hour, the team moved rapidly down the slope, toward the valley floor. A wide rocky stream meandered down the center of the valley, and one by one Thibodaux and the lead element began crossing. The gurgling stream drowned out the other sounds, and two men were mid-stream when the chopper suddenly reappeared, flying low and fast. Too late, they tried to escape the stream and reach the cover of the jungle, but their efforts were futile. Spotting them, the chopper climbed, spun about, and returned, this time dropping a red smoke grenade on the far bank as it passed low overhead.

Martin gazed up at the men standing in the helicopter door as it thundered past. It was Liegeman and Postiche.

"They're marking our position for an airstrike," Sky Soldier shouted from the far bank.

He had already crossed the stream with T-Bo, Lugo, and Gopher. Gopher, the jokester in the unit, would not be outdone as he gave the chopper occupants the best salute he could muster—a middle finger raised high.

"Go, go!" Martin shouted. "Hurry. Keep going and spread out. We'll stay over here."

He turned to Gautier. "Let's go back up the slope. Take the rest of the team and find cover. Spread out and stay down. I'll try to contact the X-ray team and see if they can tell these guys we're friend…"

He stopped mid-sentence as it dawned on him. Liegeman and Postiche probably thought he and his team were with the Montagnards. He followed his men up the hill as the roar of propeller-driven aircraft engines echoed from the north. These were likely Douglas A-1 Skyraiders flown by the Republic of Vietnam Air Force. Fighter bombers supplied by the United States, the aircraft had four wing-mounted 20mm cannons and lethal 7,000-pound payloads, which included bombs, napalm canisters, and rockets. The roar of their radial engines echoed off the far mountainside as the Skyraiders came down the valley single file. There was nothing Martin could do but join his men as they burrowed into shallow ravines on the mountainside.

The shock waves from 250-pound bombs blew through the jungle below as the aircraft roared by one at a time dropping their payloads. They were concentrating on the opposite bank where Sky Soldier, Thibodaux, and the others had taken cover. The three aircraft with Vietnamese Air Force markings climbed and circled before diving again into the valley. This time they fired rockets and strafed the jungle with their machine guns. So badly Martin wanted to take the M-60 and fight back, but that would draw fire to the men around him.

The radio broke static. "Ghost, this is T-Bo, we got hit. We need help ASAP. Over."

"Roger T-Bo. Who's hit? Over."

"Sky Soldier and Gopher are down, Sir. I'm hit too, and so is Lugo. We need a dust-off."

"Roger, T-Bo. Stay down and treat the wounded. I'll get a medevac coming our way. Standby."

He switched frequencies and contacted the relay team. Within minutes, they confirmed a Pink team was enroute escorting a medevac chopper out of Phu Bai. Their ETA was forty-five minutes, but there again came the sound of a lone helicopter somewhere up the valley. The black Huey was returning, this time low and slow as it came down the valley from the north.

First Sergeant Gautier crawled up beside him. "It's that damned black chopper. They're coming back for damage assessment."

Martin's head pounded with adrenaline-fueled anger. "Give me the damned M-60," he said.

"What if they simply mistook us for the enemy?" Gautier asked.

Martin shook his head. "Yeah, if it was a mistake, it was because they thought we were the Montagnards."

"Sir!" Gautier said, "you need to think about this."

Martin was incensed. "Come with me."

He threw a two-hundred round belt of 7.62mm ammo over his shoulder and walked to a nearby tree. Bracing against the trunk, he pointed the big gun out across the valley.

"Load this belt and feed it for me, First Sergeant."

"Sir, no matter what's happened, right or wrong, if you shoot that chopper down it'll only make things worse and give them the high ground."

"Load the damned weapon, First Sergeant!"

Gautier raised the cover and attached the belt as the chopper approached. Slowing even more, it came to a broadside hover only a hundred meters away. The helicopter was a fat duck sitting on a pond. Sighting carefully down the barrel, Martin wrapped his finger around the trigger.

"Holy shit!" one of the men muttered. "The captain's really gonna do it. He's gonna shoot down that damned chopper. He's gonna shoot those assholes right outta the sky."

A bead of sweat trickled into one eye as Martin stood unmoving, while gently pulling the slack from the trigger. The glistening black chopper made such an easy target, it would be hard to miss as it hovered above the stream. Its downdraft sent sparkling ripples across the water. Liegeman and Postiche were there, still standing in the open door, intent on searching the far bank. They had no clue Martin was behind them with the M-60 braced against the tree, and with one more gentle squeeze of the trigger could shred them and the chopper to pieces. He could send them all to hell where they belonged, but Martin gritted his teeth instead and slowly released pressure from the trigger.

"You're doing the right thing, Sir. We'll catch them when we get back," Gautier said. "I promise, and if Colonel Duggin doesn't call for an investigation and general court martial, I'll raise hell all the way up the chain of command."

After a while the chopper tilted forward and circled slowly, climbing up the far mountainside. Martin lowered the M-60 and gave it to the first sergeant.

"Let's get down there fast and find our men. We'll need to establish an LZ for a dust-off."

"Better wait a minute," Gautier said. The first sergeant pointed across the valley. The helicopter had slowed and was circling the far slope over a kilometer away. A moment later another canister streamed red smoke as it dropped from the chopper.

"That sonofabitch must have seen the Montagnards," Martin said. "He's marking their position."

"I should have let you shoot them out of the sky," Gautier muttered.

The men watched helplessly as the chopper climbed away and the Vietnamese Skyraiders returned from the north. This time they dropped tumbling canisters that Martin realized were napalm, and the jungle on the far mountainside erupted with billowing orange flames. It was his vision, and although he couldn't hear their voices, Martin sensed the cries of fear and pain. Many of the Montagnard people who had put their trust in him were now dying on that far mountainside. After a while the flames disappeared, and the smoke dissipated as he stood in silence.

"We need to go now, Sir," First Sergeant Gautier said. "We need to get down there and help our wounded."

He was right, but by the time they found the wounded, Thibodaux was the only one still alive. The Skyraiders attack had been lethal with Sky Soldier, Lugo, and Gopher all dead—their bodies riddled with shrapnel. Martin sent men out on the flanks to provide security, while he wrapped T-Bo's wounds and applied a tourniquet to his leg. The young soldier stared at him while he worked.

"What the hell happened?" T-Bo asked. "I think that was one of our own choppers."

"I know, and we'll figure out what happened later. I should never have asked you guys to come on this mission. I should have known—"

"Ghost, Sir," T-Bo interrupted. "You don't have to apologize for nothin'. I'd go through the gates of hell with you."

"T-Bo, I appreciate it. Now, lay back and rest. We've got a dust-off coming, and we're using det-cord and C-4 to clear an LZ over there by the creek, so don't let the noise spook you."

Twenty minutes later, two slicks hovered overhead while the medevac chopper positioned itself over a hole blown through the jungle canopy. Martin had made up his mind. He was extracting the entire team—all but himself. Leaves and small branches scattered in the main rotor's wash as he stood with the first sergeant, watching while his men guided the chopper into the narrow opening. The rest of the team stood by with T-Bo and the three bodies wrapped in ponchos.

"What will I tell Colonel Duggin?" Gautier asked.

"Leave me one of the radios and the extra battery, extra rations, frags, C-4, some smoke grenades and a couple claymores. Tell him we were close when we got hit by those planes. Tell him I'm not getting any more of our men killed. If he's still alive, I'll find Bushmaster and call for extraction when we're ready."

"What about that chopper?"

"Tell him everything and tell him we think it was probably an agency asset. Tell him I'm certain I saw Liegeman and Postiche onboard."

Once the team was extracted, Martin began working his way across the valley, searching for signs of the Montagnards.

Now riddled with self-doubt, he realized just how close he had come to becoming a part of the insanity that was this war. He was a heartbeat away from shooting down a "friendly" chopper—such as it was. And he wondered if he too was becoming lost in the insanity of a world where men sold their souls by rationalizing criminal acts as being patriotic and defending the better good of the nation. He wondered now if he could ever go home, and for a moment, he thought of Kania—beautiful Kania. He would likely never see her again. With every new day in the Nam, the burden of sanity was becoming more difficult to bear.

Crossing the valley late that afternoon, Martin moved with caution. NVA troops were in the area and certain to have sent scouts to investigate the air strike. Despite a thorough search he found no evidence of casualties in the napalmed area. Bushmaster had likely moved the Montagnards rapidly and escaped into the next valley. Within an hour he picked up their trail, but the sound of rolling thunder came from beyond the mountains, somewhere to the west.

A heavy storm could rapidly wash away their tracks. He moved faster. If he could catch them, his radio would enable him to bring air cover and hopefully a path to freedom for everyone, but the sound of the booming thunder was growing too fast.

This time it was Mother Nature's show as a towering wall of purple nimbus turned the sky black and a powerful wind poured down the mountainside. Within minutes a drenching rain was gushing through the jungle canopy. The wind, cracking thunder, and rattling raindrops muted all other sounds, and Martin relied solely on his eyes, but the tracks were rapidly washing away. Walking parallel to the trail, he followed it until he spotted what he dreaded most—new tracks made by booted soldiers.

The NVA had entered the trail and were now following the Montagnards. There were at least ten of them, a small patrol, likely dispatched by a nearby main force. With them between him and the fleeing villagers, his position was now even more tenuous, but Bushmaster's was worse. With over two hundred refugees in his charge and the North Vietnamese closing in, he would have no choice but to turn and fight.

Increasing his pace as much as he dared, Martin continued

following the trail up the mountain. After a while the rain ceased, leaving gurgling rivulets, dripping vegetation, and birds again singing in the trees above. The trail turned toward the top of the steep ridge and the Laotian border. As the tracks grew fresher by the minute, he studied both the trail and the jungle ahead. He was drawing closer, and when he saw muddy water swirling in a boot track, he froze mid-stride.

The enemy patrol was only seconds ahead. He focused on the thick cover to his front, but a strange sound came from behind him, down the mountainside toward the valley. It grew steadily louder until he realized it was the sound of more men sloshing through the mud as they followed the same trail up from the valley.

Moving out into the jungle, he knelt and waited. The sounds of their rattling equipment and heavy breathing grew steadily louder, and within seconds, more NVA soldiers began streaming past at a steady pace. Hidden less than thirty meters away, he counted until the last one passed—fifty-four NVA regulars. The crest of the mountain was now only a couple hundred meters away. Just beyond was Laos.

He had one last hope. If he could raise Colonel Duggin at Command & Control North, he might get a couple of Cobra gunships to support Bushmaster and the Montagnards. Using parachute-cord, he raised the long-distance radio antenna high into the jungle canopy. The X-ray relay team answered almost immediately but their transmission was garbled with static caused by the storm that had now moved over their position.

After several minutes and several apparent failed attempts at communication, his hopes were fading when the relay team came through crystal clear, "…advises you switch to Alpha Foxtrot: One-Charley-Charley-Bravo. Contact call sign Heavy Drop for new orders. If you roger last transmission, break squelch twice. Over."

Martin keyed his handset twice and waited.

"We read your Roger Lima Charley, Ghost. Good Luck, brother. X-Ray Papa Bravo-7 Out."

The relay team had told him to switch to an alternate frequency, and contact Heavy Drop, a name he'd been given during his briefing with the S-2 officer at Command and Control-North. Removing his ops notebook from a plastic bag, he thumbed through the pages until he found it. Heavy Drop belonged to C&C-Central. This could only mean he had reached the farthest southern reaches of the Laotian border and was no longer in FOB-One's AO. Beside the note were the coded digits for Heavy Drop's frequency. Martin unlocked and twisted the knobs on the PRC-25.

"Heavy Drop, this is Ghost One-Zero. Over."

"Roger Dakota One-One, Hatchet Niner is on the ground and moving your way. Be advised, approximately sixty November Victor Alphas approaching to your echo. Over."

A stressed voice and the rattle of automatic weapons came over the radio before becoming lost in static.

"Ghost One-Zero, identify yourself. Over."

Martin keyed his handset. "Heavy Drop, this is Ghost One-Zero, I have to communicate in the clear. I am a team out of Foxtrot Oscar Bravo-One following a CIDG with women and children." He continued transmitting also giving his coordinates in the clear.

"We know who you are, but I've got bad news for you, partner. You've walked into a world of shit. We've got a hatchet team in heavy engagement with November Victor Alphas to your whiskey with more approaching from your echo. Over."

"Ghost One-Zero, this is Bushmaster."

Martin could hardly believe his ears. It was Zeke.

"Go Bushmaster."

"This radio is about dead. Hold your position. The shit's about to hit the fan. And thanks for coming for us, boss. It's good to hear y—"

The transmission broke into static and faded, but Martin had no intention of waiting. He moved to the crest of the mountain. Several choppers crisscrossed the sky above the next valley. He knew now that Bushmaster had turned his Montagnards about and set an ambush for the approaching NVA. If it was successful, the enemy would likely retreat the way they came, back up this same trail. He went to work.

Before the team was extracted, he had taken up a collection: two claymores, seven frags, three squares of C-4, detonators, and five hundred rounds of 5.56 mm ammo. Setting the two claymores thirty meters apart, he aimed them up the trail in the direction the retreating enemy would come. Afterward, he rolled out the wires, connected the clackers and removed the safety pins. There would be no hesitation when it was time. Hunkering down, he waited, but it was only seconds before the jungle a few hundred meters down the ridge exploded with Bushmaster's claymore detonations and showers of red tracers.

The angles of the tracer rounds told the story. The NVA had run into the kill zone of an L-shaped ambush, and Bushmaster was having his way with them. There were sixty-four NVA and likely fewer than fifty Montagnard soldiers, but the advantage of surprise came with the ambush. The firefight, brief but fierce, raged for a minute before it became apparent the NVA were retreating. Martin hunkered down with a clacker in each hand.

Ten or twelve men came up the trail past the first claymore. Martin waited. Six more approached carrying wounded comrades. He mashed both clackers repeatedly and the trail exploded into a cloud of smoke, leaves, and human body parts. Instantly the zip and crack of bullets and green tracer rounds came from beyond the carnage as more retreating enemy soldiers arrived. They had been chopped up badly in the ambush but remained willing to fight. Scrambling on all fours, Martin crawled into a nearby ravine and followed it down the mountain, until he was no longer in the hornet's nest of NVA regulars. There he waited for nightfall to swallow the jungle in its opaque darkness.

CHAPTER THIRTEEN

The Ghost Comes to Visit
The Laotian Border

A wet ground fog draped the mountain jungle that morning, and Martin was as soaked as the surrounding vegetation. Shortly after first light, another firefight broke out somewhere to the west on the Laotian side of the border. He switched on his PRC-25 only to realize it had gone silent—dead battery. After installing the fresh battery, the radio still refused to come to life. Whatever the problem, his radio had joined the casualty list—something all too common with the 25s and the reason they usually carried two. Truly on his own now, there would be no cavalry coming to his rescue if the enemy found him.

It was time to consider his options. He inventoried the remaining equipment—starburst flares, three blocks of C-4, detonators, plenty of ammo and nine frags, two smoke grenades, and a few more lurp rations. Retreating wasn't an option. His best bet was to cross back over the mountain into Laos and search for Bushmaster and the Yards, or possibly contact the hatchet team that had been there the day before.

By late morning the ground fog lifted, and he was well down into the next valley. According to the map, this was Laos, but the jungle was the same—thick canopied walls of vegetation, bamboo, banyan trees, and the ever-present heat, insects, and steep mountain terrain. It was quiet until afternoon when another distant firefight echoed from somewhere in the hills to the west. It had begun with echoing booms—claymores, he figured, detonated at the start of an ambush. It lasted little more than a minute before silence again returned.

Crossing trails and roads cut with tire ruts, Martin moved westward in that direction. This was the infamous Ho Chi Minh Trail. He searched for signs of Bushmaster and the Montagnards, but there were only the NVA bata boot tracks—hundreds of them. He was creeping deeper into the lion's den and feeling more like a chunk of red meat with every step.

Paralleling one of the more heavily traveled trails, he reached a place where the valley turned south and split into two narrow passes. Both passes were ideal locations for ambushes, but one was overlooked by a high rock shelf. He moved that way. If he could reach the shelf, it would provide a sweeping view of the entire valley.

By midafternoon he had climbed the mountain ridge to the west and circled back toward the rock shelf. It was somewhere below. Pushing through the thick undergrowth, he began easing downhill a step at a time, stopping and listening until he found what he already suspected would be there—a trail leading down to the shelf. It wasn't well-defined, but clearly indicated someone else had the same idea about the overlook. The question was who—an American SOG team or an NVA reconnaissance unit.

Weaving his way down the narrow trail, he expected to break through the wall of green at any moment, but something stopped him. It was the faint scent of human body odor, and perhaps that of moldy canvas. He waited as a slight breeze stirred the undergrowth and the scent momentarily increased before fading entirely. Someone was already there just below him. Carefully easing ahead and parting the vegetation with his left hand, he held his CAR-15 at the ready.

Two steps away, an enemy soldier was curled up on the ground, hugging an AK-47. He was sleeping soundly. Ten meters below at the edge of the cliff sat two more men with a radio. One wore a sidearm and was glassing the valley with binoculars. Their pith helmets lay on the ground beside them. Martin slowly drew his knife from its shoulder sheath and eased forward until he was standing over the sleeping soldier. With their attention focused on the valley below, the others remained oblivious to his presence.

The sleeping soldier died quickly and quietly on the razor edge of Martin's knife. Without hesitation, he moved rapidly toward the others. The one with the radio looked up at him as he stepped close and with a lightning slash, he severed the man's jugular. The other lowered the binoculars, apparently unaware of what was happening as his look of puzzlement morphed to one of terror. Martin plunged the knife into his neck. It was over in seconds, and he used the men's canteens to wash the blood from his hands and face.

Searching through their papers, he found a treasure trove of intel, including a map with various routes sketched along the Ho Chi Minh Trail. There was also a booklet with various notations, including what appeared to be radio frequencies. Folding the papers, he shoved them into a cargo pocket, and gazed about for a place to hide the bodies. He glanced over the ledge—an ideal place for their disposal, he figured, until he spotted something in the gorge several hundred feet below. At the base of the cliff a platoon of NVA soldiers lay prone among the rocks and trees. None of them were moving, and it became clear they were waiting in ambush.

Glancing up the gorge, he spotted their intended victims.

Three hundred meters to the north, a small column of soldiers was weaving through heavy cover, coming into the narrow valley. They were only minutes from walking into the kill zone. Quickly pulling several grenades from an ammo pouch, Martin lined them in a row on the ground, and studied the troops below. His first targets would be the RPGs and heavy machine gun. He began rapidly pulling pins and tossing the frags. The booms echoed from the far side of the gorge, and the airbursts were fearsomely lethal. After tossing six grenades, he emptied his CAR-15 into the carnage below.

When he was done, he pushed the three bodies over the cliff's edge along with their radio and other equipment. With NVA reinforcements likely enroute, escaping the immediate area was his first concern. He began a rapid ascent back up the mountain and again turned southward. Remaining on the high ground, he moved several klicks before stopping late that afternoon. The gorge below had opened into a broad grassy plain where the silvery ribbons of several tree-lined streams snaked their way toward the southern horizon.

No longer holding any hope of finding Bushmaster or the Montagnards, Martin planned to turn west and make his way back to Vietnam, but the sun would set soon, and he was exhausted. He needed rest.

Crawling into a nearby thicket, he poured water into a lurp ration packet and devoured it in seconds. When he was done, he reloaded the empty CAR-15 magazine and wiped down the rifle. It would be dark soon, and he crept to the edge of the thicket for a final scan of his surroundings and the grassy plain below. The sky turned orange, then purple, and rapidly faded into a dusky gray. The tall yellow grasses reflected what little light remained, and he was about to retreat into the thicket when he spotted movement.

They appeared as mere shadows moving slowly out of the

gorge below—a column of soldiers. Over four hundred meters away, they were moving toward the thick cover along one of the streams. He counted them as they disappeared into the trees— twelve in all. It was the SOG Alpha-team he had seen earlier. Their NDP was chosen wisely, deep in the bend of a creek where they had water on three sides. He decided to pay them a visit and was backing into the thicket to gather his gear when he spotted more movement.

Another line of soldiers, also little more than shadows, was spilling out of the gorge and moving rapidly out into the yellow grass. These wore pith helmets—NVA regulars. There were at least forty of them deploying along a tree line opposite the creek where the SOG team had hidden. The grassy area between them was likely a previous extraction point, and the NVA were preparing to ambush anyone attempting to use it. The moon was rising as darkness came, and Martin began moving down the ridge to the valley below—a slow and tedious process in which a single misstep could prove fatal.

When he reached the edge of the plain, he stopped inside the trees and studied the open terrain. It had taken several hours to reach this position, and a nearly full moon now hung high and silvery in the night sky. The NVA had likely placed OPs out in the grass, and crossing the open ground would be foolhardy, if not suicidal. He moved along the edge of the trees toward the creek, stopping a hundred meters upstream from where the Alpha-team had disappeared.

Martin studied his options. Approaching a SOG team's position in enemy territory was a dicey proposition at best. He had to move slowly, but walking directly into the trees most certainly would be detrimental to his health. But they wouldn't expect someone to come out of the water—at least not without making some noise. If he crossed upstream first and circled behind them, he might have a chance.

Wading into the stream, he sank up to his chest in the sluggish water. Carefully, one step at a time, he crossed to the opposite bank where he sat and ran his hands over his skin. He was searching for what he knew was there—leeches. The little bastards were everywhere in Vietnam. Finding the first one, he pinched it from his skin before tossing it into the brush.

When he was done, he had found five in all and began moving again. Circling toward the creek bend where he hoped to find the SOG team, he crept forward in absolute silence until again wading into the murky warm water. If his calculation was correct he would come out of the water right behind them. It wasn't as deep here, and he held his CAR-15 at chest level as he crossed.

So far, so good, but halfway across the stream the silvery moonlight reflected movement in the water. It was only a few feet from his elbow. Martin froze. A four-foot-long snake with black and white bands swam languidly over his right arm and slithered onto the stock of his CAR-15. When the giant viper reached the rifle's forearm, it paused and raised its head. Martin dared not so much as a blink.

A banded krait, the deadly reptile was the one grunts called "Mister Two-Step" because its venom seldom allowed the recipient more than two steps before the onset of paralysis and death. The pit viper seemed to sense Martin's body heat as it coiled and tensed. Sweat dripped down his face and he held his breath as he prepared to grab it behind the head before it struck. Slowly loosening the grip of his right hand on the rifle, he prepared to make his move.

There was no room for error. He either nailed it with an instant grip behind the head or else got bitten. The world stood still as he opened his hand and cupped his fingers. The snake's body again seemed to tense, but it extended its head forward toward the end of the rifle. Martin hesitated, and a moment later, the reptile slithered off the end of the barrel into the water and swam away. Martin sucked down a breath of relief and tried not to exhale too loudly, but he was certain his thudding heart could be heard ten feet away. He began moving again.

By the time he reached the far bank his heart rate had eased, and he slowly stood upright a few inches at a time until the excess water had drained quietly from his gear. The SOG team had to be somewhere in the undergrowth to his front. Shedding everything but his knife and CAR-15, he crawled forward—searching the ground ahead with his free hand while moving only inches at a time. The moon had moved across the sky and was now obscured by the trees. He inched forward and after an hour he had moved little more than thirty meters. Either the team wasn't here, or he was damned close to them.

Back along the creek, frogs croaked, and from all around came the drone of insects. He listened and inhaled through his nostrils hoping to gain the scent of the men, but the night refused to reveal its secrets. Moving ahead, he reached out with his free hand, but this time he touched something—something that moved. It was a boot. Someone whispered something, but it wasn't in English, and the thought occurred to him: what if this wasn't an Alpha-team? What if it was another group of NVA soldiers? Apparently satisfied that he was one of them, the soldier rolled over and went back to sleep.

Martin's mouth was dry and filled with the metallic taste of an adrenaline overload. He again began crawling forward, but again his hand touched something. This time it wasn't a person, but a weapon. He ran his fingers along its surface. It was an American

M-16. He was tempted to declare his presence, but the M-16 might be a captured weapon. He reached out again, this time touching a man's head. The soldier rolled his way.

"What the fuck? That you, Boot Legger?"

Martin breathed a sigh of relief. "No, it's the Ghost," he answered.

"Don't be a dumb fuck. That you, Russell?"

"Not me. I'm over here," came a whispered voice from the darkness.

"Boot Legger, I'm gonna kick your ass when we get—"

"I'm back here."

The night sounds of the jungle suddenly seemed louder than ever.

"Chief, he say he Ghost. I know he say truth. Bru named Khonsu tell me yesterday he come." It was the voice of a Montagnard.

"Son of a bitch," the American whispered.

"The Montagnard call me Ghost, but if it makes you feel better, I'm Martin Shadows, Captain, United States Army. Who are you?"

"Chief Warrant Officer Dan Kirby, 5th Special Forces. Where in the hell did—how did you—I mean—?"

"I came in the back door from across the creek. What are your plans when it gets light?"

"How in the hell did you find us? I mean, this is totally insane."

"I was on that mountain over there, and I saw y'all go in here at dusk. And not long after that, I also saw maybe forty NVA go into those trees out there on the other side of this field."

"Holy shit," Kirby muttered.

"We're gonna have to move to an alternate extraction site," Boot Legger whispered.

"I told you I thought we were being followed," Russell said. "We need to do some serious E&E before daylight."

"I don't know. Moving in the dark is damned risky," Kirby said.

"Can I offer a suggestion?" Martin asked.

"Go ahead."

"The NVA aren't much more than two hundred meters away across that field. If we don't di di mau right now, we're going to be trapped here when the sun comes up. Let me take point. We'll move slow. All we need to do is get across that creek and put some distance between us and them."

"Makes sense," Boot Legger said.

A single thread of moonlight found its way through the treetops, reflecting in Chief Kirby's eyes. They were hard black eyes that Martin recognized, because he had seen them before in his own mirror—those of a combat veteran.

"Okay. Russell, you remain at tail gunner. Ghost, take point. Boot Legger, you walk slack for him. Let's move."

Walking back to the creek bank, Martin retrieved his rucksack and web gear before wading across. When he reached the opposite bank, he glanced back to see if the team was following. Just behind him were mere shadows moving in absolute silence—not a footfall was heard, and not so much as the snap of a twig or a drip of water as they climbed out beside him. *These guys were good.*

After several hours the sky began to gray, and the stars faded. The moon had set, and the birds began fluttering and chirping in the treetops. The patrol had moved at least a klick, and Martin had found another broad plain of yellow grass extending several hundred meters to the next tree line. He dropped to a knee and began a systematic visual dissection of every hump, stump and bush that lay ahead. Kirby eased up beside him.

"What'cha got?"

The chief warrant officer gazed steadily at him. With the growing light of dawn, it was the first time they could actually see one another, and Martin too was studying his counterpart. The camo face-paint disguised some features, but Kirby's eyes reflected a calm intelligence mixed with a confidence bred from experience.

Martin pointed out to the open ground. "This looks like it could be an alternate extraction site. Your call."

"You Indian?"

"My father is full-blooded Lakota Sioux."

Kirby turned and studied the distant tree line.

"The NVA have trail watchers around all these areas."

A Montagnard soldier came up and knelt beside them. His gaze was one of wonderment as he studied Martin.

"This is Hong. He's the leader of the Montagnards here."

Hong displayed a nervous smile and nodded.

"You say you spoke with Khonsu?" Martin asked.

"Yes, he say they go Cambodia."

"Did you see an American with them?"

"That'd be Zeke Anderson," Kirby said. "He was medevaced the day before yesterday—shot up pretty bad. I don't think he made it. He was a good man. Worked with him up in I-Corps a year or so back."

Martin gritted his teeth and nodded before turning his attention back to the waist-high grass and the dark silhouette of the tree line. A surge of anger and regret welled deep in his gut. Another of his men had gone down, and for what—a war effort that had been executed without any real intention of winning—a war and a people that were now being abandoned.

"What the hell happened?" he asked.

"We were on the run in the next valley up north of here, trying to break contact with a company of NVA when we got word there were sixty more coming at us from the other direction. It just so happens that Zeke, or Bushmaster as we called him, and his

Yards had set up an ambush. He saved our butts, but that's when he got hit. A hatchet team swept the area afterward, and it looks like Bushmaster and his Yards cleaned house. There were enemy bodies and blood trails all the way back over the mountain into Nam."

"What happened to the Montagnards?"

"Don't know. There was maybe a couple hundred of them. Hell, they had kids, and chickens and pigs, but they disappeared into thin air. And we need to do the same thing. This valley here has a lot of bad juju for our teams. We've lost some good men here. Now that it's getting light, I'm calling for extraction."

The Special Forces team leader deployed three two-man Observation Posts—one on each flank and one to the rear.

"When these choppers show up, I can about guarantee the shit's going to hit the fan. We've never had a cold extraction anywhere in this area."

An hour later the rhythmic thump of helicopters echoed in the hills to the east. Boot Legger removed a smoke grenade from his rucksack while Kirby whispered into the radio handset. The surrounding area remained peaceful, but if Chief Kirby was right, it was likely a counterfeit calm. Martin glanced about at the others. They reminded him of the wild turkeys back home rubber-necking the area for coyotes.

"The two slicks will fly by to the south before turning in on us. The Cobras will stay up high till they're needed," Boot Legger explained. "The Covey leader is going to buzz that tree line out there to see if he draws fire. If he does, that means we'll be exposed while we're climbing out, so we'll have to put suppressing fire in there. Put your weapon on rock and roll but hold your fire until I've emptied my magazine. Then you open up next. Got it?"

Martin nodded, and a few moments later Boot Legger popped smoke. The choppers passed nearly a klick to the south before flaring and turning back in the team's direction. The yellow smoke drifted westward as the pilots locked in on the team. It was a beautifully choreographed exercise as Kirby motioned for the observation posts to return from each flank. The first chopper's main rotor clacked loudly as it came to a hover and touched down. The second chopper was doing the same when Martin saw an enemy soldier run to the edge of the grass a hundred meters to the west. The soldier raised an RPG and sighted on the first chopper.

Boot Legger and five Montagnards had already piled into the helicopter as Martin came to his feet. It was more reflex than thought as he shouldered his CAR-15 and mashed the trigger. The tracer rounds disappeared into and around his target as the NVA soldier staggered and spun, firing the RPG skyward as he fell. The rocket-propelled grenade trailed away harmlessly over the treetops, and Martin loaded another magazine and emptied it into the tree line. A moment later a volley of rockets from a Cobra gunship shredded the enemy position. Only then did he realize the first chopper was airborne and Kirby was motioning wildly for him to come board the second. Several arms reached down and pulled him onboard as the chopper climbed skyward.

Martin stared back at the mountain valley as it grew more distant. The whining turbine and thundering rotor negated all but the loudest shouts, leaving him in the solitary world of his own thoughts. There were many. *Why had he even come here? Several of his men had died needlessly, and the Montagnard people he hoped to save were now lost forever. To understand God, the spirits, and to understand something more about life had been his hope, but it all now seemed to have been a hopelessly selfish endeavor.*

"Where are we headed?" he shouted into Chief's ear.

"Firebase Betty Lou—an absolute garden spot on the Cambodian border."

CHAPTER FOURTEEN

Assault on Firebase Betty Lou
The Cambodian Border Northeast of Kon Tum

Firebase Betty Lou was a tiny island atop a hill in the middle of nowhere. Manned by a contingent of twenty-four Green Beret SOG troops and a hundred and fifty Bahnar tribesman, it was well qualified for its description as an "outpost." Little more than a dusty red mound, its warren of sandbagged trenches and bunkers were surrounded by piles of concertina and a few hundred meters of cleared perimeter. Beyond were thousands of square miles of mountainous jungle.

The chopper landed and dropped Martin and the others atop a bunker before quickly springing nose down into the air, as it dug for sky at full throttle. This desolate little firebase was home to a Mike Force group that spent its energies obstructing the Ho Chi Minh trail. This made Betty Lou and its garrison a prime target for the NVA. It took little more than a few cursory glances for Martin to realize he was truly at the furthest reaches of the frontier and far from being safe.

"We don't particularly want to be another Lang Vei," Kirby said, "which is why we've got a recoilless rifle, and more LAWs than you can count on hand. They brought those to us a couple weeks ago when intel indicated enemy tanks south of here. We also have a bunch of anti-tank mines outside the wire. I can't believe they have armor this far south."

"Believe it, Chief. I was with the recon team out of Nha Trang that identified them. You're fighting a guerrilla war against a conventional army with armor now."

Kirby laughed.

"Yeah, well, that's kind of the way it works out, but we *do* get some pretty good tactical air support. Last month, we made shake-and-bake ovens out of some T-76s we ran into up north of here on the Ho Chi Minh Trail."

After a post-op meeting and filing their after-action reports, the men gathered in a sandbag-walled hooch—the largest on the firebase, the watering hole. The Pabst Blue Ribbon, Carling Black Label and Ba Mười Ba beers were only chasers for the bourbon, vodka, and tequila. The little bar, lit by Coleman lanterns, was packed shoulder to shoulder, and reeked of whiskey, cigarettes, and body odor. Martin looked around at walls pasted with a hodge-podge of maps, aerial photos, Playboy centerfolds, and various VC and NVA flags, uniform parts, and photographs. These boys were fighting a war unlike any others in Vietnam. Theirs was a fight where survival was victory.

The one thing different about this firebase was everyone slept with their weapons and carried them everywhere they went. Not a man in the bar was without a weapon of some sort. Most wore CAR-15s, Swedish Ks, or other automatic weapons slung across their backs. Martin didn't care, but it again sent a message loud and clear that this was an outpost and not the safest place to visit. He could only wonder where his bizarre quest would take him next. Two grizzled men wearing berets and dusty tiger-stripe fatigues sat down at the tiny table with him and Kirby.

"So, you guys had a hairy mission," one said.

"Yeah, it might have been worse, except we got dealt an ace. Meet the Ghost." Kirby raised a plastic cup of bourbon as if to offer a toast.

The two men laughed.

"Ghost, huh?" one said.

"Yeah," the other answered, "everybody wants to be the Ghost."

"I always wanted to be Zorro when I was a kid," his partner replied.

"I'm serious," Kirby said. "This is him. This is the Ghost."

They stopped laughing and one threw his head back and stared down at Martin. "So, you're the Ghost everybody is talking about?"

These were hardened warriors, and not easily influenced by war stories, rumors, or bullshit. Yet, stories were their most trusted source of information. They came from their own people—the ones they trusted.

"That Ghost thing was started by some guys with the Hundred and First that I helped up in I-Corps, but I prefer Shadows." Martin extended his hand across the table. "I'm Martin Shadows."

They shook hands as a third soldier stumbled up to the table. His tongue protruded over his lower lip, and his face glowed with a fine sheen of sweat. Bloodshot eyes and a mostly empty bottle of whiskey in one hand pretty much verified his state of advanced inebriation.

"I heard it. I heard you say this here fella thinks he's the Ghost."

"Dammit LA, quit slobbering on us," Kirby said, wiping his face.

LA braced himself with both hands on the table. "Well, I ain't puttin' up with nobody's bullshit tonight, and this little fucker ain't no Ghost. The Ghost is a fucking legend, and he ain't gonna come around a little shithole like ours."

"Dammit LA, you're fucked up beyond recognition. Go back to your hooch and sleep it off."

"Aww, Chief, I'm just trying to have some fun with the Ghost, here."

Despite his words, LA's tone remained surly. He turned to Martin. "Tell me, Ghost, do you only come out at night?"

Martin smiled at him. LA needed to be humored. "Only dark and stormy ones."

"So, it ain't dark and stormy out there tonight. That means you ain't the Ghost, right?"

"You know," Kirby said, "yesterday afternoon, someone shot up an entire platoon of NVA who were waiting to ambush us. And Hong kept insisting it was the Ghost. Said he saw the Ghost throwing bodies over the cliff. At first, I thought he was just spooked. Then we found the bodies, but I still figured it was just something he made up. Then that night you crawled into our NDP without none of us noticing.."

He stared at Martin, while LA's brows folded together in confusion.

"A three-man OP team was up there. I came down behind them and was afraid other NVA troops were in the area, so I used my knife. I was about to throw the bodies over the cliff when I spotted the ambush down there."

LA's bloodshot eyes bulged and spread apart as he swayed precariously above the table.

"Oh shit! Pardon me, ladies, but this bullshit is getting way too deep for me. So, let me get this straight. You're gonna tell us you snuck up on three gooks and killed them all with your knife?"

"Why don't you sit down and shut the fuck up, LA?" Kirby said. "I wanna hear this."

Martin kept smiling as LA drew a huge knife from his boot and held it with the blade tip pointed toward the ceiling.

"So, Mr. Ghost, self-proclaimed knife fighter, let's see if you can take this from m—"

Martin moved his left hand slightly. LA cut his eyes that way, but faster than a snake's strike, Martin's right hand shot out, grabbed LA's and smashed it down against the corner of the table. The knife clattered to the floor along with the whiskey bottles and beer cans. Three soldiers were atop LA in an instant, pinning him to the floor.

"Take that drunk bastard outside," Kirby said. "And tell him if he doesn't shape up, I'm sending his ass back to Dak To to burn shit for a month."

Boot Legger pushed his way through to the table and looked down at the pile of bottles and cans. He bent over, set the table upright, and picked up a bottle of Jack Daniels. Holding it up to a lantern, he gazed at it with a studied squint. Most of the contents had poured out on the floor. He shook his head in resignation.

"My God, such a tragic waste."

By the time he talked Kirby and Boot Legger into going outside for fresh air, Martin was feeling no pain. Only the occasional "thump" of a mortar broke the silence as it fired illumination rounds. They drifted lazily across the night sky, casting an eerie amber glow over the postage-stamp-size pile of sandbags and barbed wire that was Firebase Betty Lou. The night air was still and the jungle outside the wire was silent as they walked through the warren of sandbagged bunkers.

"I suppose you know Hong and the Yards want to put on a special meet and greet for you," Boot Legger said.

Martin couldn't help but grin. "A meet and greet? When?"

"Tonight. You want to walk down to their hooch?"

"Oh, hell no. Not tonight."

"You need to. They asked me to bring you there. They're expecting you. Besides, we've heard some wild tales about you from down at Nha Trang. Word is Luis Ravera said this Ghost busted him and five of his Montagnards out of an NVA prison somewhere off the coast. It's a hot topic among the Montagnards. They think you're some sort of a God spirit."

The last thing Martin wanted was to relive that nightmare. For months afterward his mind had drifted back to that moment when the ocean whirlpool sucked him into the cliffside cavern. It was but one of the several times he thought he was about to die.

"I'm not going to say it didn't happen, but frankly, I don't want to talk about it right now."

"Okay, Dại úy," Kirby said, "you don't have to talk about it, but I've got to keep my Yards happy, and they want you to come visit them tonight." He pointed to another sandbagged bunker. "That's their hooch over there. Be my guest."

Martin had no choice and ducked through the opening. Inside, a lantern burned back in a corner, and a circle of candles surrounded a brass urn stuffed with smoking joss sticks wafting their gentle messages to the spirits beyond this world. It reminded him of his grandfather's lodge when they smoked the pipe and shared their stories. The Montagnards' bronzed faces were raised to him as he entered, and their eyes followed him with godlike admiration. They bowed and motioned for him to join them where they squatted around a large gourd sprouting a cluster of long straws.

"That's Rượu cần," Boot Legger said, "their version of rice wine, but go easy. That stuff is more like the moonshine we have back home. It'll kick your ass."

Martin drank, and the Bahnar tribesmen began playing musical instruments—brass gongs and stringed instruments made from bamboo. He had only *thought* he was drunk before because he was now in a dreamlike state. Kirby and Boot Legger began telling stories, and he realized they were telling the Montagnards tales about The Ghost. And after relentless cajoling, Martin told them how he, Ravera, Khonsu, Brau, Katu, and Guia had escaped the island prison.

———

Martin slept all the following day, while fighting the hangover from hell, and by nightfall it had dissipated into something resembling a post-op recovery minus the pain meds. He stood with Kirby and Boot Legger, gazing into the darkness. He couldn't imagine staying in this place much longer and was thankful to be leaving on a resupply chopper coming the next day. The red dust coated his boots, and the stench from the latrines floated on the still night air. Occasional tracer rounds arced silently across the night sky, eventually disappearing somewhere in the hills beyond.

Kirby turned to Boot Legger. "Well, I thought we had him drunk enough last night to tell us who he really is, but he's the strong silent type."

"Sorry, fellas. It's just that too much of this shit turns a man's brain inside out."

"Yeah, we know," Boot Legger said. "That's why we tolerate crazy fuckers like LA."

"So, what was going on with you and Bushmaster and those Montagnards?" Kirby asked. "What the hell were y'all doing this far south?"

"My CO up at Phu Bai explained it to me this way: The Yards and Ravera were supposed to do a prisoner snatch a couple years ago, and some ARVN troops were providing backup security for them. It ended up a clusterfuck with Ravera wounded and captured along with several of the Montagnards. It was a Phoenix Program operation, but when things went sideways that night, the ARVN colonel lost his head and ordered his men to wipe out an entire hamlet. The OSA advisor running the op got with the ARVN commander and they blamed Ravera and his men for the massacre.

"Bottom line is some of the Montagnards with Bushmaster were with Ravera that night and witnessed the massacre, and when we escaped that prison, the OSA and that ARVN colonel got nervous and decided to get rid of the Montagnards. Frankly, I still can't believe Ravera hasn't had some kind of *accident*, if you know what I mean."

Silence reigned for several seconds until the sliding whisper of artillery shells came from high overhead. Seconds later, bright flashes lit the jungle west of the firebase, silhouetting the trees and hills. A moment later the sound of the explosions arrived as dull but powerful "Karoomphs."

"An LP must have movement over there in the ravine," Boot Legger said. "They come up from that valley over there in Cambodia. The bastards like to stage there before they attack. Most of the time it's just mortars or rockets, but every once in a while they come at us with half the North Vietnamese Army. Better go get our web gear."

A shout came from up near the TOC bunker as several men came running by in the dark.

"Better grab your shit and get ready!" one of them shouted. "LP says there's a whole damned NVA regiment coming up from the valley."

Men scrambled about in the amber glow of the illumination rounds as they ran to bunkers around the perimeter.

"Where do you need me?" Martin asked.

"Come with me," Kirby answered. "We're going to the TOC."

———

It had been several minutes since the initial alerts, and the artillery was now being systematically adjusted around the perimeter. Drifting parachute flares hung high in every quadrant of the surrounding hills, trailing smoke in a spooky search for the enemy. Not a single round had yet been fired into the base, but hell was coming, and everyone knew it. Martin stared out from a gunport at the shadowy darkness, searching for movement or an anomaly in the terrain—a shape, a pattern, something that might give away the enemy's position. Behind him Chief Kirby and the base commander, a captain, held radio handsets to their ears as they talked to other firebases and support units miles away.

"They're hitting the Dak Seang Camp up north of here and several others—Kon Tum, Dak To, and more down south," Kirby said. "We knew something was coming, but nothing like this."

"LP reports mortar tubes firing from the ravine," the CO shouted.

From the bunkers came shouts of "Incoming!"

Boot Legger crawled up beside him and stared out the gunport.

"Better get your head down, Ghost. This first barrage is usually the worst."

Martin ducked his head below the edge of the sandbags.

"Which direction will they come in from?"

The first mortar rounds exploded, sending clouds of red dust billowing into the gun ports as the buzzing whirr of shrapnel shredded the sandbags.

"They'll use this first barrage to get into position," Boot Legger said, "but this first attack is likely a feint. They'll hit us with the main force somewhere else. We never know where till they come at us."

Chief Kirby walked over and stood behind them.

"The command net is locked up—too many people trying to talk. I got a request through to Spooky, but they said all their assets are currently tied up."

Claymores began detonating around the perimeter as trip flares flamed to life, and the rattle of machine guns grew to a non-stop crescendo.

"Boot Legger," the CO called out, "Get on the radio, and let's start getting sit-reps from around the wire."

The CO walked over to Martin and extended his hand. "Phil Walker," he said. "I'm CMFIC here on this dirt pile. Chief here has told me a lot about you."

"Martin Shadows. It's a pleasure, Captain Walker." Martin shook hands with him.

"Call me 'Hound.' Everybody else around here does, and you go by Ghost, right?"

"I prefer Shadows, but I'll answer to most anything. Sorry we didn't get to meet sooner."

"Hound's been laid up in the aid bunker with a bout of malaria," Kirby said.

Walker's jaundiced face said it all. Malaria was kicking his ass.

"You up to this little party tonight, boss?" Kirby asked.

Captain walker pulled a small flask from a cargo pocket, unscrewed the cap, and took a swig. "I don't have much choice, Chief. From what I'm hearing on the command net, everybody is getting hit, but no one has said they're getting overrun—at least not yet. The enemy seems to be disengaging quickly in some places. I think it's a deception to make us spread our air assets to different hot-spots. The main attack will come when the aircraft return to refuel."

"Problem is figuring out which firebase will be the lucky grand prize winner," Boot Legger said. "Somebody is gonna get their ass kicked tonight. Let's hope it's not us."

Martin lit a cigarette, drew hard on it, and exhaled.

"It sounds like all the other firebases got hit before us, and all the air support is tied up with them. That kind of makes me think we might be the grand prize winner."

Kirby and Captain Walker stared at one another.

"I'll be damned, if it doesn't make perfect sense," Kirby said.

"What can I do to help?" Martin asked.

"Stay with Boot Legger," Kirby said. "There's a bunker back behind us where the quick reaction force is laid up—twenty-five Montagnards. If the enemy breaches the wire somewhere, Boot Legger takes them down to plug the gap."

These were some brave bastards, but Martin had enough experience to know they were in a bad situation. Betty Lou wasn't a firebase capable of withstanding the massive attack that was coming.

"Can you help him if it comes to that?" Kirby asked.

"Well, crap, Chief! I had an early tee-time tomorrow morning, but I suppose just because you asked…."

For a moment, Chief Kirby gazed at him with a mask of grim incredulity before his face broke with a grin. "You know, Ghost, you should put in for the schoolhouse at Bragg when you get back. S.F. could use more short-bus riders like you."

It was the first time Martin had smiled in months. Two more hours dragged by in an eternity of incoming artillery, nonstop machine gun fire, and drifting illumination rounds. Betty Lou was holding her own, until the call came in from LA. He and his men were in hand-to-hand combat with the enemy. There was a hole in the wire, and his machine gunner's barrel was glowing in the dark. The bodies were stacked three and four deep in the gap, but they were still coming—hundreds of them.

"Showtime," Boot Legger muttered.

Martin strapped on his web gear and grabbed several frags from an open crate. Stuffing them into his spare ammo pouches, he followed Boot Legger. They ran through a deep trench and rousted the reaction team. The brown faces of the Montagnards glistened in the glow of the lantern. They were already loaded and ready to go.

"Just tell them what you want," Boot Legger said. "They understand enough English to know what you're saying."

Stooping low, Martin ran with them toward the perimeter. The night air was a choking fog of dust and smoke glowing with the amber light of the illumination rounds. The hazy silhouettes of men were barely visible as they crawled from the frontline bunkers and engaged the enemy at point blank range. Matters had already gone to hell on the perimeter as hundreds of NVA regulars streamed through the wire and over the bunkers.

Martin stopped as Boot Legger went to a knee in front of him, likely trying to make sense of what he was facing. To their front, less than a hundred meters away, the wire was breached, and the enemy was crawling over their dead, coming in by the hundreds, coming for them and willing to die. It was a strange memory that flashed before him at that moment, but as the enemy climbed over their dead and rushed toward him, Martin remembered a book he once read about a hundred and fifty British troops facing thousands of Zulu warriors at Rorke's Drift in South Africa. The Brits survived, but he was struck by the similarities. The current situation said Betty Lou was doomed, but like the Brits, he would fight to the bitter end.

Boot Legger turned to him and shouted, but his voice was nearly lost in the din. "We have to move fast. Take four men and go with Phau to that berm to cover the right flank." He pointed to one of the Montagnards carrying an M-79. "Tell him to start putting flechette rounds into that gap as fast as he can. I'm taking fifteen more with me down to the bunkers. Five more are setting up an M-60 here in case we can't stop them."

Boot Legger sprang to his feet and used hand signals to split the men into groups as five enemy soldiers ran out of the darkness.

Martin hit one in the face with his fist. The fight was furious, and the enemy soldiers were killed within seconds, but not before one rammed a bayonet into Boot Legger's lower back. Martin snatched the field dressing from his web gear and ripped it open.

"No!" Boot Legger shouted. "I'm okay. Go. Go now. Take the men down to the bunkers. We've got to stop them."

He was right. Martin gave the dressing to one of the Montagnards, and motioned for the others to follow him as he sprinted down to the bunkers. Screams of agony and shouts of anger came from below as men fought with bayonets and used rifles as clubs. Others fired point-blank into the surging wall of enemy soldiers. Atop a bunker, LA stood alone and weaponless as he took an AK-47 from a lunging soldier and killed him with it. Three more leapt atop the bunker as the big soldier lost his footing and fell backward to the ground.

Martin fired his CAR-15 killing two, while the third jumped from the bunker and stumbled away into the darkness. LA leapt to his feet. The whites of his eyes shone brightly in the darkness as he stared at Martin as if to say thanks.

"Better reload that AK, I don't think we're done yet," Martin shouted. "I'm going back to find Boot Legger. He got bayonetted in the back."

LA took a magazine of ammo from one of the corpses and shoved it into the AK-47. For the moment, the human wave attack had been stopped, but enemy soldiers remained everywhere inside the wire.

"I'm taking ten men to sweep the base for the ones that got past us," Martin said. "Stay here and reorganize your men."

"Hey," LA said. He paused for several seconds. "I owe you one, Ghost."

"Buy me a drink later, and we'll call it even."

Martin spread ten Montagnards online and began a methodical

search inside the wire. By the time he reached the TOC bunker an hour had passed. They had killed eleven enemy soldiers and captured three. One was an officer. Inside the TOC, a Coleman lantern burned dimly, and Captain Walker sat in a jaundiced sweat, talking calmly into a radio handset.

"This is a Broken Arrrow situation. Repeat, our perimeter has been overrun."

"We stopped them down at LA's position," Martin said.

Captain Walker's bloodshot eyes said it all. Feverish and exhausted he refused to give up.

"Doesn't matter. They'll come at us again. They always do."

Chief Kirby stood beside his Captain and took the radio handset from his hand as there came another transmission. He twisted the volume knob on the radio.

"Roger Betty Lou, we have Spooky enroute to your....." And as with all the transmissions that night, this one was lost in a garbled hiss of static. "I think they've finally diverted one of the C-47s. It's probably coming out of Nha Trang," Kirby said. "It should be here in the next half hour."

After a moment he looked up and gazed at the prisoners. "Sonofabitch! You captured a damned colonel!"

"I'd like to take the credit," Martin said, "but Pau here captured him."

"Trung tá." Pau said. "He colonel. He big catch, but Đại úy not say truth. They attack us. He kill two with knife. Trung tá only surrender then."

One of the radios hissed and blared a garbled transmission. Captain Walker grabbed the handset and pressed it against his ear.

"That was LA," he said. "They're coming at him again. There's a couple hundred more rushing the wire."

The North Vietnamese Lieutenant Colonel blurted something at them.

"What's he saying, Pau?" Kirby asked.

"He say we surrender now, they not kill us when they take firebase."

"Tie these bastards with parachute cord," Kirby said. "And tell the colonel to shut the fuck up. You stay here to guard them. I'm going out and light the strobes for Puff and shoot some azimuths."

"Have you seen Boot Legger?" Martin asked.

"Not since y'all went down to help LA. Why?"

"We ran into a bunch of the enemy coming up the hill, and one came up from behind us. He got Boot Legger in the back with a bayonet."

"It'll be light in a few hours. We'll look for him then. Can you take the rest of these men and go back to help LA?"

"On my way."

Martin motioned for the remaining Montagnards to follow as he ran toward the perimeter. The flashing trails of rocket-propelled grenades arced into the bunkers below as showers of red and green tracers clashed, making him wonder how anyone could survive. Atop the bunker where LA had stood earlier there was now an enemy machine gun emplacement. It was firing a steady stream of grazing fire across the firebase. Dozens more of the enemy were taking cover behind a berm inside the wire.

Martin spread his men online and began pouring fire into the troops below. There was no way they would be stopped. LA and his men were likely dead, and Martin figured he and the six men with him were next. After emptying five magazines, his CAR-15 jammed, and he began flinging frags one after another down the hill. A trail of sparks shot up the slope and an RPG exploded a few meters below. It was as if someone put a double-aught 12-gauge load into him, as it delivered stinging blows to his shoulders and left hip.

When he regained consciousness, Martin had no idea how

long he had lain there, but the sounds of the battle raged as he recognized the burping roar of a minigun coming from above. He opened his eyes to see an unbroken stream of tracers impacting into the wire—only a few hundred feet away. It was what they called "danger-close."

The bullets splashed in a sparkling shower of bouncing, ricocheting, and spinning lead. Facing a near hopeless situation, Walker had called for the fire at the very edge of the perimeter, and Puff the Magic Dragon was shredding the enemy troops at the gap in the wire. The attack ended in seconds with the bloody remains of the enemy attackers hanging in the wire. Lit by the requiem candle of a drifting parachute flare, the carnage was a nightmare Martin knew he would never forget.

Daylight came to Betty Lou as the morning sunlight replaced the illumination rounds. A shroud of red dust and smoke hung over the little hilltop outpost as men searched the firebase bunker by bunker. With the help of two Montagnards, Martin hobbled to the aid station where he found Boot Legger lying against a wall of sandbags. The medic was popping him with a morphine syrette. Others were helping aid the wounded by attaching IVs and plasma bags.

A couple hundred feet away the first medevac chopper was hovering down as the more seriously wounded were carried forward. The constant thump of rotors came from gunships circling the perimeter while searching for enemy stragglers. And thousands of feet above the firebase, the morning sunlight flashed against the plexiglass canopies of fighter jets as their contrails crisscrossed the sky. The numbness in Martin's left shoulder was now replaced with a searing pain, and his fatigues were soaked with blood from his hip wound. The medic hit him with a morphine syrette and began scissoring away his shirt sleeve.

"You're lucky," he said. "I don't think either piece of shrapnel hit an artery. I've got dust-offs stacked up out there. We'll get you out on the third or fourth lift. Just hang tight. You're going to be okay."

"What about him?" Martin motioned toward Boot Legger, who had not opened his eyes.

"He's a little worse off—took a bayonet in the lower back, but it mostly went down into his hip."

"You don't worry about me," Boot Legger muttered without opening his eyes. "It's gonna take more than a bayonet to get me draped with a flag."

"It's good to hear your voice, you cantankerous bastard. Have you heard anything from LA and the men in the bunkers that got overrun?"

"LA, Fred, and Sparky," Boot Legger paused, drew a deep breath and slowly exhaled. "None of them made it—them and nineteen of our Yards, they're all KIA, and we've got several more in bad shape."

The pain intensified and Martin grew nauseated. Good men had died, and again he was asking himself, for what? Despite his pain, the morphine and exhaustion slowly dragged him into unconsciousness.

CHAPTER FIFTEEN

Rest, Recovery, and Back to Square One
8th Field Hospital, Nha Trang

Martin awoke that morning as he had so many times in the days since he was wounded. It was well before dawn, and he was drenched in sweat. Again and again, he watched those South Vietnamese SkyRaiders come down the valley, their radial engines roaring as they strafed and bombed Sky Soldier, Thibodaux, Lugo, and Gopher. And again, when they returned dropping napalm on what must have been the fleeing Montagnards, he watched helplessly. It was his fault.

He had followed his visions of spirits needing help—visions that once seemed so real but had now faded with doubt and failure. His vision—if that's what it was—had driven him to take risks for the Montagnards, risks that were all for naught. He was a fool. He had saved no one, and it cost good men their lives. Sitting up on the edge of his bed, he lit a cigarette. The hospital ward was quiet except for a nurse making her rounds.

"Put out the cigarette, Captain."

She was a comely woman, neither gorgeous nor ugly, but her smile made her seem like the sister he never had. Her O.D. fatigues did their part to leave her without identity. Martin gazed at her and nodded as he pinched the cigarette out with his fingers. The nurse wore a black bar on her collar—a First Lieutenant.

"I need your help," he said.

She shoved a thermometer under his tongue and raised her brows. Martin pulled it out.

"I need you to send a message to Colonel Duggin at I-Corps Advisory Command up at Phu Bai. Tell him I'm here and that I will return when I'm released."

"That shouldn't be a problem," she said. Taking the thermometer from his hand, she shoved it back in his mouth. "I'll show you how to send the Telex yourself. Oh, by the way, I think you'll be released today or tomorrow."

It was great news, and none too soon. He had been thinking of going AWOL as soon as his hip healed. Boot Legger had disappeared a week or two back. Later they said he caught a chopper back to Dak To and eventually Firebase Betty Lou, but he left Martin with gifts—his knife, CAR-15, and a bottle of Old Forester. These Special Forces guys had big balls, but he decided to avoid complicating matters further with an AWOL charge. He would wait for a response from Colonel Duggin.

The next afternoon the nurse came to him with a message—not from Duggin, but from MAC-V command. It said:

REPORT TO COMMANDER MAC-V HEADQUARTERS INTELLIGENCE, SAIGON UPON RELEASE FROM ARMY 8TH FIELD HOSPITAL, NHA TRANG.

He immediately began writing his after-action report. If he had to meet with Krieger again, he would be prepared.

After showing his orders to the clerk at MAC-V that morning, Martin was motioned toward a chair. "Have a seat, Captain. I'll tell the colonel you're here."

"If you don't mind, I'll stand. I took some shrapnel in my left hip and the bus ride from Tan Son Nhut was a bitch."

"No problem, Sir."

The Spec-4 clerk probably realized officers were a dime a dozen around this complex, and a captain's rank was something bordering on peon status. Martin was inclined to agree. He backed into a corner and leaned against the wall. Colonel Krieger had been a hard ass during their first meeting, and he expected more of the same—especially since the SNAFU with Pham at the Montagnard village. His only hope was that Krieger had spoken with Colonel Duggin.

Less than a minute later, he was called in. The colonel returned his salute and invited him to sit. He did, but not without an involuntary flinch from the pain.

"Hemorrhoids?" Krieger asked with a smirk.

"A steel one from an RPG, Sir."

The colonel's face reflected a mild regret for his remark.

"Sorry, Captain. It's good to see you on your feet again. So, why don't we begin with you telling me everything that's happened the last couple months. By the way, Colonel Duggin has been recalled and his unit is now deactivated. We've begun deactivating units all over the country. This war will no longer be ours in a year or two."

Martin opened his battered valise, removed the after-action report, and handed it to the colonel. It was ten printed pages he typed at the army field hospital.

"I can give you a verbal summary, if you want, Sir."

"That won't be necessary. I'll read it."

Martin waited while the colonel began slowly flipping the pages as he read.

"You know the more I read these reports the more I think you must have some serious talent for doing things the hard way. You claim here to have jumped an NVA recon group and killed them all with a knife, then attacked an NVA platoon that was about to ambush a SOG patrol. Why didn't you just shoot the recon group, and how in hell did you take on a whole enemy platoon?"

"Colonel, I only quoted the Distinguished Service Cross recommendation written by Chief Warrant Officer Kirby and his commanding officer Captain Walker as a matter of verification. And to answer your questions: there were NVA troops in the area. I used the knife so I wouldn't have to fire my weapon, and the enemy platoon was at the base of a cliff below me. They were sitting ducks."

A hint of incredulity creased the colonel's grim façade.

"So, these officers witnessed this?"

"Chief Kirby saw the bodies with the knife wounds, and I gave him and Captain Walker the maps and documents I took from the NVA officer's body. A Montagnard soldier named Kong witnessed me throwing the bodies from the cliff."

Krieger slowly turned his gaze back to the report and continued reading. After several minutes, he set it aside and gazed across the desk at him.

"I'll approve both recommendations, but I want to talk about this black helicopter that you say marked your position with smoke for the Vietnamese Air Force. Friendly fire?"

"I think not. I believe they mistook us for the Montagnard villagers who were fleeing with First Sergeant Anderson."

"Yes, Colonel Duggin reported that, but a CID investigation concluded it was a friendly fire incident. Why else would they strafe and bomb Montagnard civilians?"

"With all due respect, Sir, I believe you should talk some more with Colonel Duggin. He did an investigation and discovered the

OSA is undermining MAC-V's investigation of certain incidents that occurred during the Phoenix Program. An OSA operator who was directly involved in the incident near Qui Nhon later worked with a Vietnamese colonel named Pham to eliminate witnesses who could implicate them. Those witnesses are several Montagnards who were the intended targets of that so-called friendly fire incident."

"You're making some serious allegations, Captain. Would you be willing to make a sworn statement to that effect?"

"Yes, Sir, and I would encourage CID to interview Special Forces Sergeant Luis Ravera at the MAC-V Recondo school in Nha Trang. He and Colonel Duggin together have enough firsthand information to likely convince you what I'm saying isn't simple supposition."

"This OSA advisor—you know him?"

"We've met."

"His name Liegeman?"

"Yes, Sir, and I saw him standing in the door of that chopper the day they marked our position for the airstrike."

"Glad-handing son of a bitch," Krieger muttered under his breath.

"Captain Shadows, I believe I may have misjudged you in the past. After my initial meeting with Colonel Duggin, I ordered CID to complete their investigation based on the assumption of a friendly fire incident, but it seems there's quite a bit more to it than I first understood. As much as I don't want to believe any American would do such a thing, you have presented some pretty incredible circumstantial evidence that requires we dig deeper into this matter.

"For now, I want you as far away from Saigon and these Agency people as I can get you. You have quite a bit of time left on your tour of duty, and I've got a commander with the Hundred and First up in I-Corps with an urgent need for LRRP team leaders. I'm sending you up to Camp Eagle. Give me a written statement on what we have discussed here, and I'll have your orders cut later this afternoon. Questions?"

"Sir, my hip is still in bad shape. I can walk, but I could use a few days R&R to get it healed, and I haven't received any mail in nearly seven weeks."

"I'll get you a room at a BOQ downtown and find your mail. A courier will deliver it along with your orders when it's found. You've got three days. Keep a low profile and get well, and if you need anything, call me."

Martin stood and saluted, and when he reached the street below he found a driver with a jeep marked with full bird colonel wings waiting for him. He had apparently cracked Krieger's granite façade once and for all.

———————

Early that afternoon after reaching the BOQ, Martin stood in a hot shower for a half-hour, drank a half pint of bourbon, and lay on a bed with a real mattress. He set his forty-five automatic on the bedside table with his wristwatch and stared up at a dusty black ceiling fan turning lethargically overhead. It took only a minute before his aching butt made him roll over onto his belly. It was afternoon—nearly fourteen hundred hours, and there were things he wanted to do, but exhaustion induced by too many sleepless nights and adrenaline-driven days nailed him. It was as if he were succumbing to a surgeon's anesthesia.

When his eyes opened, the lights in the room were still burning, the fan was still turning, and he was in the same position, face down on the bed. Momentarily disoriented, he reached for his watch on the bedside table and glanced at it—2330 hours. The second hand was still moving, but he shook the watch anyway as he sat up on the edge of the bed. He hadn't had this much uninterrupted sleep even in the hospital. Nine and a half hours was the longest he had slept in months.

Walking to the refrigerator, he found a tray of ice and broke it over a bowl. It was his thirst and aching hip that had awakened him, and he addressed both with five aspirin and two glasses of ice water. Afterward, he noticed a small desk in the corner of the room. On it were several sheets of stationery and some envelopes, apparently left by the last occupant. It was a divine message—time to write letters to his mother and Kania.

June 1970

Dear Mom,

I know you got the telegram from the army about me getting wounded, and I want you to know it wasn't anything serious. I just got a little shrapnel in my butt. Life here in Nam has been consuming every minute I have, and I am sorry for not writing sooner. I have not received any letters from anyone back home in the last seven weeks. There's a colonel looking for my mail, so I hope I will eventually get your letters. There has been a lot that has happened, but as usual, I can't tell you much about it. I am being re-assigned to the 101ˢᵗ Airborne Division up at Camp Eagle near Phu Bai. Please send me updates on Dad, Grandpa, and Grandma when you can. And check on the girl I told you about, Kania. I'm pretty sure she thinks I've forgotten her, and I can't blame her. I sleep in the rain, eat in the rain, and patrol in the rain, and paper and pens don't do well in the rain. I am in Saigon now on a three-day R&R, so I will write her a letter as soon as I finish this one. Please give Dad, Grandpa and Grandma my love. Please, send me some of that southern fruitcake from your friend in North Carolina and some of Dad's venison jerky. There's not a lot I can say about this war, but hopefully, I will be home soon.

Love,
Martin

After folding the letter and addressing the envelope, Martin lit a cigarette. Kania was young, and they weren't yet locked into a life relationship. His letter to her needed to be somewhat more to the point. It had to address the reality of his situation, yet not so much so that he left her horrified or in a state of hopelessness. He began writing.

June 1970

Dear Kania,

I apologize for not writing sooner. I know this is a pretty weak statement after those days we spent together, but you must know how much you mean to me. This war has been crazy, and I have very little time to myself. If you have written more letters, I haven't received them. I haven't gotten mail in over seven weeks, but they're looking for it. In the last letter I got from you, you said your father had taken a turn for the worse. I have offered more prayers for both you and him, and I only wish I could be there at a time when you need someone. These are only words, but Kania dear, if I come home, I will be there for you from that day forward. I mean it. And if you choose to move on, I will always be your friend. I say this only because of the "Dear John" letters that so many soldiers over here get from women who can no longer stand to wait for a man who may not come home. I also say this because I don't think people back home understand just how bad it is over here. Only to you, I will say that coming home is not guaranteed. There's only so much I can say, but there are a lot more men paying for Americans' freedom with their lives than I think people realize. The problem with this war is both sides think they're right, and I'm not so sure they aren't. It's the politicians who are the problem. I suppose this is enough whining for one night. It's nearly one o'clock in the morning here in Saigon. In a few days I am on my way to another assignment. Take care of your father and visit my grandparents when you can. I will try to come home with at least some small part of my sanity intact.

Love,

Martin

After addressing the envelope, he placed the folded letter inside and began writing the report for Colonel Krieger. It was nearing dawn when he finished and went back to bed.

CHAPTER SIXTEEN

The Devil Comes Calling
Saigon, June 1970

Martin awakened late that morning after another nearly pain-free six hours of sleep. He had never slept so much, and only now did he understand just how debilitated he had become—both physically and mentally. And he couldn't help but speculate about his psyche. He had maintained his equilibrium and rationality, but how much of it was reality and how much was delusion? Questioning his sanity was now something he could no longer avoid. He had three days of freedom in Saigon, and despite Krieger's warning, his only thought was to return to the Continental Palace Hotel where he hoped to find Liegeman.

The word "obsession" was creeping about in the back of his mind, and Liegeman was the cause, but going back to the Continental was a bad idea. Nothing good could come of it. Killing the sorry bastard, which is what he deserved, would likely result in a life sentence at the military prison in Leavenworth. Two days passed while Martin rested and only occasionally visited the restaurants in the area. After purchasing new tiger-stripe fatigues, he left them at a shop to have them fitted. He planned on picking them up the next day.

It was after dark when he walked down Tu Do Street toward the BOQ, and the evening air hung still and heavy with the stench of the rivers. As he approached the Continental Palace Hotel, he wondered what the latest news was concerning the war. The press always gathered there at the rooftop bar after the five o'clock follies. There had been no sign of Liegeman, and he needed to know what people outside of the military were saying about the Paris peace talks and the possibility of the war ending.

After all, the evidence was everywhere. Saigon was changing. The city was a person with a terminal disease, a city no longer relishing its warm evenings with crowds of bar patrons. The rooftop was occupied by an anemic few with only a scattering of diehards drinking quietly and listening to a radio tuned to the AFVN. Martin ordered a bourbon over ice and glanced around to see if any of the patrons might be correspondents.

And he was there! It was Liegeman sitting alone at a table. He had already spotted Martin, and despite the dim lights it was obvious that his tanned face had become pale white. Martin killed his drink and stood. His every instinct and rationale said this was folly. It said he should walk away, but he walked toward him, knowing at that moment but not caring that he might kill the worthless bastard in the next few moments. Liegeman slid a hand inside his jacket and affected a lame grin.

"I'll be damned, Shadows. You *really* might be a ghost. Last I heard you were MIA somewhere on the Laotian border. Colonel Krieger at MAC-V said you were caught up in a friendly fire incident by the gook air force."

Liegeman's voice was shaky, and his stupid grin did little to hide his fear. Martin focused him with the eyes of a cougar—one that had its prey dead to the rights.

"And 'damned' you may well be, Liegeman. When was the last time you spoke to Krieger?"

"It's been a week or two. Why?"

"Because I told him the last I saw of you was when you and Lieutenant Postiche flew over us in that black Huey and marked our position with smoke for that airstrike."

Liegeman's lips parted slightly as he fought to maintain his grinning façade.

Martin leaned close to his face. "Don't worry. If I was going to kill you, I'd have done it that day when your chopper came back for damage assessment. I was on the side of the mountain with an M-60 pointing at you and Postiche both standing in the door. You were close—real close, and if I had wanted, you would have been among the MIA."

"Uh, I don't know what the hell you're talking about, Shadows. You better get your story straight and stop spreading lies, because those are some damned serious allegations you're making."

"You killed good men that day, Liegeman, and it was no accident. I've given a full report on the incident to the colonel. Your day of reckoning is coming. Sooner or later, it's coming."

"You crazy bastard. You don't know what you're talking about. That was a friendly fire incident, and those were…." Liegeman went suddenly silent—likely realizing he'd just admitted he was there that day.

"Do you mean your friendly fire was meant for those innocent Montagnard refugees instead? Is that what you're saying?"

"You're a damned fool, Shadows. I told you before, you don't know who you're fucking with. We are the most powerful organization in the world. This was our war and if the army had let us run it our way, we'd probably be winning by now."

And it suddenly dawned on Martin that arguing with this delusional fool probably made him the bigger fool. He turned to walk away but stopped and looked back.

"You'd better believe the spirits of those men you murdered will someday hold you accountable, Liegeman, because if they don't, I will."

Liegeman's face darkened.

"Are you threatening me?"

"Of course not. Threats are for fools. I'm saying that this is the way the soldier's world works. We stand with our brothers. Like I said, you will someday face a reckoning of your own making, and it will be with the spirits of those men standing in judgement."

By the time he arrived back at the BOQ that evening, Martin was regretting his foolish encounter with Liegeman. He hoped to increase the pressure on the pompous ass and put him on notice. That much he accomplished. Liegeman was clearly scared shitless, but it would likely make CID's job more difficult, and if Colonel Krieger learned of the meeting, another ass-chewing was surely coming.

That following day Martin picked up his new fatigues, packed his duffle bag, and prepared to depart for Tan Son Nhut the next morning. He lay back on his bunk and closed his eyes, knowing it might be his last good night's sleep for a while. Fading into a restless sleep he was awakened sometime in the night by a slight scratching sound. He sat up and listened. It came again. There was a metallic click. Someone was trying to pick the lock to his room.

Grabbing his forty-five automatic from the bedside table, he tiptoed to the wall adjacent to the door. It had to be Liegeman. He was the only person who could bluff his way past the MPs guarding the building. Martin thumbed the pistol's safety and cocked the hammer. If it was Liegeman and he stepped into the room, he would die. With his back to the wall, Martin waited until the knob slowly began turning. The bolt clicked. He raised the pistol.

The door opened no more than a few inches—and there came a metallic ping and a muted pop from out in the hallway. A tennis-ball-size fragmentation grenade rolled through the opening—immediately followed by the sound of someone running away down the hallway. The grenade rolled beneath the bed, and Martin snatched open the door. Diving into the hallway, he rolled away from the open door as the grenade exploded. The concussion from the explosion momentarily stunned him as the person disappeared down the stairwell while smoke and dust billowed from the room.

Martin came to his feet as doors up and down the hall began opening. Standing in the debris of the shattered door, he was still wearing his boxers and holding the pistol. Army officers, most armed with forty-fives, began emerging from their rooms. The dusty chemical odor of explosive filled the hallway, as the building lights flickered. Everything went black. He'd caught only a glimpse of a man's back, but his every instinct said it was Liegeman. The bastard was terrified and would stop at nothing to cover his tracks.

Only now did Martin fully realize he was engaged in a lethal game for which he was ill-prepared. As a military officer he had to follow the Military Code of Conduct. This left him at a decided disadvantage because people like Liegeman had no rules.

CHAPTER SEVENTEEN

A Call for Help
Camp Eagle, Late June 1970

After two days of questioning by the CID, Martin boarded a C-130 bound for Phu Bai and the One Hundred and First Airborne at Camp Eagle. He'd received the expected ass-chewing from Krieger, and as expected, Liegeman had secured a lock-tight alibi when he was found on the beach at Vung Tau where he had supposedly been for two days. There were witnesses, two Vietnamese prostitutes and a Vietnamese house maid, almost certainly well-compensated for their testimonies. Army CID said there was little more they could do. Such was the slimy world of dark ops and righteous psychopaths.

After his arrival at Combat Base Phu Bai, Martin and several other soldiers boarded a Huey bound for Camp Eagle. The afternoon sky was a hazy yellow, as the sprawling complex of buildings and tents came into view. South of Hue and northwest of Phu Bai, Eagle was now home to the 101st Airborne Division (Airmobile). Reporting to the division HQ, he was directed to see Colonel Thomas Lee, who greeted him with a salute and handshake. The colonel was lean and wearing jungle boots scuffed and worn—another warrior who led from the front.

"Captain Shadows, you were highly recommended by Colonel Krieger, but I put out some inquiries on you anyway. You've got a helluva reputation, and that comes from some men I respect. Your experience will likely help us, but I won't bullshit you. Where I'm sending you is in the devil's own backyard. You're going up to Firebase Ripcord to lead a lurp team. Here's the skinny.

"Ripcord is one of several fire support bases supporting Operation Chicago Peak, our planned offensive against the 803rd and 29th NVA Regiments in the A Shau Valley. There are no roads and no airstrips near Ripcord. It's remote, only twelve miles from Laos, and the only way in or out is by helicopter. We have outposts on four hilltops in the immediate AO, but things have been heating up.

"We first began reopening the firebase in mid-March and it's grown into a non-stop engagement ever since. We secured the hill in mid-April, but despite our air and artillery strikes as well as continuous patrols out to three thousand meters around the base we continue to receive constant incoming. They're hitting us with everything including 60mm and 82mm mortars, recoilless rifles, RPGs, machine guns, and small arms fire. And they're mobile. They shoot and scoot. By the time we have a fire mission on them, they're gone.

"The problem we face now is a large-scale escalation by the enemy. We believe there are nine enemy battalions with over thirty thousand NVA troops moving into the AO around Ripcord. I think the Communists are planning another Dien Bien Phu. They want to annihilate us like they did the French in '54. They've built reinforced bunkers into the sides of the mountains and they're using 12.7mm anti-aircraft guns to shoot down our helicopters.

"The Second of the 506th has done their best, but they've begun losing men as fast as we can replace them. A few days ago, we had a lurp team go missing. The enemy hit them so quickly they barely had time to call in contact before their radios went silent. We don't know if they're still escaping and evading or if they're POWs, but we're still looking for them.

"Captain, I don't know how the enemy is doing it, but S-2 believes they may be utilizing hunter-killer teams with directional antenna radios to specifically target our lurps. They got the jump on some of our best warriors. That's why I'm sending you up there. Our recon platoon and other long range recon patrols have been kicking ass, but they're spread thin and there's tremendous pressure on them and everyone else around Ripcord.

"You can handpick your team from the battalion lurp platoon. Use as many men as you want. We're inserting you into the same area where the missing team was last reported. Your primary mission is to locate enemy assets and target them for artillery and air strikes, but I also want you to find that NVA hunter-killer team and, if at all possible, our missing men. Otherwise, I strongly discourage you from initiating direct contact because that's what the missing team did just before disappearing."

"I need two days with these men before we go into the bush, Sir. I want to see them fire their weapons, and we'll need to work on our immediate action drills."

After studying topo maps of the terrain around Ripcord with Colonel Lee, Martin was introduced to an NCO wearing a Combat Infantry Badge with two stars and Master jump wings. Barely five-foot-seven, Sergeant Major Austin was lean and looked as if he hadn't smiled in months.

"That missing lurp team belongs to one of Sergeant Major Austin's platoons," the colonel said. "So, as you might surmise, he has a vested interest in your success."

Martin shook the sergeant major's hand.

"Sergeant Major Austin has a good bit of experience. He made three combat jumps during World War II, served in Korea, and has one prior tour here in Nam before coming to my outfit as a Sergeant Major. I'd listen to what he says, Captain."

"I'd be a fool not to, Sir."

Leaving the battalion HQ, Martin walked with Austin up the dusty road between rows of sandbagged tents. It was an abnormally mild day with a light breeze, scattered clouds, and strings of Hueys coming and going in the distance. Several Chinooks were also lifting away in a roaring clatter from an LZ nearly a quarter mile away.

"It's a beautiful day, Captain."

Martin answered with a nod.

"Better enjoy it while you can, because where you're going, every day will be hell."

"So I've been told, Sergeant Major."

"Colonel Lee thinks a lot of you, Sir. He told me to give you only my best men for your team."

Martin said nothing.

Austin cast a sidelong glance at him. "I'm assuming you've had considerable experience leading lurp teams."

"I've worked with some recon teams."

The sergeant major's misgivings were evident as he scratched his chin but refused to make eye contact.

"You know it might be better if you let me put an experienced team leader with you for a while. Matter of fact, since Colonel Lee is so uptight about what's happening at Ripcord, I might be able to get his approval to do it myself. We'll see. That might be a dogfight."

"What did the colonel tell you about me?"

"He said you came highly recommended from Colonel Krieger at MAC-V, that you've been through Recondo school, and that you're highly decorated."

"Is that all?"

"Well sir, he did mention some pretty far-fetched stuff, but I more or less wrote it off as war stories. You know how they are—I mean…they get exaggerated more with every telling. I don't mean any disrespect. It's just that—"

"No problem, Sergeant Major. I'm going to take you up on your offer to help lead the team, but I will be the One-Zero and call the shots. And since you know the men, it would be very helpful if you choose six more to accompany us."

"Calling yourself the One-Zero tells me you might have worked with SOG."

"Some."

Austin cast another sidelong glance at him as they walked through sandbagged walls into a cavernous tent with rows of cots. Mildewed canvas and body sweat were the odors of the day. A couple naked bulbs suspended from wires burned dimly. Twenty-one men were scattered about, sleeping, playing cards, or cleaning weapons.

"Ten-hut!" the sergeant major shouted.

"As you were, men," Martin said.

All eyes were on him.

"This is Captain Shadows, men. He and I are taking another team up to Ripcord to hunt NVA and search for our missing boys. I'll be volunteering six of you to join us."

"Are there any particular talents you're looking for, Sir?" Austin asked.

"I want an RTO with FO skills who can call in artillery and airstrikes accurately, two grenadiers who can put at least three M-79 rounds in the air before the first one lands and be on target with every round. I want a point man who misses nothing, and I want men who know how to move through the jungle without being seen or heard."

The sergeant major gazed pokerfaced at him for several seconds before giving a knowing nod.

"I believe you have more experience than you've admitted to, Sir."

A shirtless soldier walked up to them. With a typical flak jacket tan, his arms and face were deeply bronzed while his torso was pale pink, and his eyes told of too many days in combat.

"Captain Shadows, Sir, are you the one they call the Ghost?"

The soldier's voice was low, almost spooky sounding.

"I've been called that. What's your name?"

"Manny Jacobie, Sir. I'd be honored to be on your team, and I can shoot the hell out of a thump gun."

"The Ghost?" Austin said with a skeptical squint.

"I'm not sure how that got started," Martin said. "I think it was a company of Hundred and First guys I met one time while they were out on patrol in the highlands."

"I was there," Manny said. "You saved our asses that day."

Martin looked him over carefully.

"Yes. I remember you. You were the point man for the company that day."

Manny grinned.

"You just appeared there in front of me and whispered to me. I thought you really *were* a ghost. And if you hadn't warned us about that NVA ambush, we'd have been shot to hell that day."

By now, Sergeant Major Austin was staring in wide-eyed wonderment at him. "Gather your gear, Manny. You're going with us," he said. "Where's Tadpole?"

"He's got the malaria pill trots. Been at the latrine all morning."

"Okay. When he gets back, tell him to get his shit together and come to the TOC." The sergeant major turned to Martin. "Tadpole is our best RTO. He can read a map and regularly calls in artillery and air support. I'll carry the second radio if it's okay with you."

"You got it."

"Bill Wolf, get your gear. You're point man for this little soiree."

A buck sergeant sitting on a cot nodded and grinned. Martin studied him. With a hawk nose, brown eyes, and black hair, he looked Indian.

"And go over to the other tent and tell Enzenauer, Pop, and Thok they volunteered for this team. Tell them to be at the TOC in fifteen minutes and bring their gear." He turned to Martin. "Thok is one of our scouts. He's Montagnard and speaks both English and Vietnamese. He knows the highlands and he's a hell of a fighter."

"Pop's been around forever. He's probably our best lurp. Enzenauer is fairly new to the unit. His primary MOS is medic, but he's pretty damned handy with a CAR-15."

"I'm not sure we need a medic," Martin said. "I'd rather have an experienced lurp."

"Oh, he's already served ten months with an infantry platoon, and he proved himself on his first recon mission when he saved one of our best team leaders. The guy took a big chunk of shrapnel in the groin. It severed a major artery. They tried direct pressure, but he was bleeding out when Doc comes out of his bag with some forceps and a scalpel. He opens the wound, finds the artery, and pinches it off with the forceps. I've never seen a medic do that, and the guy is back in the States recovering. I'd like to keep Enzenauer on the team, Sir."

"Okay. We keep Doc. What kind of weapon does the scout Thok carry?"

"Usually, a CAR-15."

"Do any of your men carry an RPD?" Martin asked.

"No, Sir. We carry only authorized weapons."

Martin had seen Montagnards carrying the Russian light machine gun. Its drum held one hundred rounds of 7.62x39 ammunition. Light enough to be carried by one man on a fast-moving lurp team, it was a game-changer when firepower was needed.

"Can you get one for us? I want Thok to carry it."

"Will do, Captain."

Two days later, Sergeant Major Austin presented him with a fully modified RPD light machine gun. The barrel and the butt stock had been shortened. A canvas sling was attached, and Austin produced two additional drums and five hundred rounds of ammunition. He also awarded him with several cases of lightweight lurp rations and a bundle of letters.

"The team missed mail call yesterday," Austin said. "I believe there's one in there for you, too."

"Thanks, Sarge. Distribute the mail and the rations. And tell Thok to disassemble, clean and test fire the RPD."

"That's already been done, Sir. Did it myself."

"Outstanding, Sergeant Major. I am in good hands. We'll do a final inspection of the men and their equipment at sixteen-hundred hours. Tell them we're heading to Ripcord in the morning, and I want them and their gear to be ready."

Martin went to his hooch where he opened his letter. It was from his mother.

June 1970

Dear Martin,

We received your letter today and it was the best day I've had in months. We got the telegram from the army when you were wounded, and I was so much more relieved when I got your letter.

It's good to know you are doing better. I called your grandparents out in Montana to tell them about it, but I am afraid I have bad news for you. They said Kania's father passed away. They had the funeral several days ago and Grandfather Two Shadows presided over the ceremony. They also said that several letters Kania sent you were returned and stamped as undeliverable. It seems she is beside herself worrying about you. She's not the only one. I hope you will write to us again soon. Your dad is doing well, but he seems worried too, even after he read your last letter. He's always been a quiet man, but I've never seen him this quiet, ever. I also sent you a package when I dropped this letter at the post office. There was one bag of venison jerky left. I am sure Dad will smoke some more when he gets another deer this fall. I sent the jerky along with some fruitcake and other goodies. I also sent a letter to my friend in North Carolina and requested more of her fruitcake. I'll send it to you when it arrives. I pray for you every day and look forward to seeing you again next spring. I keep your bedroom upstairs clean and dusted, and I hope you will spend some time with us when you come home. Write to me again soon.

Love You Always,
Mama

He folded the letter and returned it to the envelope. At dawn he would meet with his men on the chopper pad and disembark for FSB Ripcord. The sit-reps coming from there were lousy— constant incoming, constant contact, and growing numbers of casualties. The numbers were sobering, and it seemed the NVA might accomplish what Liegeman had failed to do.

CHAPTER EIGHTEEN

Into the Maelstrom
Fire Support Base Ripcord, July 1970

Martin leaned out the door and looked ahead as the Huey dove toward Ripcord that morning. The cool mountain air raised goosebumps on his arms, and most of the surrounding valleys remained filled with a thick morning fog as the chopper dropped rapidly with its main rotor cracking and turbine whining. Perched high atop a mountain, Ripcord appeared as a tiny brown collage of sandbags, howitzers, and barbed wire surrounded as far as the eye could see by mountains and jungle—a repeated location strategy the army seemed to love.

His first impression was that this firebase was in a totally untenable position. At least it seemed so if the enemy didn't want it there. Towering mountains covered with thick jungle canopy surrounded it, and they offered close and easily concealable observation points for anyone peering into the firebase—or firing into it. A long ridge led up to the base perimeter, allowing an enemy attacking force the advantage of avoiding the steeper parts of the slope. Whoever ordered this place occupied was supremely confident in American military might or else had not the slightest clue about what happened at Dien Bien Phu.

The battered remains of a Chinook helicopter lay upside down on the side of the mountain—no doubt the victim of the enemy's fifty-one caliber anti-aircraft guns. The slope below the perimeter was a dusty graveyard of skeletal trees and stumps. If hell could be encapsulated with a snapshot, this was it. The chopper barely touched down as the team jumped clear and the pilot pulled pitch—rolling and diving off the side of the mountain. A scattering of green tracer rounds followed him down the valley. Within seconds the only remaining sound was the eerie moan of the wind in the conglomeration of long-distance antennae sprouting from the TOC bunker.

The team squatted along a sandbagged wall below the chopper pad.

"Damned!" Manny said. "This place is spooky as hell. Where is everybody?"

"Probably where we should be right now—inside a bunker somewhere," Tadpole answered.

Tadpole was the smallest man on the team beside the Montagnard scout, Thok. Having been a tunnel rat before volunteering for the LRRPs, Tadpole had seen some of the worst of it. He said after several subterranean close calls, he figured 1049ing to the LRRP platoon gave him a better chance of survival. Now, he said he wasn't so sure.

Martin told him he had simply traded skillets. The little RTO grinned and nodded.

"Sergeant Wolf," Martin said. "Take the men to that bunker over there and hang out while the Sergeant Major and I check in up at the TOC bunker. Tadpole, you come with us."

They wove their way through the bunkers toward the one with the mass of antennas.

"Why do they call you Tadpole?" Martin asked.

"Back when I was with the line company, I saw something strange one day while we were walking on this rice paddy dike toward a small hamlet. A few feet off the dike there was this circle in the water where there weren't any plants growing. They were thick everywhere else, so I knew right off something wasn't right, and I waded out to it and fell in a hole—dang near drowned till the guys pulled me out. The sarge, he pulled all my gear off, and I went down again with my forty-five and flashlight and found a tunnel that came up under the dike. It led to the hamlet. They'd dug it when the paddy was dry, and when it was flooded it was dang near invisible. Pretty smart, huh? It was their escape route.

"Captain Warner hid a squad on the other side of the dike, and we went in to search the hamlet. While we were in there, all hell broke loose out on the dike. Ten VC had come up out of that hole in the rice paddy. Our boys killed six and captured four. They called me Tadpole after that 'cause I swam through that underwater tunnel and got covered with green slime."

"That's a pretty good way to get a name," Martin said.

They walked into the command bunker where a lieutenant colonel and several others were monitoring radios and scanning maps. The colonel looked up. His eyes said it all. He and his men were fighting for their lives at Ripcord.

"Come on in, men. Colonel Lee told me to expect you guys."

He shook hands with Austin. "I can't believe the old man let you lead one of your teams."

"Always helps to keep a blackmail file. I told him it'd be in *Stars and Stripes* the next day if he held me back."

"Damned! I always thought Lee was an altar boy."

"Don't let the old man fool you. Like most altar boys, he's been in the priest's wine a time or two."

After introductions the commander got down to business as they discussed possible enemy positions, call signs, map coordinates, and myriad other details. Martin took notes, as did Sergeant Major Austin and Specialist Tadpole.

"The missing lurp team was up here in this area. We've done almost non-stop flyovers, hoping they'd pop smoke or fire a starburst, but the enemy keeps us bobbing and weaving with their antiaircraft fire. I have two companies in the AO, but constant contact keeps them from doing much searching. The NVA have heavily reinforced bunkers built into the mountainsides up there and they're interconnected with tunnels. If those boys were captured, I suspect they're being held in one of those bunkers.

"We've held off using nape for the time being, at least until we get a team up there to look around. It's a long shot but we're still hoping they're hunkered down somewhere. If you need air cover, the helicopter gunships get the best results. Problem is they have to come in low and slow in the valleys, and the enemy's fifty-one cals are playing hell on them. One golden BB in the wrong place can flat knock a Huey out of the sky."

"FSBs Airborne, Katherine, and Bradley also give us artillery support with their 105s. Their call signs are there on those papers I gave you. The 158th Aviation Battalion, the 'Redskins' from Camp Evans, the 101st Aviation Battalion as well as the 'Hawks' at Camp Eagle all provide support for us. We're loaded for bear, but so are the NVA. They're coming for us, and I don't know how all this is going to turn out, but we're fighting those bastards with everything we've got.

"I'll be airborne in my loach 'most every day. I can offer you and your men my support, but you're going into a dogfight—a bad one."

The more the lieutenant colonel spoke, the more Martin realized this was a commander dedicated to his men and his mission. He was a true warrior, but it didn't take an expert to see he was dealt a bad hand. Ripcord was Bastogne on steroids.

The Germans couldn't afford to lose hundreds of their men with frontal assaults, but the NVA didn't care how many they lost, and this officer knew it.

"Colonel, Sir," Martin said, "We will do everything we can to find those men. I'm not sure how much we can accomplish, but I ask only that you keep the friendly fire off of us."

"I'll monitor your location closely, Captain, and we'll give you all the support we can. Keep in mind though that the enemy is monitoring our radio frequencies, and we can't hardly answer a fire mission without drawing rockets and mortars on our gun crews."

"I understand, Sir." Martin pointed to the map. "We'll depart the firebase over here, and move—"

"I thought we agreed you were going to head the other way and move out toward this hill over here," the colonel said, pointing to the map.

"Yes, Sir. That's right, but I figure the enemy is watching, and if we leave the firebase that way, they'll be waiting for us. As soon as we reach the bush below, I plan to swing back and circle toward the objective. It shouldn't cost us more than a couple hours."

The colonel threw his head back and inhaled deeply through his nostrils. "Damned good move, Captain."

"And Sir, one more thing, do you by chance have any extra helmets around?"

"I'm afraid so. Most of them are used or in pretty rough shape. They belonged to men we've medevaced out. They're in a CONEX outside. Why?"

"That's okay. We can pick through them. I only need eight. We're going to wear them till we reach the trees down below. If the enemy sees us coming down the mountain in boonie hats, they'll know we're lurps. With the helmets, they'll think we're just another perimeter patrol."

"Impressive, Captain. I like the way you think."

"That's why they call him the Ghost, Sir," Tadpole said.

A flash of recognition showed in the colonel's eyes, but he said nothing as he fixed Martin with a steady gaze.

"It's a nickname, Sir, but since ghosts normally represent the deceased, I'll stick with the call-sign, Shadows."

"I was a battalion XO when I heard about one of our companies about to be ambushed by the NVA a year or so back. The way I heard it, this Ghost crawled out of the bush and up to their point man and warned them, then disappeared."

"You're talkin' to him, Sir," Tadpole said.

Martin raised his hand to silence his RTO. The Ghost thing had developed a life of its own, but he didn't need the distraction at the moment. "War stories can get stretched if men tell them enough."

Sergeant Major Austin cocked his head to one side and shrugged. His jury was still out, but the colonel's wry smile said more than words could express. He was a believer.

"Well, just the same, I wouldn't mind hearing that war story someday. Good luck, Captain, and good hunting."

By mid-morning Sergeant Wolf was on point and the team was strung out down the mountainside as they worked their way toward the jungle below. In front of Martin, Thok walked slack with the Russian RPD. Both grenadiers had their thump guns loaded with buckshot rounds, and everyone carried extra ammo for the machine gun. Most of the morning fog had burned away, but the sun was partially obscured by high level clouds drifting in over the mountains. The men wove their way around stumps and shell holes as they made their way down the desolate hillside.

Upon reaching the jungle at the base of the mountain, the

helmets were buried, and the men applied camouflaged face paint. No one spoke above a whisper, and there was absolute silence when they began moving again. The jungle was unusually quiet—no birds, nothing that broke the silence until there came the thundering booms of the 155's at the top of the mountain. The roar of the big cannons on the firebase echoed through the mountain valleys. Wolf went to a knee and waited till the fire mission ended and silence returned.

Martin eased up beside him. "You okay?" he whispered.

Wolf motioned toward the surrounding terrain with his hand. "We're in a bad place. There's enemy sign everywhere around here."

He was right. They had crossed several trails with fresh footprints leading up the mountain. The enemy presence was palpable as each man held his weapon at the ready and studied the surrounding bush. One tiny error, one small thing overlooked, and they could find themselves facing annihilation.

"Yeah, you're right. I've seen it. Do you want me to take point a while?"

Wolf's eyes flashed with anger.

"Sir, I can walk point. I'm only keeping you informed of the situation."

"I know, and I have no doubt about what you're saying, Sergeant. Believe me, you wouldn't be here if I didn't trust you. I'm only offering to spell you for a while."

Wolf slowly wagged his head. "Sorry, Cap. I'm just a little tense."

"No apology needed. We all are. Keep your eyes open, and let's move out."

After circling the mountain below the firebase for several hundred meters, Wolf again brought them to a stop and dropped to a knee. Martin eased up beside him.

"Commo wire," Wolf whispered, pointing to a wire extending across their path.

The sun came and went in the clouds, its rays casting spooky shadows in the surrounding jungle. Martin studied the underbrush where the wire disappeared in the direction of the firebase. Back the other way, it led to a small ravine at the base of the adjacent mountain.

"I'm going to check out who or what's out there on the end closest to the firebase. Drop back and tell Sergeant Austin what I'm doing. Y'all sit tight."

Martin began following the wire toward the firebase. He had progressed a hundred meters when he spotted a pile of brush. It was an unnatural one built by a man. In the open just beyond the tree line, it had a clear view of Ripcord. He crept to the very edge of the jungle undergrowth and peered out. An enemy spotter was sitting in the middle of the brush pile gazing up the mountain. Propped beside him was his AK-47 and a haversack.

The soldier was talking quietly into a radio phone as Martin suddenly became aware of the sound of an approaching helicopter. He glanced over his shoulder. The morning sun rays were scattered in foggy beams seeping through the jungle canopy. With the sun at his back, he stood motionless, well camouflaged, and only a few feet from the spotter.

The soldier chattered excitedly into the phone while glancing toward the horizon where a single Huey approached through the mountains. Martin drew his knife and held it at the ready, but to cut the soldier's throat now would alert whoever was on the other end. He waited. The chopper dropped nose-up toward the lower chopper pad up at Ripcord. The spotter continued talking excitedly into the handset while pointing up the mountain as if someone was watching.

Martin had no choice but to wait. A moment later he heard the thoomp, thoomp, thoomp of several mortar tubes firing behind him from the ravine at the base of the adjacent mountain. The first rounds missed the helicopter pad, exploding below the perimeter. The spotter continued chattering into the handset. Martin could only watch.

After dropping supplies, the chopper slowly rose above the pad as he silently urged it, *"Go! Go! Get the hell outta there!"*

Again, the thoomp, thoomp, thoomp came from back in the jungle as the mortars fired again.

"Please," he thought. *"Get clear."*

The skidding whispers of the mortar rounds passed overhead. The chopper seemed like a fly mired in honey as it came up slowly and tilted forward.

"Come on, dude. Pull pitch. Pull hard. Go. Go." Martin was whispering, if only in his own mind, as the main rotor clacked and the Huey dropped over the side of the mountain. It dove into the valley below, barely a moment before a flaming dust cloud spurted skyward from the firebase as three mortar rounds exploded around the helicopter pad. Several seconds later the thundering booms of the explosions echoed against the surrounding hills. The NVA spotter threw down his handset in frustration and shook his fist as the chopper escaped down the valley.

Martin smiled. And as if the enemy soldier had experienced a sudden premonition, he turned and gazed directly at him. The soldier seemed to stare through him while studying the jungle, but with his face painted green and his gear camouflaged with vegetation, Martin was invisible. After a moment the enemy soldier turned his attention back to the firebase. Martin hadn't moved, and the soldier had apparently not seen him.

A moment later the man's head jerked around as he looked again at something his subconscious had told him was there, but it was too late. It was the Ghost. Martin struck with a lightning flash of his K-bar, severing the man's jugular.

From the explosions up at the firebase, he figured the tubes were 82 millimeter, and there were likely three of them. They were behind him, in a ravine somewhere beyond a small rise. He hurried back to the team. Sergeant Austin already had the men facing the rise. Martin crawled up beside his second in command.

"They're over there, at the base of that mountain," Austin said. "We can take them out. What do you think?"

"Let's ease up to the top of that rise first and take a look at them."

The two lurp leaders crawled several hundred feet until they reached the crest of the hill where they could see the ravine below. Martin was right. There were three 82-millimeter mortars clustered below, along with twelve enemy soldiers. Like ducks in a shooting gallery, they were standing in the open, secure in the fact they were well hidden in the ravine.

"Let's bring the team up and send these boys to hell," Austin whispered.

And it seemed a logical move except for what Martin saw on the hillside beyond. At first it was only a slight movement, a bird perhaps, but he had learned long ago to trust that sometimes unexplainable sixth sense. Those tiny red flags often came and went and were nothing more than birds flitting about, anomalies of shifting sunlight, or the figment of an overworked imagination. Occasionally though, they became all too real elements of danger. And as he focused and refocused on the hillside, he began spotting what he suspected was there. It was at least a platoon of enemy soldiers. Well camouflaged, they waited for anyone who might threaten their mortar crews below.

"Look over there across the ravine," Martin whispered.

The sergeant major studied the hillside for nearly a half-minute. Martin waited patiently.

"Holy shit! I see them now. Must be thirty or more," he hissed. "It's your call, Sir. What do you want to do?"

"Let's back out and talk it over with the team."

Martin knew what needed to be done, but his men needed to learn to think for themselves. Three minutes later, they gathered below the hill while Martin and the sergeant major filled them in on the situation. They had to move quickly before the mortarmen discovered their spotter had gone silent. The men quickly reached the conclusion Martin had already decided upon.

"Okay. I agree with calling in artillery, but first, we're going to head north a few hundred meters. Otherwise, we'll be too damned close. A short round could take us all out. When we get in position, we'll set out a daisy chain of claymores facing this way, and a couple more to cover our flanks. When the barrage starts, they're going to know we're somewhere close, and they'll come looking for us. We'll be ready if they come our way.

"Once the barrage is over, or we initiate contact, I think we need to get moving again," Austin said.

"Agreed, Sergeant Major. Make your assignments."

"Wolf, you'll be first man out on point," Austin said. "Pop, you and Doc move next. If we have any unfired claymores on the flanks, you guys recover them and follow Wolf. Tadpole, you're on Ghost. You'll provide cover for Pop and Enz. Thok, you and Manny will remain in position and roll out last when I give you the signal."

The sergeant major looked toward Martin.

"Sounds good, Sarge. Manny, I want your thumper loaded with buckshot. Now, let's move out, but keep your eyes open. That bunch might not be the only ones around."

Wolf led them to a bamboo thicket beside a stream where Martin notified the TOC up at Ripcord of their location and called in the fire mission to FSB Kathryn. The team set out their claymores, and within minutes Kathryn responded with the initial marker round perfectly on target behind the hill. Martin having requested six rounds of HE, called "fire for effect." The team remained protected by the hill, but the barrage of 105 shells, only 300 meters away, was dropping danger-close as the ground shook and shrapnel whizzed and whirred, occasionally snapping limbs in the trees overhead.

When it ended, the team lay quiet as silence returned to the jungle. The colonel called for a couple of Cobra gunships to join him and twenty minutes later they were crisscrossing the impact area while he did damage assessment from his loach. Martin listened to the radio as the choppers spotted stragglers apparently attempting to salvage one of the tubes. The buzzing roar of a minigun erupted from one of the gunships, and the colonel's voice came over the radio complimenting the gunner's accuracy.

The cloud cover thickened as it dropped even lower, forcing the choppers to return to base. Now, without aircover, Martin and Sergeant Major Austin discussed their options. Moving toward the higher ridges above the blue line seemed their best bet, and the team again moved out. The torturously steep climb and ever-present signs of the enemy slowed their progress, and it was dusk when they crept into their night defensive position.

A mountainside shelf with somewhat less slope was their temporary refuge from gravity. It was still treacherous, and one slip could send a man tumbling down the slope. Somewhere in the distance a monkey howled and gave a series of bellowing grunts, likely gathering his troop for a night's rest in the trees. The mountain air became cold and clammy as a heavy fog moved in, and after setting out the claymores, the men wrapped themselves in their poncho liners while devouring cold lurp rations. Martin and Sergeant Major Austin discussed their next day's plans.

"With this fog setting in, we'll have to move in close to watch these trails tomorrow," Austin whispered. "That's taking a hell of a gamble."

"And which trail do we watch?" Martin added. "We've found at least four today, and all of them had fresh signs, including wheeled equipment."

"Thing is," Austin said, "they're all converging on Ripcord."

"Yeah, I know."

Austin was not simply an old veteran. He was sharp, and like Martin, he recognized the increasing flow of enemy troops and equipment focused on gathering around the firebase.

"Maybe we can find some sort of convergence point," the sergeant major suggested.

"Ripcord, maybe?" Martin said.

Austin's teeth shone in the darkness.

"You know, the more I get to know you, Captain, the more I realize we have the same cynical sense of humor."

"I think Nam breeds cynicism," Martin whispered. "I'll call in the sit-rep. You get some rest, you old fart."

"What are you going to tell them?"

"All roads lead to Ripcord."

Austin covered his mouth as he snorted.

CHAPTER NINETEEN

The Ghost is Coming
A Mountainside Near FSB Ripcord
Two weeks Later, Third Week of July 1970

Martin awoke as the first gray light of dawn broke. He and his men were high on the mountain, and a stiff breeze was blowing as the last stars in the night sky rapidly faded. He found himself shivering as he pulled his poncho liner tighter around his shoulders. Doc Enzenauer, the only other one awake, was leaning against a tree and spooning down a cold lurp ration. Sergeant Major Austin had been right about the medic. Specialist Enz was an amiable guy, but when he said he had to inspect your feet, it was not a request, and when he distributed the Malaria pills he watched each man as he swallowed his. Enz gave Martin a thumbs up as a chorus of morning birds began chirping and calling from high in the jungle canopy.

After two weeks of searching, calling in airstrikes and fire missions, and too many narrow escapes, they had found no evidence of the missing lurp team. The team was growing weary and in need of rest. More of the men awakened and began rolling their ponchos when a whooshing boom came from only a couple hundred feet away. A cloud of smoke spurted from the mountainside, but quickly dissipated in the breeze as the men ducked and grabbed their weapons.

Only then did they realize it wasn't aimed at them. It was an enemy recoilless rifle firing across the valley at Ripcord. The team had spent the night practically in the enemy's lap. Everyone was now wide awake with adrenaline pumping while strapping on their gear. Martin studied the situation. He was taking no chances and getting in a hurry was a sure way of making mistakes.

He turned to Tadpole. "Call the TOC and tell them not to return fire. Tell them we're close to these guys and we'll take them out. Wolf, Thok, and Tadpole, you guys come with me. The rest of you stay here with Sergeant Austin. Spread out and stay alert."

Holding onto saplings and vines, Martin led the three men across the steep slope toward the enemy position. The recoilless rifle fired again, sending another round across the valley into the firebase. This time the gun crew was plainly visible as they picked up the gun and ran across the hillside to a bunker gunport, where they disappeared inside.

Shoot and scoot they called it. Normally, by the time a fire mission was called in, they were deep inside the protective confines of a bunker. This time, though, the Ghost followed them. Crawling up to the gunport, Martin snatched the pin from a frag and tossed it inside. He ducked as smoke and dust blasted outward.

"Wolf, you and Thok stay out here. Tadpole, leave the radio with Wolf and come with me."

With that he scrambled through the gunport. Two of the enemy gun crew were dead. Another was dying. Drawing his knife, Martin quickly dispatched him and turned to look about. Wooden ammo crates were stacked against one wall, along with the recoilless rifle and more weapons. There was also another tunnel opening on one side of the bunker. He pointed it out to Tadpole.

"That probably leads to another bunker. As soon as I go in there, throw these weapons through the gunports and get back out there with Wolf and Thok. Y'all ease around the slope toward the next bunker, but don't get too close. Wait for my signal."

Stooping low, Martin eased into the tunnel, groping his way blindly toward what had to be the next bunker. His forty-five automatic was in his right hand and his knife in his left. A moment later a dim light appeared up ahead. There was movement, but he didn't stop. The excited voices of the enemy greeted him as he burst into the next bunker. Plunging his knife into the first soldier he met, Martin shouldered him aside and slashed another across the neck.

Despite the bunker's dimly lit interior, he spotted a map and two radios. He had penetrated a command bunker. With the two guards now bleeding out, an NVA colonel and a uniformed Chinese advisor stood beside a radio operator. All three stared at him in wide-eyed terror. Martin leveled his forty-five on the colonel and cast his voice toward the gunport.

"Wolf! Thok! Are you guys out there?" he shouted.

"We're here," came Wolf's voice.

"I'm sending out some high-value prisoners. Gag and tie them."

He began guiding the Vietnamese colonel with the barrel of his forty-five toward the opening, but the Chinese advisor lunged. Holding the forty-five steady on the NVA colonel, Martin met the advisor's attack with the tip of his knife blade. Skewered by the K-bar under his chin, the Chinaman went to his knees, but his bulging eyes remained on the knife blade now protruding upward through the side of his bloody jaw. It had apparently missed the main arteries, but the blood flowed freely from under his chin. Martin cast a gaze and raised his brows at the radio operator whose hand now rested on his AK-47. The man carefully withdrew the hand.

"Go!" he shouted at the Vietnamese colonel. "Go now."

The NVA colonel leapt through the opening, and Martin snatched the knife from under the Chinese advisor's chin.

"Now you—go."

The bloodied Chinaman crawled through the gunport while Thok pulled him to the outside. He pushed him down the hill toward Wolf and crawled inside with Martin.

"Now, you," Martin said to the radioman, but the enemy soldier again grabbed for his AK-47. It was a futile gesture as Martin's knife pinned the man's hand to the stock of the rifle. The soldier screamed in pain as Thok raised the RPD, but Martin shook his head.

"No! Don't kill him."

He saw the disappointment in Thok's eyes—something no doubt precipitated by a hatred for what the Communists had done to his people. Thok pointed at Martin and spoke to the enemy soldier. One word came through clearly, "…Ghost…"

The soldier's eyes flashed with fear, and Martin decided to use it to his advantage. There were likely more NVA troops coming their way at that very moment.

"Thok, tell him to take a message to his comrades. Tell them to run. Tell him we kill them all if they attack us."

Thok repeated his words in Vietnamese as he motioned toward Martin and again referred to him as "Ghost."

With that Martin shoved the soldier into another tunnel opening leading to the next bunker. Grabbing the maps and radios, he and Thok dove through the gunport and rolled down the hill, landing at Wolf's feet. Wolf was wrapping the Chinese advisor's jaw with a field dressing.

"He says he's Chinese and a non-combatant, but I told him that was too bad. He should have stayed home."

Martin gazed down at the man. "If you're a non-combatant, why were you carrying a sidearm?"

The Chinaman remained silent. Martin tossed the radio he had recovered at the soldier's feet. It was the interior of a PRC-25 rigged with some sort of electrical device, a scanner perhaps. He could hear the Tactical Operations Center up at Ripcord talking to another unit somewhere outside the firebase.

"That's okay. I know some really nasty people who will help you explain this radio and why you're here."

He looked around. "Where's Tadpole?"

"He went back inside the first bunker. Said he found a wood crate full of fifty-one caliber ammo," Wolf said.

"Radio One-One and tell him to bring up the rest of the team. Then notify the TOC that we have two high-value prisoners we need to extract."

Enemy mortars at the base of the mountain were raining shells into the firebase, and a fifty-one-caliber machine gun further up the mountain began firing as well.

"I'm going back to that first bunker to get Tadpole."

Sergeant Major Austin arrived with the rest of the team.

"You *do* realize we've stirred up a hornet's nest, don't you?" he said. "The bastards are everywhere around us."

"Yeah. I know, Sarge, but I need you to take these two prisoners and get moving while you can. I'm going back to that first bunker to find Tadpole. Leave Thok with me. Give him a couple extra claymores and any frags you can spare. Leave me a radio, too, and take the rest of the men with you. Get moving.

"After we find Tadpole, we'll set up a delaying action while you take the prisoners and the rest of the team back down the mountain. When you're able, get Doc to look at that Chinese advisor's face. I want him brought back alive. And call for extraction when you can. As soon as we find Tadpole, we'll follow, but don't wait on us. Radio me if you're extracted before we get there. If we have to, we'll E&E back to the firebase."

"Sir, I think we should all—"

"It's not up for discussion, Sarge. Go now, while you can. I'll see you back at the firebase."

Their eyes met. The old sergeant major's forty-something years had caught up with him. He nodded slowly. "Good luck."

———

Martin motioned for Thok to follow, and they climbed back toward the first bunker. Besides the 100-round drum attached to the RPD, Thok also carried two more in his rucksack along with two ammo pouches full of frags. Martin had his CAR-15, eighteen 20-round magazines and one ammo pouch of frags. His rucksack was stuffed with claymores, wire, detonators, a flashlight, and the radio.

After climbing up the steep slope to the bunker, he shed his rucksack and left Thok outside while he crawled through the gunport. The smell of death permeated the fresh dirt, as he looked around. Tadpole wasn't there. Only then did he notice an open trap door. Beside it was a wooden crate. Using his flashlight, he carefully peeked over the rim into the hole. There was a makeshift ladder extending down to another tunnel opening.

"Tadpole!" he shouted.

His echoless voice was deadened by the bunker's interior, yet from somewhere far below a voice answered. It was barely audible. Martin prepared to descend the ladder, but from outside the bunker came several explosions, followed by Thok's RPD firing almost non-stop. Scrambling through the gunport, he found the Montagnard warrior on his knees firing up the mountain.

"We go now!" Thok shouted. "They too many come fast."

He was right. At least a dozen or more enemy soldiers with camo-painted faces and soft hats were coming down the mountain.

These were likely one of the specially trained hunter-killer teams that had been homing in on the LRRP radio transmissions.

After emptying a magazine at the approaching enemy, Martin motioned to Thok. "Let's go."

The two men dove down the mountainside, tumbling, falling, and dodging trees as grenades exploded behind them. Desperate to break contact, they held their fire and angled first one way then another as they tried to lose their pursuers. A sudden whooshing sound came down the mountain followed by an explosion in the jungle canopy above. Martin's back was stung by the impact of tiny shards of shrapnel, and Thok dropped to his knees.

A larger piece of the RPG had struck his upper leg, and blood had immediately begun soaking through his trousers. The enemy was rapidly overtaking them, but the bleeding had to be stopped. Martin twisted a piece of claymore wire above the wound and lifted him over his shoulder.

"No, Dai uy. You go. I stay. I kill many enemy. They will not follow."

"No. You're going with me."

Martin again started down the mountainside, and after several hundred meters found an area of dense vegetation where he burrowed deep into the undergrowth. There he waited and listened while pressing a field dressing against Thok's thigh. The young Montagnard's face was graying from the loss of blood. Martin opened a blood expander kit. After inserting the needle into Thok's arm, he tied the bag to a tree, and pulled the radio from his rucksack.

It took several frustrating seconds twisting knobs before he realized there was a jagged hole in the casing. It was caused by shrapnel that would have gotten him had it not been for the radio. It was now useless, and his only viable option was to remain in the thick undergrowth until nightfall.

Thok's head nodded, and Martin lifted his chin. "Try to stay awake," he whispered.

Thok opened his eyes. "Dại úy brave soldier. I too stay brave."

It was clear Thok had lost too much blood, and if they waited until nightfall, he might not survive. Martin put the RPD machine gun in the little man's arms and gave him a fragmentation grenade.

"I'm going to set out some claymores. Then I'm taking a look around. If I don't see any NVA, we'll try to make it to the base of the mountain, maybe pop smoke and get a medevac."

They were in trouble and Thok knew it, but he gave a grim smile. Martin turned away lest his eyes betray him further. With slow and deliberate stealth, he placed claymores in a large circle, strung the wires back, and gave Thok the detonators with the safety pins removed. Afterward, he eased out through the undergrowth.

It was nearly sixty meters to the more open area of the mountainside, but he had gone little more than forty when he spotted the first enemy soldier. He was standing in the heavy cover with his back to him. Intent on watching the open ground, the soldier had no clue Martin was behind him.

Setting his CAR-15 aside, Martin unsheathed his knife. One cat-like step at a time, he eased up behind the enemy soldier. It was cool in the mountains, but a bead of sweat ran into his eye as he recognized what he was up against. This was one of the NVA soldiers he'd seen earlier with camouflage face-paint—one of the enemy commandos they called Lurp killers. There was no hesitation as he moved closer, and the soldier died quickly. Martin searched for the others. They had to be close. A second one appeared only thirty meters away, kneeling at the edge of the undergrowth. The soldier gave him a wave of acknowledgement.

A clear case of mistaken identity on the soldier's part, there was but one reasonable response. Martin returned the wave and moved nonchalantly back into the undergrowth. He circled quietly and a few moments later his blade found the second soldier's throat as well.

There was likely a dozen or more of these commandos lying about, watching, and waiting for their prey to dash from cover. Killing them all was impossible, but if he put enough fear in them, he and Thok might have a chance to escape. It was time for some psyops.

To make the corpse more visible, he propped it upright against a tree with the AK-47 in his arms. Pulling the pin on a frag, he wedged it carefully beneath the weapon, booby-trapping the body.

A few minutes later, he spotted a third enemy soldier and began circling. When he was behind him, Martin tensed, and with an adrenaline-driven thrust, drove his knife blade under the base of the man's skull. The soldier didn't kick nor groan as he went instantly limp. Martin glanced about. The more of them he killed, the more fear it would precipitate, and the better his chance for escape.

The morning dragged on into afternoon as the enemy soldiers waited patiently—somehow sensing their prey was hidden somewhere nearby. Martin continued as the unwitting enemy failed to realize their ranks were being gradually thinned, courtesy of the Ghost. By the time the sun was low in the western sky, he had killed six NVA soldiers and located where several others were hidden. It was time to crawl back to Thok and prepare for the enemy onslaught when they discovered their dead comrades. They would begin beating the bushes and searching with a vengeance, but Martin had taken that into consideration.

CHAPTER TWENTY

A Friend Repays a Favor
The Mountainside Across from FSB Ripcord

The sun was setting when Martin returned to find Thok barely responsive. He opened his eyes slightly, and it was clear he was fading. After giving him more water, Martin went to work, putting two claymores back-to-back and twisting their wires together with a third wire that he began uncoiling as he backed down the mountainside. When he had gone a hundred feet, he dropped the wire and climbed back to where Thok lay. The surrounding jungle remained quiet, but time was running out.

After leaving his rucksack hanging in plain sight, Martin covered the claymores with brush and pulled Thok across his shoulders. Dusk was fading into nightfall as he slipped back down the mountainside to the end of the wire where he attached a detonator, removed the safety pin, and hunkered down. It was only minutes before the panicked shout of an enemy soldier indicated his discovery of a comrade's body. A moment later the hand grenade exploded.

Thrown into confusion, the enemy soldiers were now shouting and arguing with one another, and a few moments later there came more excited shouts as they discovered the abandoned rucksack. Martin waited, giving them time to gather as he listened to their subdued voices only a hundred feet up the slope. He sensed they were gathered around the rucksack but suspected it too might be boobytrapped. It was time.

He mashed the clacker repeatedly, detonating the claymores and sending hundreds of steel balls ripping in all directions. When the last of the debris had fallen, only the moans of the wounded remained. With the lurp killers neutralized, it was time to move. Wrapping Thok in his poncho liner, Martin lifted him over his shoulder and began making his way down the mountain.

Sometime near midnight, Martin gave out. He could go no further, and gently lay Thok beside him on the ground. The terrain had leveled somewhat, and they were near the base of the mountain below Ripcord. Thok was still and quiet. Opening his canteen, Martin tried to get him to drink, but he refused. He was dying, and there was nothing more Martin could do. He was drained. Physically and mentally exhausted, he could go no further. He gazed up the mountain toward Ripcord. There was no way he could climb up to the firebase in his present condition.

The mountaintop firebase was now clearly visible as a black silhouette against the night sky. Still under continuous fire from enemy rockets and mortars, it erupted with fiery bursts of smoke and dust, billowing skyward and giving it the appearance of a volcano. Martin pulled the poncho away from Thok's face. He'd left Tadpole up on the mountain, deep in that enemy bunker complex, and now he was about to lose Thok. Failure it seemed was his at every turn, and all he wanted now was to lie down and close his eyes.

With his back against a tree, Martin pulled Thok close, holding his head in his lap. They had done their best, but it was for naught. It was clear the enemy intended to overrun Ripcord. They wanted to score a major psychological and political victory, but there was nothing left he could do. He was spent, and Thok was near death. Martin had failed every man who had placed his trust in him, and he had failed himself.

"We hurry. We go now," Thok said in a weak voice.

Stunned by the little man's voice, Martin held him closer. Thok was growing delirious. He pulled the poncho liner tighter around him. There was nothing more he could do.

"It's okay, Thok. We need to rest."

"I tell them 'Bóng ma sẽ đến đây sớm thôi.' I say, 'The Ghost is coming soon.' I tell them they must run away quickly, but they not listen. They know now. They die. We must go now."

"We'll go in a few minutes. We need to rest."

"No. We go now. NVA not follow," he said. "Our men, they wait for us."

"I know, Thok, but I need to rest."

And there came a whispering voice in the darkness. "Ghost, is that you?"

It was barely audible, and Martin closed his eyes. He had to maintain a clear head. It had been a long and torturous day, and he too was now slipping into delirium.

"It's me, Ghost. It's Manny. I'm with the sergeant major and the rest of the team. They're down there behind me across that creek."

War, death, and fatigue colluded to drive men mad, and Martin believed he was now at the brink. It was the voice of a wishful delusion, but one so powerful it seemed undeniable. He had to gather his strength and ignore it.

"Who are you talking to?" the voice asked.

Martin remained silent. The voice was persistent, and he remembered studying about insane people who heard voices. He refused to give in. He refused to give the voice in his mind the satisfaction of a response.

"Did you find Tadpole?"

"Ghost, I know you're there. I heard your voice. Answer me."

It was a hallucination—not reality, but the voice knew so much. That's how it was with insane people, the book had said. They truly believed what their minds imagined.

"Where's Tadpole?"

Perhaps if he answered, it would go away. "I found him, but he's still up there in that bunker complex."

Several eternal seconds passed. The voice now seemed satisfied. He hoped it would stop harassing him, but a shadow of movement caught his eye. The figure of a man was kneeling over him.

"Who is this?" the voice asked.

A hand reached out and pulled the poncho liner away from Thok's face.

"Manny, is that really you?"

"It's me, Sir. Is this Thok?"

"Yeah, but he's in bad shape."

"We heard y'all fighting up there on the mountain this afternoon. You must've given those bastards hell."

"I'm sorry, Manny, but I'm too tired to talk right now."

"That's okay, Sir. Come with me. We'll go down there with the rest of the team. I'll carry Thok."

Martin's legs wobbled as he stumbled down to the creek behind Manny and within minutes they rejoined the lurp team on the other side. Doc put Thok on a fresh plasma bag, while Pop took his pulse.

"His heartbeat is weak, Enz."

"Raise his legs," Doc said. "Put something under them. Get

our poncho liners. Wrap him up. We've got to get him warmed up. Hurry."

The two men worked feverishly while Sergeant Austin mixed a Lurp ration for Martin and gave him an update. "We dodged enemy patrols all day. The prisoners slowed us up so much until I damn near was going to shoot that Chinese bastard, but we trussed them up like hogs and carried them down the mountain. The good news is I didn't kill him, and we have an extraction group coming in at first light."

Martin scooped the food from the bag with his fingers and ate ravenously. A half hour later Doc Enz crawled up beside him. The darkness of the jungle night hid the medic's face, but Martin sensed something was wrong.

"What is it?" he whispered.

"I'm sorry, Sir, but it was too late. We couldn't do anything for him. Thok's dead. Bled out."

Martin became lost in a mental haze of anguish as he gazed over at the shadow that was Thok's body wrapped in the poncho liners. And he thought of Tadpole still up there somewhere in that enemy bunker complex. He too was probably dead by now.

"Lie back and close your eyes," Austin said. "Get some rest, Captain. You've done all you can."

And that's what he did, until he heard the sounds of choppers thundering somewhere back in the mountains. They were close and Martin opened his eyes, only to find he was squinting into the full light of day. The sunshine was streaming through the treetops, and a brisk breeze was blowing down the valley. He had slept through the night with his CAR-15 still lying across his chest where it had been when he fell asleep.

"That's our extraction group coming," Austin said. "Are you ready to get the hell out of here?"

Martin said nothing as he gathered his wits and checked his

gear. After a few moments, he left the group and crawled to the edge of the rocky stream where he began refilling his canteens. The sergeant major watched him with incredulous eyes as Martin dropped iodine tablets into each one and twisted the caps. With that done, he crawled back into the cover.

"What the hell are you doing, Sir? We're getting outta here. You hear me?"

"I hear you, Sergeant Major. Give me your extra frags and your flashlight."

"Captain, please don't do this. You've already done more than anyone could ask, and that boy is dead."

Austin motioned toward Wolf. "Pop smoke, toss it out there on that gravel bar, and get confirmation."

Wolf snatched the ring from a smoke canister and tossed it to the edge of the creek. Purple smoke began spewing and scattering as the wind whipped it downstream. Austin fired a starburst flare skyward, and Wolf radioed the inbound choppers. The rest of the team scanned the mountainside for movement.

Wolf keyed the radio handset. "Eagle Wing Niner-Five-Niner, Shadow-Walker One-Two requests confirmation of flare and smoke. Over."

"I roger, Shadow-Walker. The stars are shining, and I've got goofy grape on the blue line, over."

"That's a roger, Eagle Wing. Tell your crew chief we can use some help securing two enemy POWs. We also have one KIA."

"That's a Roger, Shadow-Walker. The 101st Combat Aviation Brigade is at your service. Stand by. We're inbound and coming down—"

"Hey!" The shouts came from the men across the creek.

"We've got movement up there above us," Pops shouted. He was pointing up the mountainside.

Wolf keyed the radio handset.

"Wait!" Martin shouted. He raised his binoculars and scanned the slope, praying he would see Tadpole.

Pop and Manny came running back across the creek.

"What did you see?" Martin asked.

"Ten NVA walking across the slope up there about a quarter mile."

"You sure?"

"Yes, Sir."

Martin turned to Wolf. "Okay, let's light them up."

Wolf keyed the handset. "Eagle Wing, we have movement across the blue line on the slope above us. Can you have your boys sanitize the area? Over."

Eagle Wing's radio transmission came back garbled, but a cobra gunship thundered overhead as its rockets streaked into the slope above. The first chopper flared and pulled out as a second cobra followed firing its minigun. A few moments later a slick approached from the north.

Just above the water, it came thundering down the creek. At the last moment the pilot pulled the chopper nose-up and hovered to a stop as the downdraft sent a sparkling shower of water into the air. The helicopter's nose was emblazoned with the emblem of the Screaming Eagles, and rainbows of water were a magnificent picture of salvation as Martin signaled his men to load up.

"Now, that's what I call service," Wolf shouted into the handset.

"Damned right!" Austin yelled.

The men were exhausted and feeling the euphoria of relief, but Martin had unfinished business.

"Give me your flashlight and frags," he said.

Austin stopped and turned. He said nothing as their eyes met. The extraction chopper set down on the gravel bar as Pop and Manny ran forward with the two prisoners. Wolf carried Thok's body on his shoulder, but Martin stopped him.

"Let me carry him."

He took Thok into his arms. The little man's body was light as a feather. The crew chief jumped to the ground to assist and together they carefully laid the young Montagnard's body on the floor of the chopper.

Austin grabbed Martin's shoulder and yelled, "I'm staying with you."

Martin shook his head emphatically "No! Get on this chopper, Sergeant Major. That's an order and see that Thok gets a burial with full honors. And I doubt the army will do it, but I want you to give his family a Purple Heart and a Silver Star. Tell them he died bravely."

Austin didn't break eye contact as he handed Martin his flashlight and grenades. A moment later Wolf pulled the sergeant major onboard as the RPMs increased, and the Huey went light on its skids.

Martin saluted them, and within seconds the sound of the helicopters faded in the distance as he sprinted across the creek and up the mountainside. After climbing a few hundred meters, he burrowed into a thicket, where he waited and listened. It was quiet as a church at midnight. For the moment, not even a bird chirped.

CHAPTER TWENTY-ONE

The Last Patrol
The Mountain Across from FSB Ripcord

Martin's decision to go back up the mountain alone was one the army never wanted from an officer. An officer's path was one of leadership, but Martin's was now a different path. Or perhaps it was only a continuation of the one he'd begun when he escaped the North Vietnamese prison. After all, the spirits weren't known for following military protocol.

If he could bring Tadpole back alive, it no longer mattered if he lost his commission. He had the rest of his life to live with himself, and he would not abandon his man, even if Tadpole was dead. The odds were long, but so were the memories. He would do this, and if he died, at least he wouldn't live with regrets for not trying.

He began climbing again when a sudden burst of machine gun fire came from an NVA fifty-one caliber somewhere higher on the mountainside. It continued firing in short bursts as Martin gazed skyward and followed the track of the tracer rounds as they impacted on the firebase. It continued for several minutes until there came several echoing booms from up at Ripcord. The artillerymen had lowered a howitzer 105 and put direct fire on the enemy position.

The thudding karoomphs of the artillery shells brought immediate silence, as smoke and dust billowed skyward from the area where the bunker complex was located. A few moments later the vibrating thumps of approaching helicopters again echoed through the mountains. Gazing skyward through the jungle canopy, Martin searched for nearly a minute before a flash of sunlight reflected from a plexiglass canopy. A Huey gunship was turning into a dive toward the mountain.

Unleashing a steady stream of rockets, the chopper sent them into the bunker complex far above. Secondary explosions sent more smoke and debris skyward as another chopper followed with more of the same. The buzzing roar of its minigun echoed across the valley as it chopped the jungle into salad. Martin could only hope if Tadpole was still alive, he wasn't out in the open.

Continuing up the mountain, he scanned every detail of the terrain, every leaf, every blade of grass, every odor, every movement, and every sound. He searched for tell-tale disturbances where a booby-trap might be hidden, but he didn't stop. He moved steadily, slowly, and deliberately, watching for the shine of a tripwire or the barely noticeable impression of a boot—anything that might alert him to danger.

He was as much prey as he was hunter, but he was prepared. And it slowly dawned on him that what had been a heavily populated mountainside the day before now seemed abandoned by the enemy. It was nearly noon when he reached the bunker complex. The assault by the helicopter gunships and direct fire of the howitzers had wrecked it.

Smoke drifted across the slope carrying with it the chemical odors of the rockets and artillery shells. There were blood trails everywhere. Much of what had been the well-camouflaged bunker complex was now laid bare by the barrage. With busted stumps, skeletal trees, and smoking craters blasted into the slope, it took a moment before Martin recognized the bunker where he had last heard Tadpole. Its gunports had caved in, and the interior seemed to have collapsed as well. Tadpole was likely buried somewhere deep inside. The probability of finding him alive now seemed bleaker than ever.

Martin refused to give up as he scooped away the dirt with his bare hands. It seemed hopeless, until he thought of his canteen cup. The quart-size steel container was better than nothing. A moment later he was scooping dirt and throwing it down the slope with the canteen cup. An NVA patrol would likely show up soon, searching for their wounded. He dug frantically and after nearly a quarter-hour the dirt suddenly fell away and dropped into the bunker's interior.

An odor seeped from inside, not quite the putrid odor of decomposing human remains, but close. He wormed his way through the opening and dropped to the bunker floor where he switched on his flashlight. The interior was partially collapsed, and lying about were several haversacks and satchel charges along with a pair of legs protruding from the dirt. Thankfully, the corpse wore the boots of an NVA soldier.

The trap door over the hole at the back of the bunker had been put back in place and an ammo crate was sitting on it. This was where he had heard Tadpole's voice. Martin strained as he lifted the crate of fifty-one caliber ammunition. He set it aside, and there came a scratching sound. He listened carefully, but it was graveyard silent inside the bunker. The sound came again from the other side of the trap door. Unshouldering his CAR-15, he carefully pulled the wooden door open and shone the flashlight into the hole.

A flicker of movement caught his eye and he responded,

pointing both the light and the CAR-15 in that direction. A large rat scampered out and raced away, disappearing into the darkness. His heart thumped and Martin drew a deep breath.

"Shiuut," he muttered.

The makeshift ladder was still there, and he was about to descend into the tunnel when he again heard the scratching sound. It was followed by a dull thump. These sounds were coming from somewhere below, but his light found nothing.

"Probably another rat," he muttered, but he had to take a look. There was no time for hesitation. The enemy would likely return at any moment. Scrambling down the ladder into the hole, he found another tunnel opening, but it too was partially collapsed. The scratching sound came again. Something was on the other side, and he began digging. A small hole opened immediately. After dragging more of the dirt away, he poked the flashlight into the opening.

"Tadpole, are you in there?"

"Ghost!"

It was Tadpole's voice—raspy and stressed, but alive.

"I'm here, but my legs are buried in the dirt. I've almost got them dug out."

Working furiously, Martin began slinging dirt behind him as he opened the tunnel. A moment later Tadpole, caked with a sweaty layer of dust, squirmed from the hole.

"I knew you would come. I knew it."

"Are you okay?"

"I am now. I sure thought I was gonna—" he stopped, as if suddenly struck with a new realization. Turning back toward the tunnel he yelled, "You see! I told you assholes he would come. I told you so. And he's here."

"It's okay," Martin said.

Combat, fear, stress, and all that accompanied it did this to men. Tadpole was no doubt suffering some sort of stress-induced hallucination from being buried in this black hole of death.

"You're alive. Let's get the hell out of here."

"But we can't. We've got to go back for them."

Martin paused. Tadpole needed to be calmed and brought back to reality.

"It's okay, buddy. Slow down and tell me what you're talking about. Explain to me why you want to go back."

"It's that lurp team we was lookin' for, Sir. I was talking to them when the damned tunnel collapsed on me yesterday. They're tied up in there."

Martin pointed his light into the tunnel. Only their bound legs were visible in the cramped chamber, but their fatigues were the tiger-striped camouflage of lurps. And it hit him as a punch in the gut as he heard Grandfather Two Shadow's words: "…you freed tigers from their grave." Crawling on his belly, he entered the chamber and began cutting the cords from around their arms and legs.

"You see," Tadpole shouted again. "I told you assholes. I told you so, but you jerks said I was just a crazy Cajun who believed in Voodoo, but here he is, the Ghost. And this fucker's gonna save your doubtin' Thomas asses."

"Okay," Martin said. "That's enough. Let's get these men out of here. I'll go up top first, and you help them up the ladder."

After searching the area for weapons and ammo, Martin took inventory. They had picked up three AK-47's, one SKs, and a few hundred rounds of ammo. There was no food or water anywhere. The lurps were emaciated and dehydrated and in need of both if they were going to make it off the mountain. After splitting his rations and a canteen of water eight ways with them, he wasted no time putting Tadpole on point and starting back down the mountain.

Despite their debilitation, bare feet, and wounds, the lurps moved as if it was their first day on patrol. Cautious and alert, they ignored their pain and moved rapidly. There was no time to waste. They not only needed to escape the area before the enemy returned, but reaching the stream at the base of the mountain before dark was a must. They would not last another day without water.

The firebase took incoming all afternoon, while airstrikes set the surrounding mountainsides aflame with napalm. Anytime a chopper was nearby, Martin halted the column until it passed. The last thing they needed was friendly fire. It was dusk when he spotted the shining waters of the stream below. They had made it. After hiding his men on the opposite bank, Martin refilled the canteen.

It took a couple hours of rest before they were ready to move again. They were anxious to get inside the wire, but it would be a hard climb. Martin joined Tadpole on point and led them up the mountain toward the outer perimeter of Ripcord. After several hours they reached the first wire. Martin dropped to his knees and with his hands searched the ground for what he knew had to be there. Setting off a trip flare at night would probably be the worst thing they could do without a radio.

It took less than a minute before the back of his hand touched it—a trip wire. He had gone as far as he dared. A hundred feet up the mountain was a gate and a bunker. Somehow, he had to talk to the men up there.

Martin called out. "Lurp team, Hundred and First. We need to come in."

There was no answer. He called out again, but again was met with silence.

"Dammit!" Martin cursed under his breath. "They must have heard me."

Tadpole stood and shouted, "Hey! You dumb fucks need to let us in. The Ghost is here, and we have that missing lurp team with us."

"Get down before you get your ass shot off," Martin hissed.

Several eternal seconds elapsed before a tentative voice came from the bunker. "What's the password?"

Again, Tadpole shouted, "We don't know no damned password, you idiot. We've been in the boonies for three fucking weeks. We're tired, thirsty and a little pissed-off right now."

"Take it easy, Tadpole," Martin said.

"But Sir—"

"It's okay. You'd be doing the same thing if you were up there."

It took another ten minutes of shouting back and forth before an officer arrived at the gate. Convinced they weren't sappers, he told them to come up to the gate. They passed through one at a time while the paratroopers in the bunkers watched with ready weapons. The lurps were taken to the aid station bunker, while Martin went to the TOC and waited for the acting ground commander to return. He was out inspecting the perimeter.

Setting his CAR-15 aside, he rested his head on a table. It seemed only a few minutes had passed before he quickly sat up. He had dozed off. His equipment and fatigues were caked with dried mud and blood and streaked with the white residue of dried sweat. He gazed around while trying to regain his bearings.

"It's nearly midnight, Captain. You seem pretty exhausted. You okay?"

It was a major, the firebase ground commander.

"I'm okay, Sir. Is there any coffee to be had around here?"

"I took the liberty of washing your canteen cup a while ago and put a couple packets of C-ration coffee in it. It's sitting over there warming on a heat tab. Ought to be pretty hot by now."

"Thank you, Sir."

"I stopped at the aid bunker, and your man Spec-4 Reese filled me in on what's happened the last few days. I abso-fucking-lutely cannot believe you came back with that lurp team—alive! I see now why they call you Ghost. And those two enemy prisoners you captured—they verified what we've suspected since the first of the month. The enemy intends to make this another Dien Bien Phu.

"You made it back just in time because—well, I hate to tell you, but this entire shitshow has been for naught. We received orders today to abandon Ripcord. The colonel is putting together the plan. We're pulling out. The battalion and all our heavy equipment will be evacuated within the next few days."

Although dazed by the news, Martin was as relieved as he was disappointed.

"The decision wasn't an easy one, but it's the right one," the major said. "Ten days ago, Alpha and Delta companies had to back off Hill 1000 because it's totally covered with enemy bunkers. They're thick as fleas out there. They're everywhere—Hill 902, 805, every damned hill is infested. Just yesterday we tapped an enemy landline and gathered enough intel to know the shit's about to come down in a major way. We also recovered documents that indicated there's not just two regiments out there, but an entire division. The documents also included maps of a planned attack coming our way any day now.

"The colonel wants you on one of the first choppers out of here in the morning. He also requests you send him a copy of your AAR when it's complete. The Chinooks will probably begin lifting out the heavy equipment tomorrow and finish the next day. We'll extract our men from here on the twenty-third and Alpha and Delta Companies that afternoon from an LZ a click and a half south of here."

Martin sipped the hot coffee and remained silent as his mind absorbed all the major had said.

"Captain Shadows, we appreciate your will to continue fighting, but the Army is facing an enemy who will never stop fighting, no matter how many of them we kill. This battle will be over in a few days and the colonel and I will be recommending you for the Congressional Medal of Honor, and because you're wounded again…what is it, a third Purple Heart?"

And Martin now saw that his reality had also become the Army's reality. The pointless loss of men had apparently found its way into the upper echelons of the military. The army was giving up because they had counted statistical data—KIAs, WIAs, MIAs—until it was too late. Winning battles based on statistical score cards was a losing strategy. Martin counted Bushmaster, Sky Soldier, Thok, Lugo, Gopher, LA, and all the others. They weren't statistics—never had been—and only now was the army realizing their statistics meant little to a determined enemy and the American families of these men.

CHAPTER TWENTY-TWO

A Final Good-Bye
Camp Eagle, Republic of Vietnam

Martin spent three days at the hospital in Phu Bai after a surgeon extracted several pieces of shrapnel from his back and shoulders. Having handwritten his After-Action Report, he left it with a clerk to be typed and forwarded to the command staff before rejoining his unit. As always, the division was busy with flights of Hueys and Chinooks clattering across the base while he sat with his men on a dusty hill at Camp Eagle.

The Second of the 506th was on standdown while refitting and awaiting new orders. The tired warriors smoked cigarettes and passed a bottle of bourbon. With the death of Thok and so many others, it was a mostly quiet and somber reunion.

There had been seventy-five men killed at Ripcord since the first of July, and on the last day of the evacuation the colonel and the major were both killed by an enemy rocket. As long as the politicians allowed this so-called limited war to continue, more good men would die. Martin searched the eyes of his men. Like him they were tired and wondering what would come next.

Agonizing stretches of silent introspection were broken by brief discussions or comments as they gazed out at the hazy sky.

The army might plunge them into another senseless battle or perhaps suddenly realize what everyone else had already known for a year and send them home. No one wanted to be the last man killed in this inglorious epic of FUBAR military failure. And, as always, the rumors flowed through the ranks as men swore they'd heard an officer say this or a friend who claimed to have heard something else.

Martin tried to make sense of it, but for now, it was clear the army was pulling back but not quite sure what to do next. The bright side was the same general who ordered the assault on Hamburger Hill had apparently come to his senses and ordered the men off FSB Ripcord. Seventy-two men died on Hamburger Hill, and the last count at Ripcord stood at seventy-five. Of course, that was only since the first of July, but perhaps it was a victory of sorts if you weren't one of the seventy-five. The numbers mattered only to bureaucrats. For the men who were there, it was about their brothers who were among the wounded and dead.

Reports were steadily coming from all over the country about firebase closings and handoffs to the ARVN. Word was that Special Force's Firebase Betty Lou on the Cambodian border had been abandoned, and the Recondo School at Nha Trang was closing as well. It was also rumored that hundreds of Montagnards were moving toward the coast in hopes of catching boats to God-only-knew-where—the Philippines maybe. Perhaps the military *really was* disengaging.

The bourbon had little effect on Martin's anger and sadness. It was the right thing to do, but it begged the question why they were here in the first place. Like so many others, he and his men had been taught if they had to fight, they should fight to win, but this war had never been about winning. Cigarettes and bourbon could assuage their frustrations only so much. Martin wiped the back of his hand across his mouth and passed the bottle to the sergeant major.

"Where's Doc Enz?" he asked.

The Sergeant Major raised the bottle to his mouth but stopped. "He's gone back to the states."

"I thought he still had a month left till his DEROS," Martin said. "Something happen?"

Austin shrugged. "I don't know. His orders came from MAC-V, but they originated from the Secretary of the Army."

For the first time in a while, Martin felt a grin crossing his face. "Well, I'll be…that letter must have helped."

"Letter?"

"Yeah. I knew he was way above average, but I figured it was a long shot when he asked me to write a letter of recommendation for him to the Military Academy."

The Sergeant Major's face shone with incredulity. "Are you talking about West Point?"

"Yep."

"Well, I'll be damned! We're finally getting some good officers in the pipeline."

Several of the men glanced toward Martin as Austin's face suddenly clouded. "Oh crap! Sorry Captain. I didn't mean any offense."

"None taken," Martin said.

Austin held the bottle high. "Here's to Enz and the best soldiers I ever served with, and here's to you, Ghost. You and these men made a good account of yourselves, and I am proud to have been with you."

It was a hell of a compliment from a warrior who had seen so much and lost so many friends over the years.

———————

Near sundown Martin returned to his quarters and began writing letters to Kania and his mother. As an officer he had to be careful about what he wrote, and there was only so much he could say. It was a struggle to write anything pleasant. After several false starts, he set his pen aside and lit a cigarette, but there came a voice from outside the hooch. A runner was telling him the brigade commander wanted to see him ASAP.

Brigade commanders seldom called for junior officers unless it was critically important. Martin grabbed a wrinkled tube of toothpaste, his toothbrush, and a canteen. At least his fatigues were clean, and he hoped the toothpaste would eliminate the bourbon on his breath. It was nearly a half-mile jog to brigade headquarters, where the colonel was apparently awaiting his arrival. The sun had set when he stepped inside. The colonel was there alone.

"Come in, Captain. Take a seat."

Picking up a paper from his desk, the colonel studied it for what seemed an endless minute or two.

"Before your CO and his S-2 were killed in action on July 23rd, I received this message from them. It's a list of men they were recommending for commendations. They were recommending you for the Congressional Medal of Honor."

Martin said nothing while the colonel removed his reading glasses, folded them, and set them aside.

"That's one helluva honor, soldier. Problem is there's no write-up. That was supposed to come later. I've done my homework. I spoke with Sergeant Major Austin and a couple others including Colonel Krieger at MAC-V. Captain Shadows, we all agree you're somewhat of a maverick, but I do believe you're the kind of man this army needs right now. We've got enough 'yes men.' What we need are men who make us old farts uncomfortable. It makes us think, and we need a lot more like you, because this war has taken us down a path the Army has never been on."

The colonel took a red and white pack of Marlboros from his pocket and shook two out.

"Join me for a smoke?"

The colonel lit one and passed it across the table to Martin. After lighting his own, he tossed his Zippo on the table. It was embossed with airborne wings and the screaming eagle logo of the Hundred and First.

"I'm damned proud to have had you in my outfit, Captain Shadows, but you've been issued new orders. You're being relegated to a non-combat role back at MAC-V headquarters in Saigon. It seems you're caught up in some sort of unsavory business with the OSA and one of our own officers. The CID is requesting you as a witness to whatever all this involves, and Colonel Krieger could tell me only so much."

Martin inhaled deeply from his cigarette and nodded.

"You don't have much to say, do you, Captain?"

"Sorry, Sir. It's just that I've learned the less I say, the less likely I am to put my foot in my mouth."

The colonel laughed.

"You know, in another war and another time we might have had some pretty good conversations, Shadows. Pack your gear. My jeep will be at your hooch at oh-eight-hundred hours in the morning to pick you up. A chopper will carry you to the airstrip at Phu Bai to catch a flight down to Saigon."

"Is that all, Sir?"

"Only that I want to tell you the commander of the Hundred and First Airborne Division sends his personal regards and sincerest thanks for what you did up at Ripcord."

Martin walked out of brigade headquarters and stared out at the orange afterglow above the mountains in the west. It was somewhat rewarding to be recognized by these great warriors, but a somber requiem all the same.

Martin reported to MAC-V in Saigon late the next afternoon where he spent the rest of the day meeting with Colonel Krieger and two Criminal Investigation Department officers. He was assigned as an analyst to MAC-V S-2 while the CID continued its investigation of the so-called friendly fire incident that killed Sky Soldier, Lugo, and Gopher. The colonel made it clear the scope went far beyond Liegeman and Postiche, and included the hamlet massacre near Qui Nhon, and Colonel Pham's attack on the Montagnard village south of Phu Bai.

The problem he faced was a political minefield of powerful bureaucrats trying to hide the sins of their underlings. The top army brass was incensed with both the ARVN and the OSA for what appeared to be stonewalling and a massive coverup, but Krieger made it clear the investigation was classified. Martin, now the ultimate cynic, knew this meant it might all come to naught and be buried forever like so many other political debacles. Yet, if he hoped to ever again see his family and Kania, he had to play the game.

Another meeting was arranged with the two CID investigators at the end of the week, and Krieger sent him to the armory to draw a forty-five which he was cautioned to carry at all times. The forty-five automatic was a welcome addition to his knife, but having to carry either was an indictment of the architects who created this insane war. The OSA and their political cohorts in D.C. were still stonewalling and impeding the investigation in hopes of cleaning up the crime scene that was Vietnam. Martin already knew this could include the elimination of witnesses.

While riding to the BOQ in an aging Renault cab, he was lost in thought as he gazed out at the old city. With the Americans now leaving, Saigon would someday be ruled by the Communists from the north. There wasn't a doubt in his mind. Until then, there would be more bloodshed and afterward the killing would become wholesale as the Communists took control with an iron fist. They would seek to stamp out every remnant of French and American culture, every element of religious influence, and every person who believed in individual freedom. People would die by the thousands.

That purge would almost certainly include a focused extermination of the Montagnard peoples who had so loyally supported the Americans. Martin could not shake the thought that he had betrayed the very people he hoped to save. Khonsu, Brau, Katu, and Guia were somewhere in Cambodia with their families and fellow Montagnard villagers, likely facing the Communist Khmer Rouge—guerrillas as ruthless as the Vietcong. Sky Soldier—Whit Porterfield was killed in action, and Bushmaster—Zeke Anderson was also reported as likely killed while trying to save them. And there were so many others.

After writing letters to his mother and Kania, telling them of his new non-combat analyst role and anything other than the true nature of the war, Martin spent two more long days meeting with the CID investigators. They left no question unasked, but it seemed as if they were at an impasse.

Besides himself, witnesses were few and far between. Postiche, who was already in restricted quarters at Long Bhin, was saying nothing, and Liegeman was an agency man beyond army jurisdiction. His accountability would have to come through other channels. That these two murderers could possibly escape punishment was ludicrous, and it only compounded Martin's sense of defeat.

The following week, Krieger gave him a five-day in-country R&R, with one limitation: he had to stay away from the Continental Palace Hotel. That wasn't a problem, because Martin knew if he saw Liegeman again, he would kill him and likely end up in prison at Leavenworth. Instead, he visited Vung Ta for several days—afterward returning to Saigon and visiting popular venues around the city. He took photos, hoping to preserve memories he could share with the family back home, but the intuitive feeling that he was being watched never left him. His recreational sojourns became fewer, and his trips back and forth to the MAC-V compound never took the same route.

The weeks turned into months, and the CID investigation moved at a miserably slow pace with only occasional updates coming from the investigators. Martin's intelligence analyst assignment also contributed to his frustrations as everything learned about the enemy was turned over to an ARVN leadership riddled with spies. MAC-V had soon as printed the intelligence reports on leaflets and distributed them in the streets. His only solace was his DEROS was a little over sixty days away. By the end of January, he would be homeward bound.

It was approaching nightfall that day as he walked along a crowded avenue, taking in the sights. The sun had set, and the afternoon breeze had stilled, leaving the city permeated with the stench of the rivers. The amber streetlamps—those that hadn't been obliterated by the war—glowed to life, along with colorful paper lanterns hanging along some of the store fronts. Women in flowing áo dàis averted their eyes as they passed him on the sidewalks, but their counterparts leaning against storefronts in colorful miniskirts hawked their wares with nasally voiced promises of the "best boom-boom" in Saigon.

The city still wore vestiges of its previous French influence with sun-faded billboards advertising products now found only on black-market tables in the alleyways. There remained the stately European style mansions, graced with gardens and wrought iron fences along tree-lined avenues. Some wore the scars of war, and a few were only burned-out hulks, long abandoned by their owners. No longer was Saigon the Pearl of the Orient, but much like Margaret Mitchell's *Gone With The Wind* and the city of Atlanta, it was a bloodstained and war-torn caricature of itself. And as nightfall came, Martin began making his way back to the security of the BOQ.

The crowds and traffic had thinned, and the amber glow of the streetlamps was quickly lost in the nighttime shadows as he instinctively touched the forty-five beneath his shirt. Unsure what prompted it, the feeling was one he normally experienced only in the bush—one that brought his senses up to an adrenaline-driven level of awareness. It made no sense other than he had stayed out too late. Liegeman and his ilk had been on the defensive and lying low for months. It would be colossally stupid for them to try something now, but Martin couldn't shake his paranoia.

Having turned down another street, he glanced back as a buzzing motorcycle with two riders rounded the corner a hundred feet behind him. Both wore baseball caps and gold wire-rimmed aviators, earmarks of the ones called "Cowboys," the thugs of Saigon—always after easy pickings from unaware GIs. It dawned on him that he had seen these two several times that afternoon riding in the traffic along Tu Do Street. They had been watching him and were likely coming for his camera.

Their little Honda motorcycle accelerated as it approached, and the driver leaned low over the handlebars while the rider in back brandished what appeared to be a club. Martin stepped back as the speeding motorcycle swerved closer to the sidewalk and the passenger leaned out, poised to swing the club.

At the last possible moment, Martin stepped inside the swing and wrenched the rider from the motorcycle. The driver lost control as the careening Honda slammed into a lamppost, while Martin planted his knee into the back of the rider. The motorcycle exploded into a shower of parts and the driver's body cartwheeled down the street. The streetlamp flickered and went dark. When the rider felt Martin's forty-five pressed against the base of his skull, he stopped struggling.

Cowboys were known for their snatch and grabs of cameras, purses, sunglasses, and other objects, but a strong-armed attack with a club wasn't their style. These two were clearly bent on clubbing him into eternity, but why?

"Who sent you?"

"You don't kill me. I give you American dollars. I swear. I tell you everything. Please. I—"

"Shut up!"

"Please. I—"

"Shut the hell up! Where is the person who paid you to do this?"

"He pay much. I give all to you."

"Who is he? Where is he now?"

"King Bar, Tu Do Street. He important American. He wait for me to bring him your I.D. card. He give me more money. I give you. I—"

"Shut up."

Using his belt, he hobbled the man and brought him to his feet. "Try to run and I'll kill you. Do you understand?"

The cowboy nodded rapidly. "I no run. I promise. I no run."

Martin held the pistol beneath his shirt. "Good. Let's go."

When they reached Tu Do Street he spotted what he had hoped to find there—American MPs sitting in a jeep. After giving them the CID investigator's contact card and explaining the situation, Martin watched as they cuffed the cowboy, but it was an hour before the CID investigators arrived. Martin suspected Liegeman was involved and hoped he didn't have lookouts nearby. Otherwise, he was long gone by now. They stopped a block away from the King bar.

"Do you have men in the back alley in case he tries to run?" Martin asked.

The MPs and CID investigators glanced at one another.

"Never mind, I'll go into the alley and cover the back entrance. You guys go in the front door. Whatever you do, don't let this guy flash an I.D. card at you and walk. And be careful. He's likely going to be armed and desperate."

The jeeps stopped in front of the King Bar. The windows and door were decorated as playing cards with the King of Clubs facing the Queen of Hearts and the King of Hearts courting the Queen of Clubs. Out front stood a bellman wearing a well-worn red jacket with black slacks. The Saigon night had grown stifling. Martin leapt from the jeep and sprinted down a side alley. Liegeman was a cagey bastard. He would bolt out the back door as soon as the MPs came through the front entrance.

Easing up to what he determined was the back entrance of the bar, Martin tried the door. It was unlocked. That made sense. Liegeman probably arranged his escape in advance in case it became necessary. Carefully, he cracked open the door and peered inside. He was looking through a back storage area into the bar. Amber and vanilla lights backlit the patrons sitting at tables, but the front door was still closed. Someone on a keyboard was playing something resembling a Mamas and Papas tune, "California Dreaming." If he was in there, Liegeman was not visible.

Martin pulled the cuff of his pant leg up and drew his knife. A moment later the front door slammed open as the CID investigators and MPs charged inside. A woman screamed and the music ceased. Too many Tet Offensives and too many lost buddies left the MPs with an uncompromising mindset as they stared down the barrels of their M-16s at the bar patrons.

"Nobody move!" one shouted. His voice boomed with authority.

"Dừng lại," the second one yelled.

Sweeping their rifles side to side they stood inside the front entrance searching the tables for their man. The bar was silent except for the sound of the patrons diving beneath the tables.

"Do you see the man who paid you?" an investigator asked the cowboy.

The boy pointed to someone sitting to one side, who wasn't visible. An MP swung his rifle in that direction.

"You there, stop! Sit back down."

"I am an American."

"I don't care who you are. I said stop."

Liegeman appeared, darting into the back storeroom as he hurried toward the back door. Martin stepped back into the darkness. Liegeman dashed through the door into the darkened alley, but such was the world of the Ghost. The Agency man, momentarily disoriented, slowed, but Martin kicked his legs from beneath him and planted a boot on his chest. Bending over, he pressed the knife against his throat.

"On your way to hell, I want you to think about the good men you slaughtered. I only wish you could live long enough to realize just how much better men they were than you."

The ambient light shone through the open doorway in Liegeman's eyes. Wide, glassy, and terrified, they were no longer the icy blue reflections of his pompous and overblown ego, but mirrors of what he must have known for months. The Ghost was his reckoning.

"You can't kill me. I work for the United States government and the most powerful organ—"

"Shut the fuck up."

"You'll hang."

And Martin recalled his grandfather's words, "...*in the end you will not use your knife to slay your greatest enemy. The spirits of those who have gone before you will dictate the way he must die.*"

Martin reached inside Liegeman's jacket and retrieved the pistol he knew was there.

"Oh, so you think you can make it look like suicide?"

"Shut up."

Pressing the release, he dropped the magazine and ejected the shell from the chamber.

"Now, get up and take this." He shoved the pistol into his hand. "Go back through that door and surrender to the military police."

He jerked Liegeman to his feet and shoved him toward the door.

"Go now before I decide to kill you!"

The OSA agent didn't hesitate as he ran inside, but there immediately came two pops accompanied by bright flashes inside the bar. The Tet Offensive had left the MPs with a permanent hair-trigger edginess. A moment later Liegeman stumbled backward out the door—staring down at his chest before collapsing into a pile of trash in the alley.

CHAPTER TWENTY-THREE

Return to The World
The Journey to Hart County, Kentucky

Despite the Medal of Honor still lost in army bureaucracy, Martin was awarded the Distinguished Service Cross for his actions at Firebase Betty Lou along with another Purple Heart and several more commendations, not the least of which was a letter of recognition from Krieger for his part in the CID investigation. As a result, his DEROS was moved up two months. He was catching the freedom bird out of Tan Son Nhut and headed back to the States. The army also granted him another thirty-day leave. He was going home for Christmas, but it happened so suddenly he hadn't sent a letter to his parents telling them he was on the way.

It occurred to him that it might be better this way. At least he would have a couple days to adjust without a loud family celebration when he arrived. His purple shrapnel scars were healed, but there were deeper scars, unseen and much more painful. Those would take time. Gazing out the aircraft window at the sparkling South China Sea far below, he was filled with somber reflection and wondering if life could ever again be the same, or if those unseen scars would ever heal.

Putting the war out of his mind, he slept most of the way across the Pacific, and it was afternoon the following day when the bus from Louisville dropped him off six and a half miles from home. It didn't matter. He was home and the hike was nothing compared to climbing the mountains in Nam. Inhaling the sweet Kentucky air and soaking up the winter sunshine, he set out. It had been ten months since he'd last seen his family, and nothing could dampen his euphoria.

He was barely a half mile off the highway when an old pickup truck stopped beside him. The old man at the wheel rolled down his window and pushed up the bill of his cap.

"Where you headed, soldier?"

"My mom and dad's farm down on the river."

"Get in. I'll take you there."

With the gears grinding, the man pulled the shifter down and engaged the clutch. A pool of white exhaust drifted across the road behind them as they pulled away.

"By the looks of that tan on your face, you must've just got back from overseas. Vietnam?"

"Yes, Sir."

"I see you're wearing a Combat Infantryman's Badge and some serious fruit cocktail above your pocket. Bad war that one—not that any of 'em is good, but we lost a nephew over there a couple years ago."

Martin didn't know what to say. The old man had the truck heater roaring. He rolled down his window slightly and loosened his tie.

The old man shrugged. "Sorry. I reckon I'm talkin' too much."

"Oh, no Sir! I just—"

Martin was again at a loss for words.

"It's okay. I know. I was with the army in the Pacific for three years during World War Two. Ain't much you can say but let me tell you this: Don't expect things to be the same now you're back. Find you something to do and stay at it. And stay off the liquor. It got me for years, but I'm okay now. That's all I'm gonna say."

"Thanks. I appreciate what you're saying."

Fifteen minutes later the old man wished him luck and dropped him at the end of the drive. The walk up to the house brought on a flood of emotion along with a strange déjà vu of his high school and college years. It gripped him. And the old man's words returned: "Don't expect things to be the same." And they weren't. Those years not so long ago now seemed part of a life that was strangely foreign. It reminded him again that he could never go back to the world he had left before Nam.

The change was jarring. Difficult as it was to believe, he was here—home again—no longer part of the killing and chaos, and yet he was an interloper in a place where he no longer belonged. It seemed he must turn and go back, but he continued walking toward the house.

And it wasn't so much the time he'd been away as much as all that had happened since he was last here—the men he'd seen killed and those he had killed himself. He forced himself to grasp the moment and the reality of being home again. Finding some remnant of the old was all that was needed to verify this was all real. The aged farmhouse was a welcome sight, but there were no cars in the driveway. The door key was hanging there on the front porch behind his mother's "Home Sweet Home" plaque.

The house was quiet as he lugged his duffle bag up the stairs to his bedroom and tossed it on the bed. A disquieting silence filled the house, and he stood wondering what to do next. There was no welcoming committee, but that was okay with him. The bedroom looked the same as it had when he left for Nam. His bed was carefully made, and his collection of model aircraft was still lining the shelves above his desk.

He walked to them. Each plastic model, part of his childhood fascination with military aircraft, had been painstakingly assembled and painted with unerring detail. A P-51 Mustang, a B-17 Bomber, an F-100 jet fighter, and perhaps a dozen more were poised in flight along the shelf.

Reaching up, he randomly grabbed one. It was a Douglas A-1 Skyraider and it struck him as an unfortunate coincidence. His throat clotted with a lump of emotion. It was the same aircraft the South Vietnamese Airforce used to bomb and strafe Sky Soldier, Thibodaux, Lugo, and Gopher, and to drop napalm on the Montagnards. At this moment, it was a reminder he didn't need.

Walking to the window, he gazed out at the Green River and the tranquil rolling hills of the rural Kentucky countryside. Less than 48 hours ago he was listening to the booms of rockets and artillery impacting somewhere outside Tan Son Nhut Airbase. Now there was only an interminable silence. The plastic Skyraider snapped and crumbled in his hands. He looked down, unnerved by what he had done.

All his dreams and visions of kindred spirits and even his life had fallen into a shambles of failure and regret. He tossed the pieces of the model airplane into the wastebasket and sat on the bed. Two Shadows was the only one who could provide answers. He had always made sense of things, and there was Kania. He needed to see them both, but not before seeing his mother and father. From somewhere outside came the sound of a car door shutting, and a moment later the back door opened. He walked to the top of the stairs.

"Who's there?" came his mother's voice.

Martin bounded down the steps. "It's me, Mom."

He swept her up into his arms and held her tight while she buried her face against his shoulder and wept.

"It's okay, Mom. I'm home now."

Looking up at him with teary eyes, she drew a quavering breath. "You're skinny as a scarecrow, Martin. Do you have to go back?"

"Not to Vietnam."

"Where then?"

"I've got a thirty-day leave before I go to Fort Bragg. Where's Dad?"

"He's gone to take a load of hay to the cattle. Come sit down and let me fix you something to eat. Have you been to see Kania yet? She actually got our phone number from Grandfather Two Shadows and called here."

"When was the last time she called?"

"Oh, well, I'm afraid it's been a while—nearly two months. She mentioned getting a letter from you. Poor thing was worried and wanted to know if I could tell her anything more about you being wounded. I told her about the telegram the army sent us, but it said about the same thing your letter did. She's staying at her family's place on the reservation, but the phone service there has been disconnected. So, how are you doing now?"

"I'm mostly healed. She hasn't called or written you since then?"

"No, but I think Dad has talked with your grandfather about her. He said since her father passed away, she has no family, and Grandmother Shadows has been looking after her. It seems you've finally met a really nice girl, and she really cares about you."

"I've got to drive out there and see them."

"When?"

"I'll leave in a couple days."

"But the weather out that way—they've already had quite a bit of snow, and it's such a long way."

"I have to go. Don't worry. I'll be careful."

Martin had been behind the wheel of his pickup for two days and a night, when he left the highway and turned north onto the Fort Peck Reservation. It was nearing sunset, and he now drove faster because of the cauldron of purple storm clouds boiling on the western horizon. A Montana blizzard was the last thing he needed to face this far from civilization. The refrozen snow crunched beneath his truck tires, and despite the exhausting drive his mind raced with anticipation.

He had called Grandfather Two Shadows, who assured him that Kania was doing well and would welcome his return, but he said she was busy tending to personal matters. The old man seldom spoke in simplistic terms, and true to form, he remained more cryptic than ever when pressed. Out of respect, Martin didn't press him further.

The storm front was coming on fast when he spotted his grandparents' house on the distant hilltop beyond Wolf Creek. The sun had dropped into the purple clouds turning them into a flaming iridescent orange river that flowed through the distant hills—and he saw a figure standing in the distant doorway of the cabin. It all but took his breath as he realized it was the figure from his vision. The pickup crossed the creek and struggled up the steep grade, but the person turned away and closed the door. The golden sky had given way to nightfall.

After following the long drive between barbed wire fences up to the house, he stopped the pickup out front. Here at last, he took a deep breath and exhaled. The porch light came on. The only sounds were those of the frigid Montana winds and the metallic ticking of the truck's rapidly cooling motor. The door opened again, but only slightly this time as the dim outline of a woman's face appeared. She was looking out at him through the narrow opening—his grandmother, he assumed.

He stepped from the truck and reached back for his coat as

the front door swung wide and the porch light lit her face, but it wasn't his grandmother. It was Kania. Charging across the porch, she ran barefoot down the steps into the snow. Her yelps of joy answered whatever doubts had plagued him as they embraced, and their lips met in a passionate greeting.

Time stood still as he stared into her eyes and she into his. He didn't know if it had been two minutes or ten when his grandparents stepped into the open doorway. Two Shadows called out to them and motioned for them to come inside. Only then did Martin realize the winter storm had arrived as huge clots of snow blew sideways around them. Kania was wearing a light dress, and he wrapped his coat around her shoulders.

"Now, go inside, while I grab my duffle bag. I'll be right behind you."

She turned to go but stopped instead and leapt back into his arms. With groaning passion, she kissed him again and again. When she finally broke away, she was breathless and staring up at him with tearful brown eyes. "Grandfather Two Shadows always said you would return."

"I am glad you listened. Now go," he said, "before you get frostbite."

Two Shadows fed several pieces of wood into the iron stove while Martin's grandmother made hot tea. A cozy warmth soon returned to the house, and after pouring the tea, she grasped Two Shadows by the arm. "Let's go to bed, old man. I am sure Martin and Kania have a lot to discuss."

And there *was* much to talk about, but Martin could only hold her tight as they sat on the couch and enjoyed the warmth of the wood stove.

"I know you must be tired," she said, "but your grandmother is right. We need to talk."

"I agree. So, let me go first. And forgive me if I'm too blunt, but the way I see it, there's only one thing remaining that needs to be done, and that's for me to ask you to marry me, right?"

She drew a sudden breath and hesitated as she stared into his eyes. "I have hoped and prayed you would."

"That's what I'm doing. I'm asking you now. Will you…marry me…I mean?"

It was a stuttering proposal, but one which Kania answered with a whispered "yes" and another passionate kiss.

"We have a lot of decisions to make."

"Such as?" she said.

"Such as where we'll live, and how many children we will have, and what we will do to make a living."

"I have only myself to offer," she said, "and I will go with you wherever you go, and as for children, well…."

She stood and pulled him by the hand from the couch.

"Come with me."

For Martin, there was but one thought—the one and only first time they had made love was near heaven. Even though he was severely under the influence then, he remembered it as if it was yesterday. And now he was cold sober. This could be the best homecoming present ever, but the wooden floor creaked beneath his boots, and he paused.

"My grandparents are probably not asleep yet," he whispered.

"It's okay," she said as she led him into the bedroom.

Turning on a bedside lamp, she bent over a crib beside the bed and lifted a baby to her breast. She turned to face him and gazed into his eyes. Kania was a remarkably beautiful woman, and her eyes were pleading and vulnerable. A baby had been the last thing on his mind.

"He's ours and he's only three weeks old."

She put the sleeping infant in his arms, and Martin was at a loss. It had been nearly ten months since that first and only night they had spent together. She smiled.

"I've never been with another man, and I had no idea it would happen the first and only time. He's the reason I didn't go back to school after Dad died."

Dumbstruck, Martin looked down at the baby. Kania clearly wanted him to say something, but his throat was knotted. He drew a ragged breath and exhaled. His whole world had changed in that moment—a realization so overwhelming he could think of nothing that would express his true feelings.

"He's so tiny."

"Don't worry, he'll grow big and strong like his father."

"But why…?" Martin struggled for the right words.

Kania cocked her head to one side. "Why…?"

"Why didn't you write and tell me?"

She gazed into his eyes. "Martin, I wanted you to come back because you wanted me, not because you had to, and when I got your letter saying you loved me, I didn't want you to worry about us while you were fighting in the war."

———————

Kania and baby Martin were a restorative that took Martin's mind away from the war, but as the days passed, the dreams returned to haunt him. While Kania remained in Montana to finish her studies in Missoula, he returned to fulfill his military obligation at Fort Bragg. It was this separation that allowed the memories and questions about the war to creep again into his psyche, but there came a reprieve. The military began offering early separations from service, and Martin submitted his request. His was accepted and by early May he was on his way back to Montana, but he planned one stop before Missoula. That was to visit Grandfather Two Shadows.

____

His grandmother baked biscuits and fried slices cut from a country ham while Martin sat at the table with his grandfather, sipping black coffee. He wanted to ask him about those past visions and the things that happened in Vietnam, but his grandmother's presence held him at bay. They talked instead about Kania's upcoming graduation ceremony and their future plans.

When breakfast was done, what little conversation there was had dwindled to silence. Two Shadows fixed him with a hard stare. "You are troubled, Martin."

"Yes, Grandfather, I am. I'm hoping you will help me understand the things keeping me awake at night."

"Are they about the war?"

Martin nodded.

"Fighting in a war causes many men to question what they have witnessed. Your father was the same when he returned from World War Two. There are no simple answers, but we will go to my lodge on the creek later today and smoke the pipe. There we can discuss these things."

____

The drive was a pleasant one, and the early May sunshine was glorious, but there was still a chill in the air. This made Two Shadows's lodge all the more inviting as he kindled a small fire and unsheathed his pipe. Having stopped by home in Kentucky, Martin brought with him a supply of the old man's favorite fresh twist Kentucky tobacco. After they smoked a bowl in silence, Two Shadows set the pipe aside.

"Tell me, Martin, about what it is that troubles you."

Where to start, that was the problem, because there were so

many things—the deaths, the losses, the betrayals and lies, the evil—all of it.

"Many things, I suppose, but I'll try to explain them as simply as I can."

He gathered his thoughts and began. "When I made up my mind to go back to Vietnam, it was because I had dreams and visions about a people there who were a lot like the Lakota. They're called the Montagnard, a mountain people shunned by others in their country. They are mostly peaceful, but can be fierce warriors, and they sided with the Americans against the Communists. There were five who escaped the North Vietnamese prison with me, and I hadn't heard from them since our escape.

"I interpreted my vision to be that they were lost and suffering and that someone was trying to kill them and all their people. Later when I found them, I discovered it was a high-level Vietnamese Colonel who hated the Montagnard. I wanted to save them from this man and others who were going to harm them. At least that's the way I interpreted it, and there is more, but this is where I failed.

"The Montagnards I tried to help, more than two hundred of them, fled Vietnam into Laos and down to Cambodia. In my efforts to save them, several men in my unit were killed or wounded. I suppose that's the heart of the matter. I got my own men killed for nothing more than my dreams of doing good."

Two Shadows repacked the bowl and relit the pipe. After passing it to Martin, he closed his eyes for a while. When he reopened them, Martin passed the pipe back to him.

"So, you believe these people escaped into Cambodia?"

"As far as I know."

"Then why are you sad?"

"Because I failed to save them. Much of Cambodia outside of its cities is under siege by the Khmer Rouge. They're a ruthless

Communist regime that's slaughtering everyone, and I don't think the Montagnard people will survive."

"Martin, I believe you have not failed them. They escaped the colonel who you say was about to kill them. And these men who died, your fellow soldiers, they have not given their lives in vain. You fought your enemies bravely, and in the end, that is all that matters, because we do not always win. Look toward your Lakota blood for understanding. We too have suffered greatly, but we cannot change where in this life the Great Spirit takes us. We can only change how we react to it.

"Our people fled our homelands. We went north into Canada, and even when we returned years later, many were slaughtered at Wounded Knee or died from starvation. As with your ancestors, you have found a place of sadness and loss, but we survived and so have you. Wakȟáŋ Tȟáŋka only gives life. It is up to the people to live it as a gift when we can. Now, take your gift of life and live it knowing that you will fail only when you no longer try, and perhaps someday you may again see these people."

Martin would never say it to his grandfather, but he saw his words as no more than a means of encouragement—helpful words but with no substantive answers to his angst. Yet, it was as if the old man was telling him something more—a truth or a lesson that came from a world beyond this one. Perhaps he was right. And perhaps someday he would see them again, but it was time to move on with his life. Looking back solved nothing, and his wife and son needed him.

"There's a lot to think about in what you say, Grandfather. Thank you for your help."

"Your doubt shows, Martin, but someday you will understand."

CHAPTER TWENTY-FOUR

Twenty Years Later
December 1992, Near Missoula, Montana

Martin and Kania now had three children, the younger Martin and his two sisters, Caroline and Maggie—all students at the University of Montana. Settling near Missoula, Martin had joined another Vietnam veteran, Buck Marino, to establish a guide service for hunters and fishermen, and Kania had become a registered nurse. She and Marino's wife, Janie, who had been an army nurse in Vietnam, were best of friends.

For Martin and Kania, their daily lives had become what some folks might consider "being stuck in a rut," but it was one combat veterans and their wives considered a blessing—normalcy. It was a time where they could breathe, and no longer fear what might come the next day. A December snow was falling and piling in drifts along the fences and against the front porch, but Martin was in his easy chair reading, while Kania was curled up in a blanket on the couch. As he often described it, she was purring like a kitten while she slept. A fire burned in the fireplace, and he too was about to doze when the sound of a vehicle came from out front.

This was strange. No one in his right mind would attempt to

travel rural Montana in what was bordering on a blizzard. His first thought was one of the kids had come out from Missoula, but it was mid-week and they had classes. Besides, they knew better than to drive in such conditions. Hunting season was over. It could only be someone lost or seeking help. He stood and went to the window. The sun had dropped behind the mountains and snow was swirling from a dusky gray sky. A black Chevy Suburban was parked in the drive, and there came a knock at the door.

The cold evening air flooded inside as he opened the door and faced the man standing on the porch. Martin found himself mired in a stunned trance as the icy snowflakes swirled about. He recognized the face, familiar yet aged, but it was one from twenty years ago—one belonging to a man killed in action in Vietnam. He squeezed his eyes shut as his head spun, but he couldn't muster a greeting of any sort.

"Ghost?" the man said.

Martin gazed into the eyes of a warrior, a Green Beret, one who had followed him through the gates of hell, and only after several long seconds did he find his voice.

"They told me you…they told me you wouldn't make it. All this time, I thought you had died."

"Rumors of my demise have been greatly—"

Martin leaped forward, wrapping his arms around the man's neck, and for the first time since childhood he felt warm wet tears on his face.

"You bastard, you hard core bastard, I can't believe my eyes. I thought you were dead."

"I told you I would knock on your door someday."

The two men embraced on the porch.

"Who is it, Martin?" came Kania's voice.

"It's…it's Bushmaster. I mean, it's Zeke, Zeke Anderson. He's…he's here…now…."

"Bushmaster still works for me," he said.

"But…"

Martin was still lost in the stunning realization that Bushmaster hadn't died in Vietnam. He was here now standing on his front porch. Kania stepped into the doorway.

"Please, come inside, Sergeant Anderson. Martin has told me so much about you that I feel I know you."

Dumbstruck, Martin sat in silence while his mind raced with a thousand questions. That Bushmaster had lived was a miracle.

"I suppose you're wondering why I flew all the way out here to Montana in the dead of winter to find you."

"Well, there *are* better months to visit here."

"I have some really good news that I wanted to bring to you personally. It took a hell of a lot of calling around to find you, but the upshot is U.N. soldiers clearing mines found a Montagnard village in Mondulkiri Province in the highlands of Cambodia. There were nearly four hundred Montagnards there, and the men still had their weapons. They were still crossing back into Vietnam and fighting the Communists after all these years."

Martin's mouth went dry, and his heart was suddenly thumping in his chest. He walked to the liquor cabinet and removed two glasses and a bottle of Evan Williams.

"Now you're talking my language, Tonto," Bushmaster said.

"Kiss my ass, Lone Ranger. Now, tell me how you know all this and if our people were with them."

"Sure. You see, I live near Greensboro, North Carolina, and I began working with the Montagnard DEGA Association in 1987. Our Special Forces men who fought beside them in Nam helped DEGA and other organizations establish a Montagnard settlement there. So, anyway, some guy named Thayer wrote an article in the *Phnom Penh Post* about this lost village. That was back in September, and it was splashed across the front page. Vice-President Quayle got involved and told Ambassador Twining to bring them all to America if they wanted to come."

Martin could barely restrain himself, but Bushmaster deserved to tell the story his way.

"So, I weaseled my way on board a flight with a group that included Pierre K'Briuh, a leader of the Montagnards in North Carolina, and Don Scott, one of our boys. We met with a bunch of hotshot diplomats at the Hotel Le Royal in Phnom Penh and later took a U.N. chopper into the boonies to visit the village. It was actually five villages along a river, but anyway, they spoke with Y Peng Ayun, the military commander of the group through another guy named Y Hin Nie. He spoke English and was their political leader.

"After a lot of back and forth we finally convinced them to let us take them to a refugee camp in Phnom Penh. Bottomline is they surrendered their weapons in October and boarded flights to Los Angeles, then to Greensboro, North Carolina. We brought home two hundred and sixty-nine men, twenty-four women and eighty kids."

Martin could stand it no longer. He had to know. He killed his glass of bourbon.

"How about we cut to the chase?"

Zeke killed his drink and held out the glass. "Most certainly, but if you don't mind."

Martin quickly refilled the glass while Kania sat wide-eyed and near tears.

"And?"

"Sorry—didn't mean to be so windy. Yes, I found them. Khonsu, Brau, Katu, and Guia, and most of the other men from our group along with their families. And do you know what the first thing they asked me was? They asked me about the Ghost. Those guys still think you're the next thing to deity."

"Where are they now?"

"Greensboro, North Carolina, awaiting your return from the past. I told them I was going out to search for you."

Kania walked over and sat beside Martin, wrapping her arms around him, and pushing her warm lips against his ear.

"Two Shadows told you they would return, and now, so shall you for them."

For years, Kania had tolerated his moodiness with stoic patience. And when he went back into the mountains for days at a time, she understood and allowed him his indiscretions. Never had he fully reconciled the two cultures within, but it now seemed his Lakota half was coming home, and Two Shadows had foreseen it all.

Shortly before Christmas, Martin, Kania and their three adult children boarded a flight for North Carolina. It was something Kania had insisted upon—something about their father she said the kids needed to witness firsthand. Bushmaster was there to meet them at the Charlotte Airport, and they rode with him to Greensboro. Both men wore the brass bracelets given to them by their Montagnard friends twenty years ago.

Vehicles of every sort were parked up and down the road as the crowd spilled outside into the cold December air. The meeting hall was apparently full, and several photographers walked along with them, maintaining a constant chatter of clicking cameras. Martin glanced about at the smiling faces and grasped Kania's hand as they followed Zeke inside.

"You didn't tell me this was going to be a major affair, Bushmaster."

Zeke glanced over his shoulder. "I never knew you to get nervous in crowds—especially Asians."

"What the hell is that supposed to mean?"

"Well, you always acted pretty calm when the NVA were all over us."

"Bushmaster, you *do* know you just aren't quite right?"

"Most snake-eaters would take that as a compliment."

As if choreographed, the crowd parted, and Martin followed Zeke across the room. When he spotted them several feet away, Martin stopped. Springing from folding metal chairs, the Montagnard warriors closed around him. Reaching out and touching his shoulder, Khonsu locked eyes with him.

"Ghost!" he whispered.

"Ghost!" the others repeated.

Martin and his men embraced one another as the entire room broke into jubilant cheers and applause. Nearly three minutes passed before someone pushed a microphone into his hand, and the room fell suddenly silent. Martin glanced at the now teary-eyed Kania who smiled and gave him an affirming nod of encouragement. He cleared his throat and sucked down a calming breath.

"Twenty years ago, I departed Vietnam thinking I would never again see these men who were closer to me than brothers. Well, a few days ago, someone came up my drive in Montana in a howling blizzard and knocked on my door. I thought it was someone needing help, but it wasn't. It was Zeke Anderson. Bushmaster, we call him."

Martin put his hand on Zeke's shoulder. "I thought he had died back in Vietnam, and if that weren't enough of a surprise, he told me about more men who fought beside us—our Montagnard warriors. He told me they too were alive and living here in North Carolina.

"Ladies and gentlemen, it's been a long time since that war, and I've had more than a few restless nights when I was unable to sleep because I was thinking about these men—my friends and fellow warriors. Now, I am able to finally walk away from that time so long ago, knowing all of it wasn't in vain. And with that, I have only one more thing to say."

He turned to the Montagnards. "Welcome to your new home, my friends, and never forget that we will remain as loyal to you here in America as you were to us in Vietnam."

If you enjoyed this story

Please leave your written review of
Specter of Betrayal, A Vietnam War Story, The Ghost II at
www.amazon.com/review/create-review?asin=B0CYKCNVND.
The author and other readers will appreciate your comments. Post
your review and tell others what you like about this book.

Keep reading for a preview of another of the novels from The
Vietnam War Series, *The Gomorrah Principle*, a story about
a young sniper who becomes involved in the CIA's infamous
Phoenix Program.

The Gomorrah Principle

RICK DESTEFANIS

CHAPTER ONE

The Tennessee Overhill, 1967

Cradling the rifle in his arms, Brady Nash sat high above a cornfield with his back against an ancient oak tree. The evening, windless and still, was void of sound as a somber sun sank in the distant hills. With the fall foliage now gone, there remained only the skeletal limbs of winter and a scarecrow hanging ragged and forlorn amongst the dried stalks below. Brady pulled his collar snug around his neck. It was cold in the mountains after sunset, but it was a good cold, crisp and fresh. It made a person feel alive, and he'd never felt life as much as he did now. This was his last hunt, possibly forever, because beyond the hills, beyond the Hiwassee and the Tennessee Rivers, the world and a war awaited him.

Despite Lacey's objections, he was leaving, and she, as stubborn as she was beautiful, hadn't spoken a word to him since he enlisted. Back when Duff joined up, she'd said, "Even if he *is* my brother, he's crazy for going off to that war in Vietnam." Brady had agreed with her then, but things changed. Duff was dead and Lacey had moved off to Nashville. Now it was his turn to go, except giving her the reason for his enlistment would only make matters worse. She should already know that leaving Melody Hill was the last thing he wanted to do.

As a dusky twilight settled over the bare cornstalks far below, the faint sounds of chimes broke the silence as they drifted across the hills. They came from Melody Hill, a small settlement tucked high in a mountain valley overlooking the Hiwassee River. It was little more than a cluster of houses surrounding a gas station, restaurant, and general store, but it was home. And there was the church—the Melody Hill Methodist Church. On a rise at the far end of town, its steeple rose above the trees, a titanium spire visible from miles away to people living in the wooded hills and along the foggy river gorges of the Tennessee Overhill.

Life in the Overhill was simple. The lucky ones worked for the L&N Railroad down at Etowah or at the cotton mill up at Englewood. Otherwise, there was the copper mine, twenty miles down the highway, or one of the logging companies. Everyone did a little farming on the side and got by. It wasn't a fat life, but people here respected one another, and everyone knew right from wrong.

Earlier that afternoon, Brady had driven his truck up a rocky backroad to this remote farm. He'd come here to escape the television with its cacophony of voices telling of the chaos and conflict gripping the world, the world into which he was going. One more brief respite before leaving was all he wanted—to sit in the silence of the hills and watch the day fade away one last time. He snapped from his daydream as the yips and howls of coyotes echoed from a ravine below the cornfield. Coyotes were a species new to the Overhill, and this wasn't their normal squealing welcome of nightfall but the sounds of a chase. They drew nearer as Brady peered through the riflescope. Despite the sun having set, there was still good shooting light. A moment later, he spotted movement. A doe and fawn scrambled from the rhododendron at the far end of the field. Bounding in long, graceful leaps, the two deer came up the edge toward him. The coyotes spilled up out of the ravine behind them, streaking in hot pursuit.

Propping the rifle across his knee, he contemplated firing a round to scatter the pack, but the coyotes were three hundred yards away and too close to the deer. The howling din grew, echoing from the surrounding hills. Both deer and the coyotes came up the field and disappeared into the grass at the base of the ridge below. A few moments later, the doe reappeared as she bounded effortlessly up the mountainside toward him. The howls of the pack drew closer as she passed within a few yards, but the fawn was lagging behind.

Still a hundred yards down the mountain, the little deer had broken stride as it slowed to a tongue-lolling canter. Knowing they had their prey, the coyotes trotted alongside. Brady drew the crosshair down on a large, yellow-eyed male but hesitated as the exhausted fawn crossed back and forth through his line of sight. He needed to wait until they were closer, but the big male lunged for the fawn's throat.

The roar of the thirty-aught-six rolled down the mountainside and across the cornfield below, reverberating against a distant hillside as the predator's chest exploded. A second animal skidded to a stop, and the pack milled in momentary confusion. Quickly bolting another cartridge, Brady pulled the crosshair onto the next target. The second animal's head snapped convulsively from the bullet's impact and the pack scattered into the broom sedge. After chambering another round, he waited as the echo of the last shot faded into the distant mountains. A hundred yards below, two dying coyotes quivered, but Brady focused his attention on the high grass at the base of the ridge. This was where the rest of the pack would break from cover.

In the fading light, he detected movement as another coyote cautiously raised its head from the yellow grass. With its ears erect, it gazed back up the mountainside. At least two hundred yards away, it must have felt safe as it looked back. Brady centered the crosshairs and carefully squeezed off another round. The animal rolled and disappeared into the grass as the remainder of the pack broke from the brush at the base of the ridge, sprinting toward the far end of the cornfield.

"Aren't you gonna throw another shot at 'em?"

Brady jerked his head around. It was the landowner, Hubert Brister, standing behind him.

"Wait a minute, Mister Hubert," Brady whispered as he turned and looked back at the fleeing coyotes.

"But the rest of 'em are getting away," the old man said. "Shoot 'em."

Brady peered through the scope. By now, the coyotes were nearing the far end of the cornfield—at least four hundred yards away.

"Wait," he said. "It'd be blind luck to hit one running at this distance."

The lead coyote disappeared into the ravine at the end of the field, but one of the animals at the rear of the pack broke into a series of stiff-legged hops. It bounced sideways as it neared the field's edge. Brady waited.

"Atta boy," he murmured, "just give me a look." Bracing the rifle, he kept the animal in his sights. "It's getting away," Brister said.

"No, it's not," Brady muttered as he held the rifle steady.

He held his cheek against the stock and his eye in the scope as the coyote bounced one last time and stopped, staring back at the mountain. The wind was dead still. With the horizontal crosshair eight inches above the animal's back, Brady squeezed the trigger. The thirty-aught-six thundered again, and the bullet knocked the coyote flat in a cloud of dust.

"Damn, you're a crackerjack, ain't ya, boy?"

Brady remained silent as he stood and brushed the dust from his pants.

"So tell me," the old man said, "how did you know that critter was gonna stop?"

"I didn't for sure," Brady said. "But you know how the Bible tells when Lot's wife stopped and looked back at Gomorrah even when the angels told her not to? Well, I reckon animals have that same fatal curiosity 'cause they do it a lot."

Brister rubbed the stubble on his chin and nodded, but he said nothing more as they walked down the ridge to his house. It was quiet and the house was dark except for a single bulb burning on the front porch. When Brady opened the truck door, a hound bellowed beneath the porch.

"Hush up, Hank," Brister yelled. He turned to Brady. "Why don't you come inside and have a cup of coffee? I sure wouldn't mind some company for a little while."

Brady hesitated as he clung to the truck door. The old man let him hunt his land when he wanted, and he was a widower with all his kids having moved off to Knoxville or Chattanooga.

"Cup of coffee sounds good," he said.

———————

The aroma filled the kitchen as the percolator bubbled and hissed on the stove. Old Man Brister set two stained cups on the table. The cups, like his hands, were riddled with the lines of age, but everything in the room was neat and clean. Each dish towel was carefully folded, and each dish was washed, dried, and placed in the cupboard.

"Word is you enlisted in the army," Brister said. Brady nodded.

"Well, what's done is done, but you know that ain't gonna bring Duff back."

Brady eyed the old man carefully. He didn't want to be disrespectful. "Sounds like you've been talking to Lacey," he said.

"I went to Europe when I was seventeen years old," Brister replied. "Eighty-second Division, World War One."

The old man picked up a dish towel from beside the sink and walked over to the stove.

"A war is too big and too ugly to think you can go there to get revenge."

He was certain now that Brister had talked with Lacey.

"This isn't about revenge," Brady said. "Yeah, Duff was my best friend, and since I enlisted Lacey and I haven't seen eye to eye on much of anything, but there's more to it than…" Brady hesitated. What could he say?

Brister used the dish towel to grasp the handle of the soot-blackened percolator and walked over to the table. His hand trembled with the unsteadiness of age as he poured the coffee.

"Ain't got no sugar or milk," he said. "Black's fine with me," Brady said.

"Yeah, well, she probably doesn't want you to end up like Duff or Jesse Harper."

Jesse Harper was a legend of sorts around Polk County. He had served two tours in Nam as a forward air controller, piloting small planes over the mountainous jungles along the Cambodian and Laotian borders. He now owned a canoe and tube rental business down on the Hiwassee. He drank some, and rumor was he grew a little pot on the side as well, but his biggest claim to fame was getting drunk and landing his little Cessna on rural highways when he got lost. Everyone in the county seemed to tolerate him, and the teenagers loved him.

"What's wrong with Jesse?"

"Hell's bells—you must think it's normal to get so drunk you can't find your way home and land your airplane on a road."

"No, but—"

"No, and there ain't no 'but' to it neither. The last time Sheriff Harvey found him, Harper was slobbering and crying like a baby and saying he couldn't find his men 'cause they were lost in the jungle. You want to end up like that?"

Brady had never heard this part of Harper's antics.

"Lacey thinks I'm going to get killed, but like you said, what's done is done. I just wish she'd talk to me."

"I saw her this afternoon when I was—"

"Lacey's home?"

The old man placed the coffeepot back on the stove as he spoke. "Yeah, said she came home to see you off this weekend. Then she's heading back to Nashville."

Holding the cup in front of his face, Brady inhaled the coffee's aroma, but his mind was on Lacey. It was only two weeks ago that she said she was never speaking to him again. He'd tried to reason with her, but she was too angry, and it was all too strange—what had happened those few days after Duff's funeral.

After receiving a phone call from a stranger who said he knew Duff, Brady had driven down to Athens to meet the man at the bus stop on 411. He was a soldier wearing a uniform with the same unit crests and patches as Duff's. The man didn't introduce himself as he cast about with a nervous glance. When he seemed satisfied that no one was watching, he drew hard on his cigarette and stared at Brady with sunken eyes as he pulled a brown envelope from inside his coat.

"Look, I'm a friend of Duff Coleridge's, and I just got out of the army yesterday up at Fort Campbell. Before I left Nam a few weeks ago, Duff gave me this letter and asked me to carry it home to you. He said his mail is being read and his life is in danger—I mean from the crazy people he's working with. Anyway, just read it. It explains everything, but don't ever mention how you got it or that you ever saw me, okay?"

The veins in Brady's temples pulsed with the beat of his heart as he realized the man didn't know Duff was dead.

"Put that envelope inside your jacket and get on your way," the man said. "You don't need to be seen with me."

"Look, mister, uh…" Brady glanced at the soldier's uniform, but his nameplate was missing from above the pocket. "There's something I need to tell you."

"Make it quick. I'm catching that bus home." The man motioned toward an approaching Greyhound as it slowed to pull off the highway.

"Duff was killed in action almost two weeks ago. We had his funeral last week."

The man's face hardened, and his voice dropped to a near whisper. "Lousy bastards." He bent over and picked up his duffel bag, pulling the strap over his shoulder as the bus hissed to a stop. "Regardless of what the army tells you, Duff probably wasn't killed the way they say. Just read that letter. You can decide if you want to do something about it."

The bus driver stepped down and opened the baggage compartment, but before he stowed the soldier's bag, Brady saw the name James R. Noble and part of the serial number 410-33-. He wrote them on the envelope as the bus pulled away.

"More coffee?"

Brister's voice jerked him back to consciousness. Brady noticed his cup was empty.

"Yeah, sure," he said.

"What's on your mind, son?"

Brady glanced up. In the future, he would need to mask his feelings. But as he looked across the table at Brister, an idea came to him. And who better was there to trust than Hubert Brister?

"I've got something to show you, but first I need your word that you won't tell anyone."

The old man smiled. "Hell, son, you've been like one of my own boys. I reckon if you want it that way, you got it."

Brady stood up. "I'll be right back."

After walking outside to his truck and retrieving the envelope from beneath the front seat, he returned to the kitchen. He pulled Duff's letter from the envelope and gave it to Brister. The old man took a pair of wire-rimmed reading glasses from his shirt pocket, while Brady peered over his shoulder, reading the letter again for what was probably the twentieth time.

Brister's lip quivered as he finished the letter. He looked up at Brady with eyes wide and hard with anger. "Them bastards killed that boy. You need to take this letter to the president or like Duff said, to a newspaper or something. Them sorry bastards."

"I know," Brady said, "but I'm afraid the army might cover it up. Besides, look at this."

He turned the envelope up and emptied the contents on the table. There were several more documents, one a handwritten note on a telex message that said, "You're getting a lot of good press from the big boys in Saigon." It was signed with the name "Spartan." The telex message read, "Tell your new man job well done. Interrogation of his captured suspect proved valuable."

There was yet another note, one Duff mentioned in the letter. It was a list of Vietnamese names. Several were marked through, and a note was scribbled below, "The ones marked off are already terminated." It was the same handwriting as on the other telex message. Brady set it aside and picked up a yellow card splotched with what appeared to be dried blood. On the front of the card were the words "Phung Hoang" along with a strutting red-and-green bird carrying arrows and sticks of dynamite in its talons.

"What is all this stuff? What does it mean?" Brister asked. "And this French woman in the letter, the one he said was his girlfriend, how is she going to know anything?"

"I don't know for sure," Brady said. "But if Duff said I should contact her, then she must know something. That's why I'm going over there to try to find some of these people."

"Boy, how do you think you can ever do that? There ain't even a guarantee you'll get sent over there, and even if you do, that's a big country with millions of people."

"I already did my homework, Mister Hubert. My enlistment contract includes a guarantee of MOS training and duty station. I requested airborne ranger, like Duff, and the Republic of Vietnam. That will be my first duty station. There are only two airborne units over there, and Duff was with one of them when they recruited him."

Brister grew red-faced, and the veins bulged on his forehead as he lit a cigarette.

"Son, you're being foolish. What are you gonna do if you find them? This man in Duff's letter, what's he call himself, Spartan? That can't be his real name. You might just end up like Duff—then what?"

"That's why I'm telling you this. If something happens to me, I want you to give this letter and the other stuff in this envelope to the army and the newspapers."

"This is the stupidest damned idea—"

"There's right and there's wrong, Mister Hubert. I have right on my side, and I'm going to find those people, no matter what it takes. You gave me your word."

Brister drew hard on his cigarette, then pulled off his glasses and rubbed his eyes. After a few moments, he replaced the glasses and looked up at Brady.

"You need to think again about what's really right and what's not. Remember the Good Book says that revenge belongs to the Lord."

"All I'm going to do is get names and faces, unless they try to do me like they did Duff. Can you help me?"

Brister shook his head, then nodded. "All right, I reckon if you say I gave you my word, then I did. I'll put this letter in a safe place, but I'm telling you again, this is a stupid thing you're doing."

"You're probably right," Brady said.

It was a long shot at best, but next to Lacey, Duff had been his closest friend on Earth. If his death involved something more than an act of war, Duff deserved for someone to try to find the ones responsible.

The Gomorrah Principle is available now in
ebook and paperback.
Buy it now: www.amazon.com/gp/product/B00EUBZPU0

Glossary of Terms

APC: Armored Personnel Carrier

ARVN: Army of the Republic of Vietnam, the South Vietnamese Army or its personnel

BOQ: Bachelor Officers Quarters subsidized and managed by the Army

CIA: Central Intelligence Agency

Clacker: A handheld firing device for a Claymore mine

Claymore: A command detonated directional mine that sprays approximately 750 ball bearing-size steel pellets in a cone shaped pattern.

CMFIC: Off-color military slang for Chief M****r F****r In Charge

CO: Commanding Officer

CIB: Combat Infantryman's Badge

CIDU.S.: Army Criminal Investigation Department

CIDG: Civilian Irregular Defense Groups—villagers, Montagnard tribesmen, Thais, and other irregular soldiers who fought with American and South Vietnamese forces.

CONEXA: large metal shipping and storage container

Dại úy: Vietnamese for 'Captain.'

Dien Bien Phu: A battle that resulted in a Viet Minh victory over the French and ended the first Indo China War in 1954.

DEROS: Date of Estimated Return from Overseas Service
dừng lại: Vietnamese words meaning 'stop' or 'halt.'

E&E: Escape and Evasion, to escape and evade the enemy.

Foo gas: Fougasse is an improvised explosive device (55-gallon drum) which projects burning liquid (JP-4, Naptha, gasoline).

Frag: Fragmentation grenade, or the act of using one against another soldier.

Loach: Nickname for the Hughes OH-6 Cayuse, a Light Observation Helicopter often used by commanders for command-and-control purposes.

LRRP: Long Range Reconnaissance Patrol

Lurp(s): Nickname for members of Long-Range Reconnaissance Teams

MAC—V: Military Assistance Command—Vietnam. Controlled all military entities.

Moi: A term the South Vietnamese used describing the Montagnards as savages.

Montagnards(Mountain people—French): Tribesmen from various tribes who fought with the Americans against the Communists.

NCO: Non-commissioned Officers, also called non-Coms—the sergeants.

NDP: Night Defensive Position—usually a perimeter.

Nguoi Thuong: The Montagnards were known in Vietnamese as Nguoi Thuong

Nung: Ethnic group in Vietnam loyal to the Americans

NVA: North Vietnamese Army, often used as reference for smaller units of that army as "the NVA.".

OSA: Office of the Special Assistant, codename for CIA headquarters in Saigon

REMF: Rear Echelon M****r F*****r, a derogatory term for support troops.

S2: Army designation for intelligence operations

Snake Eater: A nickname for an Army Special Forces soldier (a Green Beret).

SOG: Acronym for Studies and Observation Group/ Special Operations Group

Special Forces: United States Army Special Forces A.K.A. The Green Berets

The Pig: A nickname for the M-60 Machine Gun

TOC: Tactical Operations Center- a headquarters center with radios where missions are coordinated.

X-Ray Relay: A radio team posted in mountainous areas to relay messages.

About the Author

Rick DeStefanis lives in northern Mississippi with his wife, Janet, two cats and a male yellow lab named Blondie. Although many of his novels cross genre lines that include military fiction, southern fiction and historical western fiction, he utilizes his military expertise to produce the Vietnam War Series. *Melody Hill* (*Book #1*) is the prequel to his award-winning novel *The Gomorrah Principle*, both of which draw from his experiences as a paratrooper with the 82nd Airborne Division.

Learn more about Rick DeStefanis and his books at: http://www.rickdestefanis.com/ or visit him on Facebook: https://www.facebook.com/RickDeStefanisAuthor/